TH
BL
CH
BO
(SU

PE(
DIS.

To: _it__ __lw.com_
Fr__ _k_
Su____ _e Na__ty and Nice Collection_

Sh____ _t giving in. What should I do? I thought of buying her somethi____ be something from the Tantalizing Thongs Collection would g____ clue and help speed things up? What do you think?

Jac

CORPORATE
SEDUCTION

A. C. ARTHUR

Genesis Press, Inc.

Indigo Love Stories

An imprint of Genesis Press, Inc.
Publishing Company

Genesis Press, Inc.
P.O. Box 101
Columbus, MS 39703

All characters in this book have no existence outside the imagination of the author and have no relation whatsoever to anyone bearing the same name or names. They are not even distantly inspired by any individual known or unknown to the author and all incidents are pure invention.

Manufactured in the United States of America

First Edition

Visit us at www.genesis-press.com
or call at 1-888-Indigo-1

DEDICATION

*To all the co-workers (attorneys and staff) in the firms
where I previously worked.
Thanks for the inspiration*

ACKNOWLEDGMENTS

I am so glad to have completed this book. I was a little nervous about a sequel but it was fun re-visiting these characters and the law office of Page and Associates.

Thanks always to Damon who, I think, enjoyed this story more than I did.

Thanks to my brother Darren, who answered my computer questions.

And last, but certainly not least, thanks to my Lord and Savior for the gift, the patience, and the strength to endure.

PROLOGUE

It was Thursday morning, and Reka couldn't wait for the weekend. Even though her weekends were now spent quite differently than in her past, she still looked forward to her personal time. Opening her Inbox, she scrolled down through her new messages and sighed as she glimpsed an all too familiar sender.

> To: *mail@passoclaw.com*
> From: *Jack*
> Subject: *The Naughty and Nice Collection*
>
> *She's still not giving in. What should I do? I thought of buying her something. Maybe something from the Tantalizing Thongs Collection would give her a clue and help speed things up? What do you think?*
>
> *Jack*

"After all these months you still haven't slept with Jill?" Reka rolled her eyes, right clicked and deleted the message. "You ask too many questions, that's your problem, Jack, ole boy."

She had to smile to herself at the latest of the sexual emails the office had been inundated with. It had started about three months ago and, at first, Cienna and Tacoma, the new office manager, had just assumed they were a joke. But then the sexually charged messages had begun appearing with more frequency and much more urgency from their originator, Jack.

Now the entire office seemed focused on these messages. Most of them wondered who they were from, speculating about the staff, as well as the attorneys, especially since love connections were known to happen in this office. Some of the more simpleminded employees, though, took the messages all too literally. On any given day talk in the lunchroom was of the steamy messages and the thoughts they provoked. Tacoma had had more than a few reports of quickies in the storage room and had even caught Nigel, from the mailroom, and Kelly, from accounting, hugged up in the stairway acting out a previous email, one entitled Exciting Edibles.

Tacoma was hyperventilating by the time Reka had made it to his office after his urgent page for her. The male/female connection was not his cup of tea, which was clearly understandable since he was now engaged to his longtime boyfriend, Terry.

Reka, however, didn't take the unsolicited emails quite so literally, but had to admit that lately they seemed to exacerbate her own situation—no boyfriend, no prospects and no inclination to find either.

Cienna Turner-Page clicked the icon that would load Microsoft Outlook onto her computer. She flipped through the day's schedule while listening to the computer go through the motions. When her screen blinked with the familiar background, she clicked into the Inbox and began a cursory glance at the subject line of this morning's messages. 'The Naughty and Nice Collection' caught her eye and she instantly positioned the mouse to open that particular message.

Cienna read the words and stifled a scream. Jack was beginning to piss her off. She had a lunch meeting with her longtime client, Johnathan Peterson, the CEO of Sensuality, Inc., a lucrative lingerie company, and planned on discussing this situation again for the billionth time in the last three months. She had no idea how the emails that had first appeared throughout his growing company had found their way to her law firm as well. But she was damn sure going to find out.

Picking up her telephone, she dialed a familiar number.

"Judge Page's chambers," Gayle, the receptionist, answered in a cheery voice.

"Good morning, Gayle. Is the judge on the bench yet this morning?"

Gayle smiled at the friendly, familiar voice on the other end. "Oh, hello, Cienna. No, he's having his usual cup of caffeine right now."

Cienna chuckled. Keith said he needed all the caffeine he could get before dealing with the lunatics that came through his family division courtroom. "In that case, I can interrupt him."

"You sure can. I'll put you right through."

"Thanks, Gayle."

"No problem," the woman said happily before ringing Keith's office to announce that his wife was on the line.

"Mornin', beautiful. You miss me already?" Keith Page looked at his watch, noting that he'd left his Greenwich Village house only about an hour ago after his lovely wife had given him a very satisfying send-off. If she didn't miss him already, he damn sure missed her.

"I miss you every minute we're apart," Cienna sighed, still helplessly in love with her husband after three years of marriage. "But that's not why I'm calling," she added quickly. Behind closed office doors, she and Keith had shared some pretty steamy telephone conversations, and this had the potential to go there, unless she cut it off quickly. "We've got a problem."

"A problem?" Keith sat up in his chair. "What's up?"

"I got another message this morning. From Jack."

Keith knew very well who Jack was, and how the pervert was wreaking havoc on the firm he partnered with his wife. "Forward it to me now."

Cienna did as he asked and waited while he read it.

Initially, Keith chuckled. "I've seen the Tantalizing Thongs. That just might work, Jack."

"Keith!" Cienna was not feeling his humor.

"Just kidding, sweetie. This is serious, I know. It's been three months now, and this guy hasn't let up."

"What are we going to do? Everybody's walking around here like they're in heat or as if they're amateur detectives trying to figure out who in the firm could be sending them. Attendance is down, morale is shot to hell since nobody can keep their mind on the business of law. I'm sick to death of the jokes and banter going around on a daily basis and, to top it off, Johnathan plans to release the new collection in four weeks. Just imagine how this thing is going to explode once the public gets wind of the collection *and* the sex-orientated emails."

"Calm down, baby. I'll take care of it," Keith assured her.

"How?"

"I've been talking to this computer guy I know. I offered him a job a few years ago but he turned me down. I'll just give him a call and tell him that I really need him this time."

"You think he'll be able to find out who's sending these messages so we can prosecute for harassment?" Cienna wasn't very optimistic, but realized this might possibly be their only hope.

"He's the best."

"Okay, when can I meet him?" she asked.

"I'll invite him over for dinner tonight. Print out all the messages and bring them home, I'm sure he'll want to see them."

"You're inviting him to our home? You know him that well?" She was a little shocked. She knew all of Keith's friends and wasn't sure she'd ever met a computer guy before.

"It's Khalil. You know, we play ball on Saturdays. I've told you about him, haven't I?" Keith asked the question although he already knew the answer. He hadn't told his wife about Khalil, mostly because a reason had never come up, but partly because of the business Khalil was in.

"I don't think so. But I vaguely remember him from the cookout last summer." She was getting a blurry picture of the friend Keith was referring to.

"Well, you'll meet him tonight, and we'll get to the bottom of this. Don't worry."

Cienna read over the message again and sighed. "That's easy for you to say. You're not going to be hearing 'The Thong Song' all day."

Seated in his high-backed soft leather chair, Khalil desperately tried to dismiss the conversation he'd just had with his mother. It was just too damned early in the morning for that type of drama. Besides, he'd made his mind up and this time, Cornelia Hughes Franklin was going to have to accept it.

He was about to go over the report a new employee had left on his desk last night when Carol, his assistant, buzzed through the speaker phone.

"Judge Page on line one," she stated in a professional voice.

Khalil grinned. He'd put a hurtin' on Keith in Saturday's game. If he knew his friend, Keith was already calling to talk trash about this weekend's rematch. "You feelin' better, old man?" he asked when he lifted the receiver to his ear.

"Feelin' better?" Keith queried.

Khalil couldn't help chuckling. "Yeah, after that butt whuppin' I served you a few days ago."

"Ah, man, please. You just got lucky, that's all. It's about time you started playin' like you had some skills. Those Ivy League schools made you soft." Keith laughed. "But that's not what I'm calling about."

"Really? What else can I do for you?"

"Remember those email problems I told you we were having at the firm?"

Khalil sat back in his chair, abandoning the reports. He remembered the problem, and didn't want to miss anything. The erotic emails his friend had mentioned a few weeks ago had sparked his interest. "Yeah. Is the firm still getting them?"

"Mmmhmm. Cienna forwarded me another one this morning. She's really upset, says everybody's more focused on who's sending the messages and why than on work now."

Khalil thought of his own non-existent sex life. "There are worse things then sex that they could be thinking about."

"I agree, but not at work. I want you to come take a look, see if you can find out who's sending them so we can prosecute."

Franklin Investigations had just opened its second office in Connecticut, so Khalil didn't need another client. It was purely personal intrigue that had him consenting to help Keith. "Sure. When can I gain access to the computer system at the firm?"

"As soon as I convince Cienna to hire you as the firm's new IT tech. I don't want her to know you're an investigator. She might get nervous."

"But I thought she wanted to prosecute?"

"She does, but ever since all that stuff went down a few years ago, the police and investigations make her a little jumpy. That's why she stopped handling complex litigation cases. I just told her that you're a computer geek and that you could probably find our culprit."

"A computer geek, huh?" Khalil shook his head at the familiar jab. Most of his friends had dubbed him that long ago. His family was very proud of his computer skills, but wished he'd use them at the family's investment company instead of his investigation firm. Sonya, however, hadn't really cared what his interests were, as long as the bank account kept growing.

Keith grinned. He knew the nickname would needle Khalil, and he so loved to keep his buddy going. "Yeah, that means you know your stuff."

"No, it doesn't." Khalil chuckled. "But I'll go along with your plan anyway. When do I start my new position?"

Keith rubbed his hands together, confident that Khalil would get to the bottom of this, and quickly. "Come by for dinner tonight and we'll talk over the logistics with Cienna."

"Now you know I don't pass up a free meal. I'll be there."

The men finished the conversation with more basketball banter before hanging up. Sexy emails being sent to an office full of lawyers. Khalil couldn't figure out the connection, but was sure there had to be one. He picked up his phone and gave Carol a list of cases to distribute among the other investigators. He needed a break from the office anyway. He'd been working really hard and, now that he had a competent staff, he could finally take some time for other things.

A simple computer case like this would take his mind off Sonya and the disaster their breakup had been, and it would probably add some spice to his otherwise boring life. Erotic emails definitely sounded like a lot of that.

1

"I know you're not wearing a dress." Reka dropped her pen and was now staring pointedly at Tacoma, who had invaded her office about ten minutes ago to discuss his impending wedding.

Tacoma rolled his contact-gray eyes. "I'm going to pretend I didn't hear that."

"Oh, okay, just so we're clear about that." Reka straightened in her chair and gave Tacoma her full attention. "Proceed." She hadn't really been listening to him when he first came in because she had been organizing a file for Cienna, and generally Tacoma just wanted to vent. Replies usually weren't necessary. But from the looks of him, she needed to throw some serious concentration his way. Her friend was definitely a little on the edgy side this Friday morning.

"I'm not sure what I'm wearing. It's a choice between this dynamite cream-colored Versace I saw in a magazine and this off-the-rack white contraption that Terry likes. I swear, he's monitoring my spending for this wedding like we're one cracker shy of starving." Nervously, Tacoma crossed his right leg over his left and rolled the end of his coral silk tie around his finger. Over Reka's shoulder he could see it was a sunny New York day outside. And to top that off, it was Friday. Still, his mood was sour and his loving fiancé was the reason why. "Nice weddings cost money, and I want mine to be fabulous! I don't know why he doesn't understand that."

"There's a difference between fabulous and extravagant, Tacoma. Terry wants to take you on a nice honeymoon, but if you spend all the money on the wedding itself, you'll be staring out the window of your apartment instead of lying on some tropical beach."

Tacoma unraveled his tie, smoothed it down and gave himself another nod of approval for putting together the ivory linen pants, melon-colored silk shirt and tie that was just a shade lighter. His Kenneth Cole butter-toned tie ups and soft beige dress socks topped it off. Since his promotion to office manager and the big fat raise that came along with it, he'd been dressing his hundred and nineteen pound butt off.

"We've been to Cancun and Jamaica and the Bahamas. I'm about beached out. I suggested Paris."

Reka watched Tacoma checking himself out and smiled to herself. No matter what was going on, Tacoma's first concern was always his looks. He primped more than she did when they went out. Though they did most of their shopping together, she'd had nothing to do with today's citrus look. "Paris isn't cheap. Why don't you cut the guest list? That'll save some money on the food."

Tacoma made a sound that was dangerously close to a screech, and Reka frowned. "I can't cut my guest list. All those people just have to come. This is my big day," he whined.

Reka pursed her lips and leaned her elbows on her desk. "Why don't you fall in the floor and start rolling around? That's all you need to top off this juvenile tantrum you're throwing."

Tacoma gasped.

Reka waved a hand in dismissal. "Save it for somebody who doesn't know you like I do. You don't even remember half those people you have on that list, you just want to show off. Cut the list to one hundred and fifty guests and tomorrow we'll go and find you and Terry nice Versace-*looking* suits. But not white. That virginal thing is so played out."

Tacoma straightened in the chair, his palms on his knees, and cracked a smile at her. That's why he so adored Reka; she knew just how to make him feel better. "Okay, shopping and lunch tomorrow. That's wonderful. Now I have to get back to work."

He stood and Reka chuckled. "You remember how to do that?"

Tacoma was about to spray her with a smart reply when her speaker phone buzzed and Cienna's voice filled the tiny office.

"Reka, I need to see you in my office, please."

Reka pressed the red button on her phone and answered, "I'll be right there."

She stood, smoothed down her own purple knee-length skirt, and walked around her desk.

Tacoma opened the door, looking back at her for a second. "Girl, those pumps are killer , but you should have worn the blazer with that outfit instead of the scarf."

"Keep walking, I've got this covered," she said as she re-tied and fluffed her lavender and violet scarf so that it hung alluringly over her shoulder. Her sheer lavender blouse was plain and buttoned almost to her neck. The scarf awakened the otherwise drab material and tied the entire outfit together. She'd received two compliments while on the subway this morning, so she knew she had it going on.

Not that she would waste her time on the two tired, jobless men that had complimented her. Those days were over. Drama-filled relationships, heated breakups and senseless sex were a part of her past. Since receiving her degree from Queensborough Community College Reka had re-arranged her priorities, putting herself first, before any man.

As a matter of fact, at twenty-eight, living alone in a lovely Upper West Side apartment that she could now thankfully afford, she felt she'd finally arrived. She was perfectly content with her life just the way it was. Gone were the days when she longed for the company of a man, any man. Now she had work that occupied her mind.

Men were definitely off limits for her.

Cienna's door was closed, so Reka knocked once before turning the knob to enter. She'd assumed Cienna was alone, so the gentleman sitting in the chair across from her desk was a slight shock. "Good morning," she said cheerfully, and looked to Cienna before taking another step. Maybe she just wanted her to get a file or locate a report for this client. She could have simply told her that over the phone, but Reka had long since stopped trying to tell Cienna how to do her job.

"Good, you're here. Shut the door and have a seat, please." Cienna grabbed a stack of papers from her printer and barely looked up at Reka as she spoke.

Reka did as she was told. She sat in the chair next to the client. His scent hit her first.

Expensive, not musk—she hated musk—smooth, almost sensual, either Dolce & Gabanna or Escada. She liked them both, so it was only natural that she check out the man who was smart enough to wear them.

Uh oh! Big mistake! Colossal error!

He was fine. No, he was *Fine*, with a capital F. From the top of his close cut, dark wavy hair, down past that excellently cut designer suit— tailored for his muscular physique—to the shiny black tie ups, he was a mouth-watering creature.

She found her voice and decided to act like the educated professional she now professed to be. "Good morning," she spoke clearly, without any hint that he'd roused hormones long dormant.

Khalil had just taken the stack of papers from Cienna and was about to flip through them when he heard her voice, which was just a trace shy of being husky, and a bit too sultry for an office worker at ten o'clock in the morning. He looked up at her, his mouth opened to speak. Then his eyes found hers and then his mouth closed abruptly— without releasing a word.

Reka raised her brows. Was he deaf, or just courtesy deficient? She couldn't tell, but no matter how good he looked, that didn't excuse rudeness. "It is a good morning, isn't it?" She rephrased her question, hoping the cute dunce would pick up on her meaning.

She'd taken him off guard—or rather those slanted catlike eyes had. Re-grouping, he realized she was being smart with her latest statement and felt the urge to grin at her audacity. She hadn't been rude, so there was no need for Cienna to reprimand her. To the contrary, that brandy-laced voice had been more than polite, more than cordial, and she'd even smiled when she'd finished, ensuring her comment wasn't taken the wrong way, no doubt. Yet a flash of mischief in those alluring eyes told the true meaning. "It's a fantastic morning—now." He did smile at her then, curious as to what she'd say next.

Cienna, who had witnessed the exchange, decided she'd better speak up now before Reka lost her little bit of polish and reverted to her true form. "Khalil Franklin, this is my assistant, Reka Boyd. Reka, this is Khalil Franklin, our new IT supervisor."

Reka sat back in her chair, a part of her breathing a sigh of relief that he wasn't a client. She was always a little worried about how far her mouth went sometimes. Well, only in the workplace. After hours, it was on. Whatever came to mind inevitably came spilling out of her mouth, and she rarely felt any remorse. He was smiling at her, a damned sexy smile at that. Her eight-hour days might have just gotten a bit brighter, she thought.

Hold up! Wait a minute! Stop the presses!

She was not looking at him like that! It was not that type of party. He just looked like he could take a joke, like he was cool to hang around. It wasn't like she wanted to get to know him better or anything like that. Because she didn't.

His eyes absorbed her entire presence in one long, heart stopping, toe curling sweep and she swallowed hard.

She definitely didn't.

"I look forward to working with you," Khalil offered when it seemed he'd been successful in stopping her quick retorts. Still, he wanted to hear her speak again.

"And you will," Cienna chimed in. "As my assistant, Reka knows just as much, if not more, about Sensuality, Inc., than I do. She can give you the rundown of the company as well as their new product line, since you think that's the link to the emails."

Cienna had given Reka the moments she needed to get herself together, and now she was ready to do business. Mr. Handsome was now Khalil Franklin, co-worker, computer guy, and she was Reka Boyd, paralegal, assistant. "Yes, the Naughty and Nice Collection is due to be released the week before Christmas. You think that has something to do with the pervert sending the suggestive emails?" Crossing her legs, she looked over at Khalil. That was a nice name, fitting for this nicely dressed, probably very intelligent man.

No, he wasn't a man, he was the computer guy or IT something-or-other, she corrected herself.

Khalil had read only two or three of the email messages sent by the person known only as 'Jack.' He'd gotten a little background information from Cienna on the company that the messages originated from and figured that working for a high-end lingerie and sexual accouterment company had to make a person pretty damned horny on a regular basis. It didn't surprise him someone had taken things to another level.

"Well, I have to admit that I've seen some of Sensuality's lingerie so I know how it could pique a person's interest, get their mind to wondering about things. I'm thinking that whoever is sending these messages has a lot on his mind right now." Khalil put a rubber band around the thick stack of messages that he'd review once he got into his office at Page & Associates. He'd make a copy and take them to his real office later this evening and begin a series of separate scans as well. But first he needed access to Page & Associates' system.

Reka chuckled. "The only thing on his mind is getting laid, and he doesn't quite seem able to do that."

"Reka," Cienna began, but couldn't help smiling herself. "I don't care if he gets laid or not. I just want him to stop sending his sick little messages to my office. Khalil, do you think you can find out who's sending these notes and make them stop?"

Khalil, who was desperately trying to squelch the effect Cienna's enticing assistant was having on him, finally looked to his new boss in response. "I'll find out who's sending the messages. Then you can decide how to deal with him or her."

"Her?" Reka asked. "Jack is definitely a man."

Both Cienna and Khalil looked at her.

"How do you figure that? Just by the familiar male name?" Khalil questioned.

Reka stood, suddenly unable to keep still beneath this man's...the IT guy's intense gaze. She fiddled with her scarf again before letting her hands fall to her sides. "No, by the fact that he hasn't figured out how to get Jill into his bed yet. You see, only a man would miss the obvious, sort of like how a dog continues to chase his own tail."

Cienna shook her head, her fingers coming up to her temple. She knew that whatever Reka was about to say was going to be way over the top—that was just how Reka was. "Maybe we don't need to hear your reasons for believing he's a guy, Reka. We'll just let Khalil do his job."

Despite Cienna's words, Khalil stood and faced Reka. Her pointed gaze made his blood pump hard, and he gripped the stack of papers a little tighter than necessary. In these few minutes he'd become more aware of this woman than any other female he'd ever met in his life. She was substantially shorter than he was, but then he stood six feet, four inches tall. He doubted if he was going to find many women he met eye to eye. Yet even with her small stature she emanated great strength and character, and he found himself more than a little curious to learn all he could about her. "It's okay, Cienna. I'd like to hear Reka's explanation."

Reka didn't miss that he'd called her by her first name, nor did she miss how her pulse quickened when he did. But she could surely ignore both. "Men play the same tired games over and over again and then wonder why they can't get a good woman. Dogs chase their tails day in and day out, still wondering why they never catch the damned thing." When he didn't respond, but only looked at her with a more heated expression, she put her hands on her hips. "If Jack were a woman she'd know just how to get her man to comply with her wishes, and therefore wouldn't need to send these juvenile messages. Instead, Jack the man continues to ask advice for his inadequate love life. Advice that I doubt he'd take even if somebody gave it to him because the male ego won't allow it. Jack has got to be a man, a lonely, misguided man."

Khalil stood quietly resisting the urge to touch the smooth looking orange tinted skin at her cheek. Her hair was an intriguing mass of auburn curls swept into some sort of twist at the back with sexy strands hanging down around her neck. She held herself perfectly still, tilting her head just a bit to stare up at him.

Something about the way she was checking him out shook his usually solid control. He was a professional, a businessman, with a job to do. This little wisp of a woman shouldn't have rattled him. Yet every time he watched those long-lashed lids close and re-open, that's exactly what she did.

"You seem pretty well versed on the laws of men and women. I think you should be the one to go over these messages with me. You know, to find common links and match them up with possible culprits."

Cienna stood, wanting this tense atmosphere lifted and taken immediately out of her office. She had enough to handle with the messages steadily coming in. The last thing she needed was Reka and Khalil going head-to-head as well. "That's a fantastic idea. Reka, you could get your files on the Naughty and Nice Collection and join Khalil when he reviews the messages. There probably are lots of similarities and references to the collection. Compiling a list and narrowing it down to a few employees at Sensuality, Inc., shouldn't be a problem." At least she hoped it wouldn't. "In any case, Khalil can come up with a firewall that will keep Jack from sharing his trials with us."

Something told Reka working with Khalil was a bad idea. Still, her big mouth was about to sign a check she only prayed she'd be able to cash. "That's fine. I'll work with him. Men tend to think alike, so having a woman on the case might prove the best route."

Khalil couldn't help it. He threw his head back and laughed. He liked this woman. She was refreshing, so different from the women he was used to meeting. She said what she meant and he had a feeling she meant what she said. She was brutally honest. Something Sonya had definitely not been.

"Then it's a deal. I'll give you some time to get your files together and then you can meet me in my office," he told her, even though he sensed she didn't like being told what to do.

"Then that's settled. You two are on the case. I'm depending on you to bring this to a timely close." Cienna walked to the door and opened it. Reka gave her a blistering gaze on her way out.

"You know you can depend on me, Cienna."

"I know, Reka." She knew, all right. She knew that before the day was out she'd have to hear what Reka really thought of Khalil Franklin and her orders to work with him.

Khalil stared after Reka, his eyes undoubtedly drawn to the sway of those purple-clad hips. His blood, which had already been pumping way too fast, simmered and boiled. He straightened his tie when he caught Cienna staring at him. "Which way is my office?"

Cienna gave a knowing grin. "Blessedly, in the opposite direction of Reka's."

Reka had a file box full of correspondence and materials from Sensuality, Inc., going back to the first thing Cienna had done for the company, the articles of incorporation. From there she'd worked on their patents and advised Mr. Peterson on office policies. Just recently she'd taken on his messy divorce case. His wife was no fool; she wanted everything she had coming to her, and then some. So they'd begun the paper war, collecting and exchanging information with opposing counsel.

Mr. Peterson always shared his new product announcements with Cienna and she, in turn, forwarded them to Reka. Before returning to her office, Reka, with Tacoma's help, brought the boxes of information from the workroom and placed them in the corner so they'd be accessible when she met with the IT guy.

Sitting behind her desk, she allowed herself five minutes to think about the IT guy. "Five minutes won't hurt," she mumbled. He was tall, oh so damned tall. Almost too tall, she thought with a frown. Considering she was barely five feet, two inches, just about any adult was tall to her. Yet when he stood in front of her, very closely in front of her, his height hadn't seemed intimidating at all. To the contrary, it made her feel almost secure. As if he were a shield, offering her protection.

His skin reminded her of her favorite candy, Milk Maid Caramels. Even though she hadn't touched him, his cheeks looked smooth. The lower half of his face was covered by a thin beard and mustache—so thin creamy-colored skin showed beneath the dark hair. His eyes were dark as they'd raked over her.

Lastly, because her five minutes were running out, his suit. Reka loved a man who could dress and, from the looks of his tailor-made suit, this brother definitely had good taste. The jacket had molded against his broad shoulders perfectly, the pants, pleated—men without pleats in their pants had serious fashion issues in her book—hung on his hips expertly, and the cuffed hem rested on those shiny shoes.

She twirled the ends of her scarf around her fingers and rocked in her chair. He was a good-looking specimen. If one were looking for a good looking specimen.

Which she definitely was not.

Donovan had been the last straw. Even thinking his name had her on the verge of screaming. His ultimate betrayal had hurt her one final, excruciating time and, from that moment nine months ago until now, she'd known that men were not in her immediate future.

Thank heaven her five minutes were over.

Something told him she wasn't coming to his office. Maybe it was because of her generally defiant air or maybe because he'd practically ordered her to come. Either way, it had been forty minutes since he'd first laid eyes on her in Cienna's office and she still hadn't appeared.

Cienna had walked Khalil to his office, introducing him to other staff members along the way. He had a desk, a computer, a telephone and a separate fax machine. That was all he needed for the moment. He'd bring in his personal scanning equipment next week so he could link it to the Page & Associates network. But since today was Friday and they were just getting started, he'd go over the mountain of messages that had been sent so far.

But he didn't want to do that alone.

Reka Boyd, Cienna's assistant. She'd awakened something in him, something he hadn't even known was there. Something about her spunky personality had unnerved him and, for some strange reason, he wanted to experience it again. He wanted to hear that voice that was so different from the sophisticated drawl he'd been used to hearing from the women he dated. She wasn't street, yet she had a definite urban-ness that appealed to him.

And that body…Damn, the man who'd originally compared the female form to a Coca-Cola bottle would have had regular dreams about Reka. She was short and curvaceous and wore clothes that emphasized her attributes. He chuckled. Maybe he shouldn't classify her as short. Petite probably sounded better to her. Even though she wore sizable heels, she'd still fallen well beneath his shoulders. But that hadn't stopped her from eyeing him down and standing her ground.

Her opinions about the email stalker being a man had been humorous, even though he'd sensed she was dead serious, too serious, as if she'd had experience with immature, egotistical men. Or had she called them dogs? Either way, he was dying to hear more, to learn just how her mind worked. He hadn't been this intrigued in a long while.

Where was she? He looked at his watch again, then decided she wasn't coming. He grabbed the emails and made his way down the hall to her office. If Mohammed wouldn't come to the mountain…

Reka was printing a particularly bothersome pleading that she'd been working on since the day before. She wanted to get it on Cienna's desk for her review before she left today. She knew she had to meet with that IT guy and didn't want this assignment to sit idle while she did. She'd just taken the papers from the printer and was about to staple them together when she heard a brief knock on her door, then watched as the door opened.

He leaned his long frame against the doorjamb. He'd removed his jacket, and she immediately noticed the bulging biceps as his shirt constricted. Beneath one arm he held a stack of papers she assumed were the infamous emails. The other hand was stuffed nonchalantly into his pocket. And he smiled.

Her breasts seemed to expand, her nipples hardening instantly, and her lips thinned in consternation. She'd given herself five minutes to think about his gorgeousness, but apparently that hadn't been enough.

"I thought I was to come to your office," she said tightly, looking away.

Khalil presumed that was all the permission he was going to get, so he entered her office and shut the door behind him. "You were taking too long." Setting the papers on the edge of her desk, he took a seat.

"Impatient, are we?" She dropped the work she'd just finished into her out basket and cleared her computer screen.

She shifted in her chair, giving him a glimpse of her plump breasts against her blouse. With much effort he dragged his eyes back to her face. "I'd say anxious describes it better."

He swept a dark gaze over her. No, it wasn't a gaze—it was more like a caress and her heart thumped in her chest. For an instant she tingled beneath his scrutiny. Then thoughts of Donovan and his bold good looks resurfaced, and her resolve hardened. "Fine. The sooner we get this over with, the sooner we can both get on with other things."

Did he make her nervous? Of course not, she was too sassy to be nervous. But he'd definitely ruffled her feathers in some way. "You don't like me, do you?" he chanced to ask.

Reka sighed heavily. "I don't know you, Mr. Franklin." For a minute she'd almost called him IT guy or worse, Mr. Handsome. "I'm sick of getting these emails, so if you can find a way to stop them, then I'm more than glad to help."

"The emails bother you? Why?" She didn't look like the type to be easily intimidated; or embarrassed, for that matter. He wondered if the emails bothered her on a more personal level. Of course, that had nothing to do with the job, but still he wanted to know.

Reka tilted her head and stared at him, wondering why he'd asked that particular question. "I don't normally like to discuss sex at the office." At least she and Tacoma made a valiant effort not to discuss sex at the office.

That was a professional response, one he should have accepted. But being a PI, he prided himself on his ability to dig a little deeper. "What does your boyfriend think of them?"

Reka narrowed her eyes, sat back in the chair. She noticed his kissable lips. Kissable meaning they weren't so thin you had to wonder if they were just slashes across his face where he stuffed his food or so thick you'd fear being swallowed during the experience.

"How old are you?" she blurted out.

Khalil blinked at the quick shift in subject. "Thirty-five. How old are you?" He'd wanted to ask that anyway; now she'd given him the chance.

Great, he was a little old, even if she was interested, which she definitely was not. Her usual age difference was limited to three or four years; seven was a stretch. "I'm twenty-eight, and old enough to know that if you want to know something you should just come right out and ask. If you want to know if I have a boyfriend, just ask me."

Khalil grinned. Damn, but he liked this woman. "Okay, do you have a boyfriend?"

Because, despite herself, his smile did something to her, she cracked a grin. "No, I don't. But if I did, I still wouldn't want to get these messages."

She didn't have a boyfriend—that was amazing. "I see your point. So why does an attractive female like yourself not have a man?" Be careful, he warned himself, digging could get him into a lot of trouble.

He had an angle, she was sure of it, all men did. If he weren't so uptight looking, she'd simply assume he was flirting and let him down quickly. But there was no way this guy was interested in her. She was clearly not his type; that's probably why he spent so much time laughing at her. Still, there was no reason not to answer his question. "Frankly put, because I'm smarter than most men out there. I know all their games because I've either played them or been played by them. And I don't have the patience to wait for boys to grow into men."

So. Her explanation about why Jack had to be a man and her clever wall of defense made it perfectly clear. She'd been burned before. He wondered briefly what idiot had been stupid enough to hurt her.

But that really didn't matter, because he had no intention of making the same mistake.

2

"Thank goodness it's Friday," Reka moaned as the bartender put her brightly colored appletini in front of her. She and Tacoma were at their favorite Friday night happy hour spot near the Village, relaxing, or at least she was trying to relax. Tacoma, on the other hand….

"Maybe he likes you," he said after sipping at his white wine.

Reka almost choked on her own drink as she cut her eyes at Tacoma. "Don't play. You know damned well a man like that wouldn't be interested in me."

Tacoma loosened his tie and grimaced. "Why? There's nothing wrong with you."

Reka had removed her scarf and unbuttoned the first few buttons on her blouse the minute they'd walked into the bar. This was a laid-back atmosphere; she didn't have to be the consummate professional here. "Oh, I know there's nothing wrong with me. I'd be a good catch for any man. Any man the same type as me, I mean. He's blue blood, old money, suit and tie. And I'm—"

"An attractive black woman, newly graduated from college and independent," Tacoma finished for her. He was in a slight state of shock. He'd never seen Reka this way before. Reka was the most self-assured person he'd ever known. Whatever you told her she couldn't do, she did, and did it so well you were left looking like a fool. But ever since leaving the office she'd been talking about the IT guy, who she practically refused to call by his name, and the way he'd asked her so many personal questions. As if she couldn't read the signs.

"I know all that, Tacoma." She rolled her eyes. "But I'm not from his world. I'm from a different crop all together." She ran her fingertip absently around the rim of her glass. "Besides, you know I'm not interested in relationships. So this entire conversation is pointless."

"Who said anything about a relationship? It sounds to me like he was just trying to get to know you better. What's so wrong with that?"

"Nothing," she said quickly, and then let out a heavy sigh. "Everything. He's too old for me, and he's all distinguished and polished. Look at me, I'm sitting in a bar on a Friday night. Do you really think Mr. IT Guy would be caught in a bar during happy hour?"

Tacoma would have answered but as his line of vision traveled just over Reka's shoulder he spotted the subject of their conversation and smiled. "To tell you the truth, I wouldn't be surprised if he walked right through that door at this very moment." Taking another sip of his wine, he tapped Reka on the shoulder and pointed towards the door.

Reka shifted in her seat to see what Tacoma was pointing at and had to catch her breath when she watched the familiar frame making his way towards them. What the hell was he doing here?

"So this is where the staff meets after work?" Khalil said, taking the empty seat beside Reka. "Thanks for inviting me, Tacoma."

Reaching behind her, Khalil shook Tacoma's hand. Reka shot Tacoma a heated look, and his smile brightened.

"No problem. After reading those raunchy emails all day I figured you'd need to unwind." And after having lunch with Reka and hearing all about the big bad IT guy, Tacoma knew there was something going on between those two and wanted to witness it for himself. The way Reka's shoulders had squared and her usual banter had ceased, he figured he was pretty close to the mark. There was definitely some chemistry going on. The question was, would either of them act on it?

"I'll have a rum and coke, please."

Reka looked up at Khalil, who was still wearing his suit jacket and tie. Another sign that he was distinguished and out of her league. Even Tacoma loosened his tie after five. "You drink rum and coke?"

Khalil glanced at her. He'd noted the change in her demeanor when he'd approached. She wasn't thrilled with his arrival. This woman was going to be a challenge. In all his years of dating he'd never had to work hard to impress a woman. Since all the women he'd dated already knew who he was and what he had, they were impressed from the moment he said hello.

But Reka didn't seem so easily impressed. Khalil took that as a good sign. "What am I supposed to drink?" He looked over at her glass. "That's cute, but looks a little too prissy for me."

Reka shrugged. "I don't know. I kind of had you pegged for a wine kind of guy, like Tacoma here."

Khalil, who'd been taking a sip of the drink in question, choked slightly at her words. Did that mean she thought he was gay? That was a possibility he hadn't considered and would not hesitate to rectify.

Something in the way he looked at her must have given away his thoughts because she grinned. "I don't mean it that way."

With a napkin Khalil wiped his mouth. He liked her smile. It lifted her already high cheekbones and caused those exotic eyes to twinkle. He decided then and there that he wanted her to smile at him more often, and only at him.

"I'm glad you didn't mean it that way."

Tacoma emptied his glass. "There's nothing wrong with being that way. Half the male population is. They're just too egotistical to admit it."

"Oh gracious, we've ruffled his feathers." Reka turned and put a hand on Tacoma's thigh. "You know I love you, darling. But you are different from most men I know."

"You're damned right I'm different. I'm better than those jerks." Tacoma smiled down the bar at Khalil. "Excluding you, of course."

Khalil tried to suppress a grin. "Of course."

"So what about those messages? Did you see the one that came just before we left?" Tacoma asked Khalil.

"I saw it and its attachment," Khalil said, remembering the message vividly.

I purchased this for Jill today and wondered what you thought. I figured a thong was a good idea, but tell me, what color do you like the best?

Below Jack's signature line were pictures of a black, a gold and a white thong, all outlined with feathery fringes that made the garments look more like costume accessories than underwear. Khalil frowned.

"What? You don't like thongs?" Tacoma asked.

Reka smacked his thigh, giving him a look that said she did not want to have this discussion in front of the IT guy.

Khalil didn't miss the implication and looked directly at Reka. "To the contrary, I love a thong, on the right woman, that is."

"Ain't that the truth," Tacoma slapped a palm on the bar, "because everything's not made for every *body*." He emphasized body by making a wide motion with his hands.

Khalil grinned. Reka rolled her eyes.

"This is why those messages need to stop. From the moment Tacoma got that message he had joke after joke. I'm glad payroll was done before he got the message, else none of us would get paid next week," Reka said in an exasperated tone.

Khalil had decided earlier today that he liked Tacoma. The guy was a riot, and was very helpful in revealing things about Reka that Khalil suspected she would never have divulged. He'd sensed right away that Tacoma and Reka were very close, so he figured he'd found himself a pretty good ally when the small-framed gentleman had waltzed into his office this afternoon. It hadn't taken Khalil two seconds to figure out that Tacoma was fishing for information about him, and because he hoped Tacoma would take the information back to Reka, he readily gave it.

"Well, maybe Jack was trying to give you an idea of what to do with that paycheck next week? You know, a little lingerie shopping." Khalil watched her carefully, wondering what she was going to say next. He'd been slightly disappointed with the way she'd stopped talking since his arrival. He'd traveled to this bar just to hear her voice again, just to be near her again. It would be a shame if she clammed up and he'd made a wasted trip.

His look startled her. It wasn't reserved or distinguished; it was downright hot, and she didn't like it. "No, I don't think so."

"Why? You don't like lingerie?" Khalil asked, mimicking Tacoma's earlier question.

Reka heard Tacoma chuckle but refused to look his way. "I didn't say that," she said tightly.

"Then what are you saying?" Khalil realized he was probably crossing the line, again. He hadn't known Reka more than a day, and already he was talking to her about such personal things as her underwear. Given the situation, they were bound to have uncomfortable conversations like this, but he had to admit that his line of questioning went well beyond the realm of business.

"I'm saying that I have better things to do with my money than blow it on lingerie." His eyes raked over her body and she shifted in her seat. Reka took a deep breath. The chemistry between them was potent and she hated it, hated the implications.

"Then maybe someone who doesn't have better things to do with his money could buy it for you." Khalil took a chance and let his hand rest on top of hers, his eyes holding her gaze.

Tacoma signaled for another drink, entirely too happy with what he was witnessing. "If I've told you once, I've told you a million times, never turn down a gift. Especially an expensive one."

Reka removed her hand from beneath Khalil's because his touch made her feel things she didn't want to think about. She made the mistake of meeting his gaze. The dim lighting gave him a devilish look. A look that promised to take her places she'd never dreamed of going. "I don't need gifts," she said pointedly.

Khalil got her meaning and leaned back in his seat. She was interesting, like the ultimate dare. She didn't want to be bothered with men, of that much he was certain. She'd been hurt in the past; her comments had proven that. But he knew she felt the same electrifying attraction that he did. The smoldering heat that she cleverly tried to disguise gave that fact away.

As tiny as that bit of hope was, Khalil grabbed hold of it, determined to let it guide him. He didn't know the whys of it, he just knew he had to pursue her. Yes, just two weeks ago he'd broken off his engagement to Sonya and yes, he had vowed to take time for himself, but he'd also vowed to find a woman that excited him, who made him think only of her every second of every day. He'd met that woman close to nine hours ago—Reka Boyd.

Before Khalil could speak again the threesome turned into a four-some when a tall, dark-skinned man joined them. From the way Tacoma stood and embraced the man, giving him a peck on the lips, Khalil surmised that this was his partner. He didn't pay that much attention, figuring to each his own, but when the newcomer to the group also embraced Reka, kissing her as well, his blood began to boil.

Good breeding kept him still and quiet, but his eyes never left the man, not until the moment he was no longer touching Reka.

"Terry, this is Khalil Franklin. He's the new computer guy at work." Tacoma happily introduced the two men, holding tightly to the arm that Terry had extended to shake Khalil's hand.

Khalil stood, pasted a pleasant smile on his face and gripped the man's hand. "Good to meet you, Terry."

"Same here. I see they've already gotten you into their Friday night ritual." Terry nodded towards the bar. "No matter how hard I try, I can't convince these two that sitting at a bar talking about people isn't attractive."

Khalil relaxed, realizing with the way Terry gazed at Tacoma that this man was no threat to him. He had absolutely no interest in Reka; he only had eyes for Tacoma. "I don't know, we've been having a pretty good time. Wouldn't you say so, Reka?"

Dammit, she'd hoped with the new male arrival it would eliminate the need for him to talk to her at all. His closeness caused her body to betray her mind, although, if she had to be truly honest with herself, there was more than Khalil's quiet sexual allure that agitated her. "Oh yeah, we're having a jolly ole time." She signaled for another drink.

"Why don't you join us?" Khalil offered politely. In truth, he simply wanted to be alone with Reka. She'd bewitched him. In the span of about nine hours he'd met her, verbally sparred with her and, now, was totally entranced by her. But that would have to wait until another time. For right now, he was content just to be sitting beside her. While he waited for Terry to answer, he downed his drink. A quick vision of Reka in those thongs they were previously discussing had caused his throat to go dry.

Terry smiled graciously. "Maybe some other time. I've actually come to whisk Tacoma off to dinner plans that I just made. Maybe you two would like to join us?" he offered.

"Yeah, that's a great idea. C'mon and go to dinner with us," Tacoma insisted.

Khalil could eat, and as he always said, he never passed up a meal. But one glance at Reka told him she'd truly detest that idea. And since he was trying to get on her good side, he figured he'd earn brownie points by turning the offer down before her. "Nah, I think I'm just going to hang out here for a little while longer, then head home."

Reka was shocked. She'd absolutely expected him to think it was a good idea. Momentarily she was at a loss for words. But she quickly rebounded. "You know, I'm kind of tired. I think I'm just going to head home." The IT guy could sit here and drink by himself.

Tacoma passed Khalil a look, then said, "Okay, then I'll see you in the morning." He patted Reka on the shoulder and dug in his pocket to pay for his drinks.

Khalil held up a hand. "I'll take care of it," he told Tacoma. "Thanks for inviting me."

Tacoma smiled. "Anytime." His smile wilted a bit as Reka glanced at him. "Don't be late. I want to get to the stores early tomorrow. Do you need a wake up call?" he asked her, quickly changing the subject.

Reka frowned. "No, I don't need you to wake me up. I'll meet you at the subway station at ten."

"Cool. I'll see you at the office on Monday, Khalil."

Khalil nodded. "See you on Monday."

The men shook hands, and then Khalil and Reka were alone.

She drummed her fingers on the bar and decided she was making too much of this minor attraction to him. So what if he had a really good body and dressed really nice and smelled even better? Her own peace of mind was more important. Besides, she wasn't his type, she reminded herself.

"So why don't you have a hot date with your girlfriend tonight?" she asked casually.

Khalil folded his arms over his chest. "I thought you said when you wanted to know something you just asked." He valiantly kept the smile from his lips. She wouldn't like being mocked.

She caught his drift anyway and pursed her lips. "I am asking. I want to know why you're not out with your girlfriend instead of sitting at this bar with me." No, she wanted to know if he had a girlfriend, and if not, why. It was foolish, she knew, but she was curious about him. And she could get to know him without wanting to *really* know him.

"Touché." He nodded. "I don't have a girlfriend. And I kind of like sitting at this bar with you."

"Why?" she asked suspiciously.

Keep it light, he told himself. She was being civil to him again. He didn't want to mess that up. "Sitting next to a pretty woman always makes a man look good."

"Or like a sex-crazed fool, take your pick," she quipped.

He chuckled. "I asked you before if you liked me and you didn't answer."

"So?" She hadn't wanted to answer him then, and she definitely didn't want to answer him now. Would he know if she lied? Probably, since he looked at her as if he could see right through to her soul. That rattled her too.

He recognized avoidance, a common ploy when you really did like someone. Smiling, he asked, "So, do you like me?"

She took a sip of her drink. There wasn't enough vodka in her martini, she thought dismally, and put the glass down. "You'll do. If you can stop those messages I'll probably like you a lot more."

Because she'd mentioned the messages again, he wondered what really bothered her about them. Just about everyone else in the office that he'd talked to, with the exception of Cienna, took the emails as an ongoing joke and didn't attach much importance to them. Yet Reka seemed really bothered by them. "The emails seem to irk you a little more than they do the other employees." For the first time he wondered if she were the one sending them, and if this was her way of clearing her name ahead of time.

"I told you, the office is not the place to discuss sex."

He wholeheartedly agreed. But they weren't in the office now. And since they were two consenting adults, talking about sex wasn't a crime. Unless you weren't getting any sex. Then that could be touchy. He had no idea if she were having sex and berated himself for even thinking of her that way. She was so much more than just a beautiful body.

He was getting way ahead of himself and needed to pull back, to remember that his relationship with her for now was purely business. And while he had already decided he would be changing that status, it wouldn't be here and it wouldn't be tonight. "You're right. That's why I'm going to concentrate on finding this guy and putting a stop to this madness."

Grateful that they weren't going to discuss those emails in detail, Reka stood, grabbing her purse so she could pay for her drinks and leave.

"I'll pay for the drinks."

"Fine." She didn't feel like arguing that she could pay for her own drinks. She just wanted to leave. She began to walk away.

Khalil hurriedly threw some bills on the bar and went after her. Outside the night air was brisk. He pulled his jacket closer and watched as she attempted to hail a cab. He went to the curb, touched a hand to her elbow in an effort to pull her back. "Let me get that for you."

Reka rolled her eyes. "No, thanks. Paying for my drinks was all the chivalry I can stand for one night." But she wouldn't deny that his touch had inexplicably warmed her.

Khalil ignored her remark and hailed a cab, satisfied when the vehicle pulled up to the curb. He opened the back door and motioned for her to get in. "I'll see you home," he said as she was about to slide into the backseat.

"Don't bother. I'm young, but I'm old enough to see myself home," she spoke harshly.

Khalil again ignored her comments and not-so-gently pushed her inside before climbing in behind her. Before she could speak, he closed the door and tapped on the window for the driver to begin moving. "Give him your address," he instructed her.

Reka opened her mouth to protest, closed it, then rolled her eyes at him again. Reluctantly, she gave the driver her address. Otherwise they'd ride around the city for who knew how long and she desperately wanted, needed, to get away from this man.

Her sanity depended on it.

3

They traveled in silence.

Reka seethed at his audacity. He hadn't known her a full day and he was acting like her long-lost friend. She didn't need an escort home. She was capable of getting there on her own. And if he thought he was paying her cab fare, he had another thought coming.

Khalil couldn't help feeling the heated vibes coming across the back seat he shared with her. She absolutely did not want to be near him. Yet there were moments when he looked into her eyes and could swear he saw something else. She seemed totally resistant to any attempt he made at simply being friendly. If he told her that he had no intention of stopping at friendship, she'd run for her life. He knew that as surely as he knew his own name.

He'd already decided that as feisty and independent as she appeared on the outside, on the inside Reka was a frightened young lady, using her prior experiences with men to dictate her future.

Though he'd figured out her problem, he was still baffled as to how to get around it.

The cab slowed and then pulled up in front of a red brick duplex. He almost smiled when he realized she was only about two blocks away from his condo. He spied the meter and quickly retrieved the money from his wallet.

At the same time Reka pulled out a twenty and was about to extend it when she witnessed the driver taking his money. Immediately she thrust her money toward him. "Here, I can pay my own way home."

"Put your money away. I know you're employed and capable of paying for things yourself." Without waiting for a reply he took the handle and let himself out of the cab.

She closed her lips tightly. He was really beginning to irritate her. Who told him he had a right to simply pay for things on her behalf? She slid across the vinyl seat and stepped out into the night air, turning to face him instantly. "Look, I'm not a charity case," she began.

Khalil shut the door of the cab and waved the driver on before taking her by the elbow and leading her onto the sidewalk.

"Where's the cab going?" She looked unhappily at the cab proceeding down the street. "And why are you still here?"

Khalil put his hands in his pockets, quite amazed that such a small person could talk so much. "First things first," he began, watching her closely. "I know you're not a charity case, but I'm a gentleman. You had a few drinks. I was there, so I paid for them. I said I would see you home, so I paid for your cab fare. Now put your money away. All New Yorkers aren't as kind as I am."

Reka opened her mouth to speak, then quickly shut it again. Realizing that they were standing outside on a very public sidewalk, the odds of someone coming along and snatching the twenty dollar bill out of her hand were a tad on the high side, so she stuffed the money into her pocket. "Well, that doesn't explain—"

Khalil put two fingers to her lips. "Next, seeing you home means making sure you are safely in your house." He looked at the building they stood in front of. "Is this where you live?"

Reka started to speak, then realized his fingers—which were quite warm and tempted her to kiss them—were still firmly planted on her lips. All that escaped was a muffled sound. Giving him an angry look, she removed his fingers from her lips, cleared her throat and spoke. "Yes, I live here. And thank you for seeing me home, but I think I can manage walking up the steps and letting myself into the building."

For the first time tonight Khalil actually clenched his teeth in annoyance. Why was he even bothering? Finding a woman had never been a problem for him. To the contrary, between them, his mother and his sister had enough friends and sisters of friends to keep him occupied for years to come. But the thought of those other women paled in comparison to Reka. "I'll walk you in." He grabbed her elbow again and they took the steps.

"This really isn't necessary."

"I agree, you're acting like a child. It's a simple courtesy to see a woman home, and you're making it seem like I'm kidnapping you or something."

At the top of the steps she pulled away from him and turned so they were face to face. "I am not acting like a child!" Because he might not have believed her, she resisted stomping her foot. This man was making her crazy. "I just mean that taking me all the way to my door like we've just returned from a date isn't necessary."

He wanted to be angry with her; he wanted to tell her and her smart remarks to go to hell and walk the remaining blocks to his condo. But she stared up at him, those golden eyes shooting sparks his way, her shoulders squared in defense. And all anger fled. She was protecting herself, an instinct most likely as natural for her as breathing.

He took a deep breath and spoke calmly, "Open the door, Reka."

Was it the way he spoke with controlled authority? Or was it the look he was giving her? The one that made her want to smile, to relax and just be herself. She wasn't sure but her hands went to her purse and she found her key, turned and opened the door.

They walked up the flight of stairs leading to her first floor apartment, pausing in front of the next door. She turned to him, ready to say goodnight, but he was right behind her so that they were now toe to toe, his eyes pinning her against the door.

"Now, was that so difficult?" he asked when she remained quiet.

His closeness surrounded her until she had to fight to breathe. "No," she responded in a voice that sounded foreign to her own ears. "Look, I'm sorry if I've been rude." Her shoulders slumped as she'd attempted to right her wrong behavior. On the trip up the stairs she'd admitted to herself that he was only trying to be nice and she was repaying him with a totally bitchy attitude. All day and all night he'd only been polite and courteous to her. It was this strange attraction she was feeling that made her so irritable. But that wasn't his fault. He couldn't change how attractive he was, nor could he change the reasons she shouldn't want him to touch her. None of what she was feeling was his fault, and she needed to stop blaming him.

"You don't have to apologize. Let's just chalk it up to a rough day at the office and leave it at that." He offered a smile in exchange for the apology he could see was hard for her to give. "Go ahead and open the door so I can be assured you're safe. That's all."

She gave him a tentative smile back. He really was being too nice to her. Had she been in his shoes she would have certainly cursed herself out about three hours ago. Instead, he stood waiting patiently for her to go into her apartment before he would leave her.

How many dates had dropped her off at the curb after securing her half of the cab fare? Too many to count.

Putting her key into the door, she pushed it open and was about to turn and say goodnight when a loud crash came from inside the apartment. She stilled.

From behind Khalil asked, "You have company?"

She turned to him, then back to try to see into the dark living room of her apartment. "No, I shouldn't have. I live alone." She'd begun to whisper, her heart beating faster at the thought that there was, in fact, someone in her house.

Khalil grabbed her by the arm and pulled her to the side. "Wait here, I'll check it out."

There was that quiet command in his voice again. She wasn't sure but she didn't think she liked it. This was her house. If anybody was going to go in and check things out it would be her. "Oh no, this is my place. If somebody's in there stealing my stuff, I want to be the one to bust his head!" Instinctively she moved to the umbrella stand by the door and lifted her souvenir Yankees bat into her hand.

Was she out of her mind? Did she have any idea how dangerous it was to walk up on a burglar? Especially in New York? The bulb from the hallway provided enough light so that he could still faintly see her as she headed towards the kitchen. In one stride he was beside her. With an arm around her waist, he turned her so that she was again behind him and he proceeded towards the kitchen, blocking her as she continued to try to get in front. At the doorway they both slowed, leaned over and peeked inside.

Khalil was confused.

Reka was relieved. "Grammy?"

The refrigerator door was ajar, a very plump, flower-clad posterior protruding from its center. Humming echoed through the small kitchen, and Khalil struggled to hold a smile at bay. At the sound of Reka's voice, he straightened and allowed her passage.

"Grammy? Is that you?"

The humming stopped abruptly and the flowered bottom turned to face them. The cherubic face was red at the cheeks, probably from her prolonged visit inside the refrigerator. In one hand full of rings she held a platter of lunch meat. Stuffed under the other arm was a box of saltine crackers.

"There you are. I was calling for you but you didn't answer. Do you have any jelly?" the woman, who looked to be in her seventies, asked.

Reka let her bat slide to the floor as she closed the distance between them. "Grammy, what are you doing here? How did you get here?"

Reka couldn't believe her eyes. What was her eighty-year-old grandmother doing in her kitchen at eight o'clock at night when she lived in a retirement center all the way across town?

"I took a cab. How do you think I got here? Now come over here and find the jelly. I don't know why you and your mother insist on keeping it in the refrigerator anyhow. It belongs in the pantry."

Reka moved to the refrigerator, retrieved the jelly and closed the door. Grammy had already moved her round body to the counter, where she deposited the other items and began to make herself a cracker sandwich. Again Reka said, "Grammy, I don't understand what you're doing here."

Slapping a piece of bologna onto her cracker, then opening the jar of jelly, Grammy took a deep breath, then turned to face her grand-daughter. "Gal, don't keep asking me foolish questions. I'm here, ain't

I? I told you I took a cab. Now if you want to make yourself helpful, put on a pot of water for some tea. I'm hungry."

Khalil had gone to shut the front door. Now that it appeared Reka wasn't in any danger he figured he should probably leave. But something told him all was not right with this picture. She'd said she lived alone, yet there was an elderly woman scouring through her refrigerator. He found himself walking back towards the kitchen to check on them.

Reka had almost forgotten about him until she'd put the water on to boil and turned to see him standing in the doorway.

"Um, this is my grandmother," she'd begun to explain when Grammy stopped fixing her snack and pushed her to the side to stand in front of Khalil with her hand extended.

"I'm Estelle Grant, and you are a very handsome young man."

Reka rolled her eyes skyward, praying her grandmother would not continue to embarrass her. Why hadn't Khalil just left when he realized it wasn't a burglar in her kitchen? This man was just too chivalrous for her.

Khalil smiled at the warmth in the woman's eyes, eyes like Reka's. He took her hand and shook it lightly. "Thank you, ma'am. I'm Khalil Franklin. I work with Reka."

Estelle held on to his hand. "Reka. Isn't that a pretty name?" she asked, then looked down at his hands. "And you have nice big hands. You know what that means," she said, casting a satisfied smile over her shoulder to Reka.

Over Estelle's head Khalil found Reka's gaze and admitted seriously, "Yes, ma'am, it sure is a pretty name."

Reka shifted uncomfortably beneath his gaze. "Grammy, Khalil was just dropping me off. He needs to get home." He needs to get away from me, and he definitely needs to get away from Grammy and her wandering eyes, she thought to herself.

This was the first time he'd heard her say his name. He liked how it sounded on her lips.

"Nonsense. You're being rude. At least offer your date a nightcap."

"He's not my—" she started to say.

"It is rather chilly outside. A cup of tea would be nice." Khalil had instantly liked Mrs. Grant. Her open smile and twinkling eyes gave him the impression that she, too, would be a good ally. With one glance at Reka's glare, he knew he was going to need all the allies he could get to win her over.

Grammy and Khalil had long since moved into the living room, where he'd so helpfully started a fire. Now they sat on the couch, talking and laughing like long lost friends, while she stood in the kitchen looking through the small opening in the wall at them.

She'd called her mother and, together, they'd discovered that Grammy had left Sunny Days Retirement Center early this morning and hadn't returned. Reka had no idea how long her grandmother had been in her apartment, nor did she have a clue as to how she got in. Her mother had said to let her stay for the night, that she'd be there first thing in the morning to take her back.

Reka sighed. She'd seen Grammy slip a brown paper bag from the pocket of her mutli-colored housecoat and pour something into her tea. No doubt it was whiskey. Grammy loved her VO.

"So where'd you take my granddaughter this evening? And why are you back so early? In my day, my beaus didn't bring me home a minute before curfew." Grammy crossed her legs at the ankles and folded her arms, rocking back against the big pillows on Reka's couch.

"Actually, I didn't take her anywhere. We were at a bar for happy hour with another co-worker. I just met her today."

"Oh. Well, you plan on taking her someplace special, right? Because my grandbaby deserves the best."

Khalil smiled, wholeheartedly agreeing with her. "Yes ma'am, she does deserve the best."

With that statement Reka made her way into the room. It was definitely time for him to go now. "Grammy, it's time for you to be heading off to bed." She walked closer to the couch, aware that Khalil was staring at her as she moved.

She'd taken her shoes off but still wore her stockings. Her scarf was gone, long since thrown into her purse, and the top three buttons of her blouse were undone so that she was now showing a considerable amount of cleavage. But she was tired and mentally exhausted. Fighting with her conscience all day over whether or not she should be feeling what she was feeling for this man had been an exhausting battle. Now all she wanted to do was climb into her bed and fall into a deep sleep, hopefully free from thoughts of Khalil.

"I ain't ready for bed. It's still early," Grammy protested.

Khalil stood, noting how Reka's steps had begun to drag. She was tired; it was written all over her face. He'd have to spend time with her lively grandmother another evening. "Mrs. Grant, I really must be going."

Grammy hustled to her feet. "Nonsense, you stay here and get to know my grandbaby better. I'm going to go on in the other room and watch some cable. You know they don't have cable at that damn psych ward her mother put me in." Grammy had already begun walking towards the curving stairs that would lead to Reka's loft bedroom.

Reka groaned. "No HBO and no Cinemax After Dark, Grammy."

Grammy waved her hand but didn't turn back. "Chile, I'm old enough to show them people a thing or two," she chuckled. "You come back and visit me, handsome."

Khalil was flattered, even though he'd told Mrs. Grant his name more than five times since he'd met her. "Yes, ma'am, I sure will."

Reka raised a brow in his direction and he shrugged helplessly.

"These steps are enough to make a person woozy," Grammy complained as she finally made it to the top and disappeared.

"Either that or all the whiskey you put in your tea," Reka said almost to herself as she removed her grandmother's teacup from the coffee table.

"You saw that, huh?" Khalil picked up his cup and followed her to the kitchen.

Reka laughed as she padded across the kitchen floor to the sink. "Yeah, but she does it all the time, so it's to be expected."

Khalil put his cup down in the sink and took a step away from her. Closeness was not good right now. He'd gotten a glimpse of the bronze-colored skin leading to her breasts and wasn't sure he could keep his hands to himself if he stood too close. "So she lives in a psych ward?" he joked.

Reka took down a glass from the cabinet and poured herself some water. She hadn't eaten yet, and those martinis had begun to rumble around in her empty stomach. She thought maybe water would help until she had a chance to eat something. "Sunny Days Retirement Center. Which is a far cry from a psych ward. Besides, the psych ward's free; Sunny Days definitely is not."

"She doesn't like it there, I take it." He watched as she took slow, steady sips of the water, holding the glass with one hand and massaging her neck with the other. A few of her curls had fallen loose and now brushed her shoulders. Her hair shone beneath the light and framed her face softly. He realized he liked looking at her, just watching her move, doing normal things. He didn't think he'd ever noticed that about a person before.

"Grammy doesn't like being told what to do."

"So that's where you get it from?"

Reka stopped rubbing her neck and stared at him. She couldn't deny the obvious. "I guess so."

He laughed. "I'm glad you didn't try to argue that observation with me."

She shrugged. "What would be the point? It's true." She emptied her glass and set it in the sink, then turned back to stare at him pointedly.

"What?" Something was going through her mind. She had a question, he could tell. "What are you thinking?"

"I'm still trying to figure out why you don't have a girlfriend."

His insides warmed. So she'd been thinking of his single status. That was a good sign. He leaned against the counter top, pushing his jacket aside to slide his hands into his pockets. "I haven't found the right woman yet. Is that so hard to believe?"

"That's a reason for not having a wife. A girlfriend doesn't necessarily have to be the *right* woman. She can just be a stepping stone on your way to Ms. Right."

"I'd rather not waste time with stepping stones. When I find a woman I like enough to spend my time with, I'll be looking at her as though she is Ms. Right." And there was a very real possibility that Ms. Right was staring directly at him.

She shrugged. "I guess that's a good way to approach it." She moved to leave the kitchen. It was too close in here, and the way he watched her was doing weird things to her already raging hormones.

Reaching his arm out in a quick, smooth motion, he stopped her retreat, holding her still in front of him. "What about you? Are you looking for a stepping stone to a husband?" He knew her answer even before she said it. But in order for him to get around her defenses he had to know why they were there in the first place. And up to this point she hadn't actually said why she was so against men. He'd only guessed at the reason.

At his touch she gasped and tried to back away.

"Come here." He pulled her closer, keeping their bodies from touching, other than his hands around her waist. "Tell me why you're so angry with men."

"What gives you the idea that I'm angry with men?"

"For starters, the comparison to dogs chasing their own tails." He grinned.

Reluctantly, she grinned back. "I'm not angry."

He arched an eyebrow, letting her know he didn't believe her.

"I'm not," she insisted. "I'm simply fed up."

Now they were getting to the root of the problem. He pulled her an inch closer, lifted a hand to finger one of those springy auburn curls. "Fed up with what? How men act in general?" He toyed with her hair until his hand was close enough to touch the soft skin of her neck. "Or how they treat you specifically?"

She frowned. Her full lips curved downward, but were no less attractive to him. She had kissable lips. Lips that a man dreamed about being all over him.

"I'm not a scorned woman or a whiner. I've just had my share of lies, games and drama, enough to last a lifetime. I'm really in no hurry to go through it again."

"Lies, games and drama shouldn't be part of a mature relationship."

"No, they shouldn't." She tried to ignore the pleasure spikes soaring through her upper body with his touch. "But, more often than not, they are."

"You said you didn't have time to wait for boys to grow into men."

"That's right." She tried to keep her eyes on him, to prove that he wasn't getting to her, but her lids felt drugged with each stroke of his finger and she wanted nothing more than to close her eyes to the comfort he offered.

"Then stop getting involved with boys," he said simply.

"And who would you suggest I get involved with?" She knew what he would say, wanted desperately to hear the words, although she knew nothing could come of them.

Khalil pulled her closer, until the tips of her breasts brushed against his chest. "I'm not a boy, Reka. I learned a long time ago how to treat a woman right." He watched the play of emotions on her face, tried desperately to anticipate her response, but was so caught up in his own body's response to her that he couldn't think straight.

For a moment she allowed herself to believe him, to believe that he could be different, but then memories of Donovan and the all-out route he'd taken to deceive her kept her strong. She straightened her back, moved her head so his hand was no longer touching her, and stared him straight in the eye. "That's what they all say."

Despite knowing her objections, knowing who he was dealing with, her words took him aback, and he stared blankly at her. He should simply walk away. He should leave this apartment and not give her another thought, since it appeared she was determined to not give another man a chance. But he wanted to prove her wrong. He wanted to show her what a real relationship was like, what it felt like to be loved by a real man. And at that moment he had no doubt that he could fall in love with this woman.

But he had to take it slow. He suspected that it had taken years to build this wall of resistance around her heart, and as good a man as he considered himself, he wasn't going to be able to knock it down in one day. With that in mind, he took his hands off her and moved toward the entrance of the living room. "I'm not like the others. Try to remember that," he said before turning and walking to the front door. He was going to leave, not because she wanted him to, but because it was the last thing she expected him to do. She thought she knew every-thing men did and said. He was going to prove her wrong.

She'd thought he'd argue with her a little more, try to convince her why he was different, like any other guy would. But he was moving so quickly towards the front door that she had no other choice but to follow him. "I didn't say you were. I was just explaining why I don't believe what most men tell me," she said when he opened the door and stepped into the hallway.

He wasn't going to repeat that he wasn't like most men. She'd heard him clearly; she just hadn't taken the time to digest that fact. "I'd like to take you to dinner." His eyes dropped momentarily to her lips before returning to her captivating eyes. Man, was there anything about this woman that didn't turn him on?

"No."

"Why?"

Reka acted as if she were thinking for a minute when, truth be told, she'd spent all day long coming up with a list of reasons why she couldn't get involved with him, why she was not his type. The most prominent came to mind and she decided to let that be her main reason. "Let me see, how I can say this nicely?" She tapped a finger to her chin. "I'm too young for you. Yeah, that's it. I wouldn't want you to catch a charge."

She was so damned pretty, he admitted to himself for the billionth time today. That beauty mark just beneath her bottom lip practically begged to be kissed. He smiled, and with a light touch, traced her bottom lip. "I'll pick you up at seven tomorrow night. And don't worry, I work for lawyers."

4

The ball bounced to the ground a few inches away from Khalil's feet.

"You plan on playing ball today or what?" Keith moved past the seemingly dazed guy who was supposed to be his opponent.

"What?" Khalil turned to see Keith retrieving the ball before it rolled off the court and into the street. "Sorry, man. I wasn't paying attention."

"Tell me about it. You haven't been paying attention for the last twenty minutes." Keith came to a stop beside Khalil, tossing the ball at him unexpectedly. "Something going on you wanna talk about?"

Reflexively Khalil caught the ball, palmed it in both hands and held it in front of him. He didn't really want to talk about it. Actually, he felt kind of embarrassed to have thought about it all night and most of the morning. He was a grown man, experienced with women and relationships. There was no reason why this one angry little woman should be affecting him like this. "Nah, it's nothing." He jogged down the court, dribbling.

Keith shrugged and jogged along with him. Something was on Khalil's mind, he could tell. And if he wasn't mistaken, it was most likely a woman. He shook his head as Khalil missed another lay-up. Only a woman could get inside a man's head like that.

Khalil bounced the ball with a fierceness that gave away more of his worries than he knew. Keith watched him, knowing he'd miss this shot as well. He'd miss every shot until he got what was bothering him off his chest.

Khalil shot the ball. It hit the backboard and bounced over the hoop, falling to the ground with a dismal thump.

"Whoever said height was all you needed to play ball didn't know squat," Keith said with a chuckle. "I'm sitting down. If you're not going to play real ball there's no sense in me running up and down this court with you while you make a fool of yourself."

Khalil grabbed the ball again. That's exactly what he was afraid of doing—making a fool of himself over this woman. He'd invited her to dinner, no, he'd told her they were going to dinner, not really leaving her a choice in the matter. And for that alone he knew he'd have to hear a mouthful from her. That thought, strangely enough, intrigued him.

She did talk a lot, and all of what she said was delivered with such attitude and such brashness that the normal person would be in a hurry to get away from her. But he wanted to be near her—for long periods of time.

"Once you sleep with her you'll feel a lot better."

Keith's words snapped him out of his Reka moment and Khalil took the remaining steps that led him to the bench where Keith sat. "What?"

Keith took a swig from the water jug Cienna had packed in his gym bag. "The woman that's got you all tied up. Once you sleep with her, you'll feel a lot better. That's how it is when you meet a new woman and haven't tasted the fruit yet." Leaning forward, his elbows resting on his thighs, Keith bounced the basketball.

"How would you know? You're married." Maybe talking about it would shed some light on the situation, maybe explain why of all the women in the world, all the women he'd been with, none of them had given him a sleepless night like Reka had.

"I wasn't always married. I know how it feels when you first meet a lady and can't wait to have her under you."

Khalil leaned back against the gate. "Was that how it was with you and Cienna?"

"Of course. But as soon as I got her, I knew she wasn't going anywhere, so I could just sit back and relax." Keith also leaned back.

"Yeah right, I seem to remember her leaving you and you burning up I-95 in search of her."

Keith waved a hand. "Whatever. So who's this lady that's got you so frazzled?"

"I'm not frazzled," Khalil defended.

"No? You're playin' ball like a blind senior citizen. That's frazzled to me."

They both laughed.

"You know, I started working at your firm yesterday—"

"I was going to ask you how that went."

Khalil dragged a hand down his sweaty face. "It wasn't what I expected, I can tell you that."

"Really? What happened? Did more emails come in?"

"A couple, but they weren't the problem."

Keith sat up, turning his head to look at Khalil. "Then stop beating around the bush and tell me what the problem is."

Khalil took a deep breath. "That's where I met her. She works for you."

Keith's eyebrows raised in question. "You've got the hots for somebody at my firm? What, did those emails get to you too? Now you're all horny like that dude Jack?" Keith grinned.

"Nah, it's not like that. She's not like that." He shook his head, still trying to get a grasp on it himself. "She's different from any woman I've ever met. She's like a breath of fresh air from all those snooty women my mom and Danielle try to hook me up with. And she's definitely different from Sonya."

"She's all that, huh?" Khalil was silent. "Well, tell me who she is. Maybe I can put in a good word for you."

Khalil doubted a good word was going to do anything where Reka was concerned, but figured maybe Keith could offer some insight, some advice that would tell him how to handle her. "She's Cienna's assistant, Reka."

Keith stood and looked down at his friend, not believing what he'd just said. "Reka? You're missing shots and looking crazy over Reka?"

Khalil couldn't tell by Keith's reaction if that was a good or bad thing. "I'm just saying that I met her and I like her. That's all," he reiterated.

Keith's head fell back as he laughed.

Khalil was offended. "When you said you were chasing a co-worker around the office I didn't laugh at you, no matter how juvenile I thought it was."

His laughter slowly subsiding, Keith sank back down on the bench. "You're right. You're right," he said, letting the last few chuckles release themselves. "I'm just laughing because if I had to pick the perfect woman for you I couldn't have done a better job. If anybody is perfect for your uptight, geeky, wanna-be-ballplayer butt, it's Reka Boyd."

"And what's that supposed to mean?" Normally Khalil tolerated the light banter from friends, but this time Keith's words seemed to strike a nerve.

"Don't get all serious on me. I'm only pointing out the obvious differences between you two. You're more mature, more focused, more studious than Reka is. Reka's…she's…how do I say it?"

"She's what?" Khalil knew his brow was furrowed, knew that his normally quiet brown eyes were darkening with anger.

Keith ignored his expression and proceeded. "She's spunky and spontaneous and in-your-face honest. Can you handle that?"

"Come on, Keith, you know me. I can handle anything. She's just a woman." Even to him that sounded wrong. Already to him she was more than just a woman.

"Then if you think that you shouldn't even waste your time with her," Keith said seriously.

"Why do you say that?"

"Look, Reka's been through a lot. She and Cienna are pretty close, so I get to hear about some of the situations she's been in. She's had it rough where men are concerned."

More about Reka and bad relationships. How bad could they really have been? "I get the impression that she's had a nasty experience. She's a little bitter, but you can't base the future on the past."

"You can if your past just keeps repeating itself. I won't tell her business but I'll say this. She's had some guys do some pretty bad stuff to her, and if you're planning on hittin' and runnin', I'm gonna have to tell you to leave her alone. She can't take that right now, and I don't want to see her hurt." Not only that, if Cienna found out Khalil had hurt Reka she'd kill him herself. Keith thought it was best to forewarn him.

"I stopped with the drive-bys a long time ago." And he knew without a doubt he wanted more than that from Reka. "I know she's different from what I'm used to. I think that's what attracts me to her the most. She doesn't have an ulterior motive. I know that if she were only out for my money she'd tell me that and still expect me to give it to her."

Keith chuckled. "Yeah, and if you didn't give it to her she'd probably take it from you. And she's not like Sonya or those other women you've dated. She's not from that crowd, if you know what I mean."

Khalil nodded. "I know what you mean, but that doesn't matter to me. I just like her. I got to spend some time with her last night and I think we'd be good together. I'm not the same when I'm with her."

"Can you play ball around her? Because you sure as hell can't now," Keith joked.

"Shut up, man. I mean, I feel different around her. Usually I'm thinking about the business, work, my family. But last night all I could think about was her and what I could do to make her happy."

Keith evaluated the forlorn look on his friend's face and shook his head again. He had it bad. "I'm just saying to be careful. Reka's not in the mood for men right now. I know because every time we're together she tells me how fed up she is. If you think you can change that, then by all means give it a try. But understand that it may not be an easy job."

Khalil heard him and appreciated the heads up. "My entire life's been easy. I was born with the proverbial silver spoon in my mouth, went to the best schools my father's money could buy, wore the best clothes, drove the best cars and even dated the best girls. I'm thinking that I'm kind of tired of that type of perfection. I want something more, something substantial. I want Reka."

"Here, this is great. You can wear it to dinner tonight." Tacoma shoved the silky black slip dress into Reka's hands.

Reka held the dress up, surveyed it a moment, decided she liked it, then decided she had nowhere to wear it and hung it back on the rack. "I am not going to dinner tonight. I told you I told him no."

Tacoma grinned as Reka turned her back and headed towards the men's section. Quickly and discreetly he pulled the sexy black number from the rack and tossed it over his arm. He had to take a few lengthy steps to catch up with her, but as soon as he did he brought the subject up again. "You also said he didn't take no for your answer. Which means he believes you're going to dinner."

"I don't care what he believes." *Yeah, right.* She'd been steadily trying to convince herself of that fact since last night. Too bad she'd been unsuccessful, else this shopping spree would have been much more enjoyable. As it was, for the last three hours she and Tacoma had been in and out of stores purchasing everything from tulle for the wedding favors, to gorgeous navy slacks and matching silk shirts for Tacoma and Terry to change into after the reception. All the while the conversation had stayed firmly on Khalil Franklin and his proposal.

"Oh, get over yourself," Tacoma sighed with a bored expression. "It's a free meal. He didn't ask you to marry him, for Pete's sake."

"I'm usually interested in the men I share meals with."

Tacoma was headed for the checkout counter. He was meeting Terry at four and didn't want to be late. "I know, the thugs, street pharmacists and wanna-be rappers really capture the imagination. But now it's time to grow up, expand your horizons. Khalil seems like a good guy."

Ignoring his jab at her ex-boyfriends' occupations, Reka frowned. "They all seem like good guys in the beginning."

Tacoma passed the black dress to the cashier and noticed that Reka was staring off into space, so he motioned for the woman to put the dress into a separate bag and took Reka's hand as a further distraction. "What are you really afraid of? That he'll turn out to be a dog and break your heart, or that he'll be so fantastic you'll find yourself opening your heart to him instead?"

Because she didn't know the answer to that question, she remained silent.

An hour and a half later, as she soaked in her bathtub, she still hadn't figured it out.

Without a doubt she knew that Khalil scared her. That was enough to piss her off—fear was not an emotion she was used to feeling.

But what scared her most was not knowing whether he was a good guy, a tall, extremely handsome, well-dressed, chivalrous good guy or, more likely, just some stuffy computer guy looking for entertainment with a young hottie.

She chuckled then. Was she a young hottie?

Still, he seemed almost too educated, too polished for her tastes.

Reka heard the knob jiggle just before the door was thrust open by a woman dressed in a floral creation with a hideous black background and another woman only a few inches taller and wearing too-tight jeans, red boots and a red leather jacket.

"You been in here forever," the lady in red chirped.

"Just like when you was a baby, didn't wanna come out 'til you was wrinkled as a prune."

That was Grammy, her words making Reka look down at her fingertips—yup, wrinkled. She frowned. "Could I have some privacy?" she said indignantly.

The lady in red, aka Janell Boyd, made her way completely into the bathroom and stood in front of the mirror lifting her hands to her hair. "Chile please, we all have the same thing."

Grammy plopped down onto the closed toilet seat, a weathered hand going to her bosom. "Yeah, but gravity's taken hold of mine."

Reka rolled her eyes and groaned. She closed her eyes, knowing the women would still be there when she finished, and stood to grab a towel.

"Grammy's going to stay with you for a while," Janell said as she followed Reka out of the bathroom.

"What?" Reka's wet feet slapped against the hardwood floors. "Why?"

Janell took off her jacket to reveal a skintight red t-shirt. "She had a little disagreement with some of the women at Sunny Days, so she needs some coolin' off time."

"Why can't she cool off at your place?" Reka whined.

"Because I'm barely there."

Reka fell with her back flat on her bed, the towel secured around her breasts. "I work too, Mama."

"Yeah, but you don't do anything but work lately. So I figured Grammy would keep you company."

"I want that handsome friend of hers to keep me company." Grammy said once she entered the room and took a seat on the opposite side of the bed.

"What handsome friend?" Janell immediately looked down at Reka, who was now groaning loudly.

She should have known that while Grammy was known to forget to wear panties she would remember meeting Khalil Franklin, only because her granddaughter wished to forget him.

"He's not a friend, he's a co-worker," Reka supplied, praying she wouldn't have to go any further, but soon realizing her prayers were rarely answered.

"They went on a date last night and then came back here for a nightcap." Grammy was going through her purse, in search of what, nobody knew for sure since she never seemed to find it.

"We did not go on a date," Reka said adamantly, then threw her hands in the air in defeat. Grammy was going to say and think exactly what Grammy wanted, and nothing Reka said was going to change that.

Janell fell on the bed beside her daughter. "You seein' somebody new? He works with you, huh? Well, you know, working with somebody *and* sleeping with him can be a pretty dangerous game." Janell put a hand to her neck. "I remember this guy, Todd. We worked together at J.C. Penney years ago. He had the biggest hands and man, oh man," Janell shivered, "in that storeroom after hours, he sure knew what to do with them."

"Mama," Reka scolded. She was used to Janell's graphic depiction of her relations with men, but she didn't think it was appropriate in front of her grandmother. Janell, however, didn't seem to care.

"But there was this other chick, Nellie. She worked in men's shoes, and she thought she was 'it,' so as soon as she found out about me and Todd, she started blabbing. Then my supervisor started questioning why I always wanted to work the closing shift. And wouldn't you know it, one day when me and Todd was in that storeroom—and I mean Todd was hittin' it somethin' good—that old battleaxe came waltzing in, screaming and bustling about like she was about to have a damned heart attack, and both of us got fired." Janell's head was tilted back as she reminisced.

Grammy tsked and shook her head, her big sponge roller curls bobbing at her ears. "If I told you once, I know I've told you a thousand times, if a man can't afford to take you to a moe-tel, he ain't worth the time it'll take you to open your legs."

Reka dropped an arm over her eyes. Her family was nuts. No wonder she didn't have any luck with men. She sat up. "Look, Khalil is just a co-worker. We're working on a project together. That's all," she said emphatically. So emphatically that two pair of eyes widened and searched her face intently.

The telephone rang. The two older women didn't move, just kept looking at Reka as if she were about to reveal the secret to nuclear fusion. Muttering a few choice words, wisely under her breath, Reka scooted off the bed and picked the phone up from the nightstand. "Hello?"

"Hello, Reka. I was just thinking about you and wondering if you were getting ready for our date."

We don't have a date, her mind screamed. But to do so verbally would most certainly amuse the two instigators in the room, who no doubt had their ears perked up. How was she going to convince them that Khalil was just a friend if he insisted on this so-called date? She gripped the phone tightly. "I just got out of the tub, and I'm trying to take a nap. Tacoma and I were out all morning."

Khalil tried not to feel the slight edge of jealousy—she'd spent all morning with Tacoma, while he'd spent all morning thinking of her. "Well, I said seven, and you have another hour, so go ahead and lie down for a bit." He paused, trying like hell not to say he was on his way. "But I'll be there promptly at seven." He knew she'd try to give him another excuse, so he hung up before she had a chance.

Setting the phone down in its cradle, he figured that was two things he'd catch hell for tonight. Closing his eyes, he let the sound of her voice replay in his mind. It wasn't so much what she said as the way she said it, with determination and attitude. He smiled. Man, he really liked her style. Her candor and her stubbornness. Well, he could forego the stubborn streak, but then that would be changing a part of her. And there was nothing about Reka that he felt needed changing.

He took that back. Her ideas about men needed changing, and he was just the man to make that happen.

Reka slammed the phone down. He had a lot of nerve telling her what she was going to do and how long she had to do it. She was about to release a few choice expletives when she turned and bumped right into Grammy.

"Was that him? Was that Mr. Handsome?"

Reka rolled her eyes. Her choices for this Saturday evening were to stay in this apartment with the two love connectors picking at her to find out about her relationship with a man she didn't have a relationship with, or go to dinner with a man she wasn't quite sure she could trust.

"Hmph, he must be a doozy if he's got you all worked up with a simple phone call," Janell added, standing to touch Reka's cheek. "Look, Grammy, she's blushing."

"I am not!" Reka pulled away from them, going to the side of the bed to pick up the bags from today's shopping spree as a diversion. "I told you he was just a co-worker."

"Mm-hmm." Janell folded her arms over her chest and continued to stare.

Reka dumped the contents of the bags onto the bed and gasped when the silky black material slid out. With two fingers, as if it were a piece of burning wood, she lifted the dress.

"Hot damn! Old co-worker's gonna score tonight!" Janell whooped.

"I know that's right," Grammy added with her own denture-filled grin.

Reka groaned again. "I'm going to kill Tacoma!"

5

At seven o'clock on the dot, Khalil raised his hand and knocked on Reka's door. Within seconds it swung open, and a slim, hippy woman smiled up at him from the other side.

"You must be the co-worker, Mr. Handsome."

She extended her hand, lifting it palm downward to signal him to kiss it. Khalil chuckled a bit to himself, took the offered hand and performed the desired deed. "I'm Khalil Franklin. And you are?"

Amazed and impressed, Janell lowered her hand slowly to her side. "I'm Janell Boyd, Reka's mother."

Damn, Khalil thought to himself, if all mothers looked like this, young boys would have a hell of a time deciding which woman to date. Luckily for him, his interest had already been piqued and, even though Janell had a pretty tight body and didn't look a day over thirty-five with her stylish hair and impeccably made-up face, there was only one woman for him.

Entering the familiar living room he spotted Grammy and went to the sofa to give her a hug. "Hi, Grammy. It's good to see you again." He liked the older woman, but wondered why she hadn't returned to the retirement home.

Grammy embraced the young man, enjoying the sexy smell of his cologne. "Hey, handsome, you smell good tonight. Where are you taking my grandbaby? You're all dressed up, too. That's a fine suit you got on." Grammy surveyed him.

Khalil felt a bit uncomfortable as Janell closed the door and began to examine him. He was being appraised, and he wondered if their approval would work to his favor with Reka. He smoothed down his tie and smiled lightly. "I've made reservations at Roth's."

Janell whistled. "That's a pretty nice spot. I've been there once. Reka likes steak, good choice." She winked at Khalil before taking a seat at the other end of the couch.

"Have a seat, handsome, and tell us about yourself while you wait for my grandbaby." Grammy motioned to the single chair that matched the couch.

Khalil did as he was told, faintly amused by these two women. He could see where Reka got her build and her catlike eyes. A pair exactly like hers was staring him down something terrible right this moment. He wasn't nervous, though, didn't feel an ounce of wariness. These women looked at him appreciatively, and he was used to that from women, almost expected it half the time. Yet when he'd met Reka, her look had been something totally different. "What do you want to know?" he asked, letting his palms fall flat on his thighs.

"Where do you live?" Janell asked first.

"I have a condo at The Zachary."

"That's not far from here," Janell noted.

"No ma'am, it's not."

"How old are you?" Grammy queried.

"I just turned thirty-five."

"Mmmm, an older man. You know Reka's only twenty-eight. Does the age difference bother you?"

He thought for a moment; he hadn't really considered it except for the comments Reka had made the night before. "No, I don't think the age difference is a problem."

"Uh huh, so what are your intentions towards my daughter?"

Reka cleared her throat even as her pumps clicked across the floor. She should have known not to leave him too long with them. "Dinner is the intention," she said to Janell. Then turning to Khalil, she said, enunciating very carefully, "And that's it."

Khalil stood, her words falling on deaf ears as his eyes lingered over her body. The black dress she wore hugged all the right places, emphasizing all the pleasurable spots and leaving her arms and neck bare so that her smooth skin tantalized him even more. The auburn curls that had been swept up the night before now hung down past her shoulders, held back at both sides with diamondlike pins that made her eyes sparkle even more. She wore light makeup, a silver dusting over her eyes, an almond glaze on her lips. Her legs were clad in sheer black nylon, and the straps of come-and-get-me pumps twined around her small ankles.

He swallowed—hard—tried to find his voice and took a step towards her. "You are stunning." That was an understatement but the curve of her lips, the twinkle in those once leery eyes, said it was just enough.

Beneath his intense gaze Reka felt her heart thud a rhythm that sounded strangely like the Ludacris song that had just been playing on the radio in her room. She'd taken a good look at him as he stood statue still in front of her. The black suit, crisp white shirt and ice blue tie looked almost regal on him. His shoulders seemed broader, if that were possible, since yesterday, his thighs, thick and muscled. Usually a beard and mustache thoroughly turned her off, but Khalil's was neat, thin and a bit sexier than she was ready to admit.

"Thank you," she said without the terseness she'd intended. "I'll get my coat and we can leave."

She moved to the closet with Khalil admiring the way the thin fabric of her dress molded over her backside, wishing he were the dark material himself.

"Dessert comes after the main course," Janell muttered from behind.

He'd forgotten the other two women in the room, so she startled him a bit, though he didn't show it. "It was very nice meeting you, Mrs. Boyd," he said as he turned to face the two women—the Mod Squad, he'd dubbed them. "Take care, Grammy." He nodded, then moved to the closet, taking Reka's coat from her hands and holding it while she slipped her arms inside.

Reka tried to squelch the fuzzy sensation rippling through her. He was a gentleman, she'd already given him that much, so his actions should not keep inciting school-girl feelings.

They left the apartment without another word, walked down the steps and out into the chilly night air, still in silence.

"Should we hail a cab?" she asked when they both stopped at the bottom of the stoop.

Khalil had been focused on the intense heat between them as they walked so closely together, so her words startled him for a second. "No, I drove my car this time." With a hand to the small of her back he led her to the curb.

Reka didn't whistle, as she normally would have, nor did she seem overly impressed with the shiny silver Jaguar parked in front of her building. But truth be told, she was bowled over by the luxurious car and was positive it had been paid for with honest money. So as she slipped into the leather passenger seat, her heart didn't thump with the fear of being arrested. Instead it beat steadily with excitement about what tonight might bring.

Khalil closed the door when she'd settled in the seat and fastened her seatbelt. He walked around the car with extra pep in his step, opened the driver's side door, and climbed in. Sensing she was still a little uncomfortable, he took her hand, rubbing his thumbs over the smooth skin. "Just relax, Reka. I promise you a wonderful evening."

In the darkness of the car, his eyes seemed more the color of coal, yet they caressed her with a warmth she'd never felt before. In that moment she could swear that all her reservations about trusting this man were bogus. More than anything she wanted to believe in him, believe that he really wanted to be with her, that he was really attracted to her and for tonight—just for tonight, she promised herself—she would allow herself to trust and to accept.

She offered him a smile. "If you promise it will be wonderful, then I'm sure it will be."

A half hour later they were seated in leather-skirted chairs, perusing the menu while a jazz trio serenaded the room. Reka was suddenly glad she'd worn the new black dress, even more grateful that Tacoma had had the foresight to purchase it. When she got home, she'd call to thank him, even though she wouldn't hear the end of his 'I told you so's. Not only was she appropriately dressed for the elegant yet casual restaurant, but Khalil couldn't stop staring at her. She knew she looked good. She purchased clothes that would accent the attributes she was blessed with, whether it was hipster jeans, corporate suits or this dress. If it didn't enhance something, she left it in the store. It was as simple as that. The dress and her heels made her appear taller, giving her legs length and grace. The deep plunge in front offered a tantalizing view of her cleavage without giving away all the goodies, and it didn't hug her butt to the point of showing a panty line. It gently covered her most prized possession. Yes, she was extremely thankful to Tacoma and to the maker of this little black number. Even if it were only for one night, like Cinderella, she planned to enjoy every minute of it.

They ordered and spent the first few minutes thoroughly enjoying their meal. Reka was sure she'd never before tasted steak so tender, so flavorful. Khalil was positive he enjoyed this meal that he'd ordered so many times much more tonight because of the woman sitting across from him.

She was lively, talking about everything from the décor to the music the strolling trio played. She professed to liking jazz, although R&B was her first love. He'd even enjoyed her impromptu rendition of Anita Baker's "Giving You the Best that I've Got." Surprisingly, she had a really nice voice, even though she swore she hadn't had any lessons and had never fancied a singing career. Now she was chewing slowly, as if she were savoring every morsel. Her eyes wandered the room in a cursory fashion, and when she caught him staring, she smiled, letting him know she, too, was happy they were here together. Still, his need to know everything about her was not satisfied, and he pushed further. "So tell me all about Reka. I know that she likes to sing, even though she won't admit it, but I want to know more."

Reka put her fork down, took a sip of the red wine he'd ordered for them and found that she actually liked it. "I'm not sure what you want to know exactly. My life's pretty cut and dried."

"Then how about I ask questions and you supply answers?" he offered.

Whether it was the wine or the ambiance or simply being with him, Reka felt agreeable. "Shoot."

"Are you part Native American?" That was his first question, because he knew it wasn't what she expected. She expected him to ask about her past relationships, about why she was so angry towards men, and he did want to know all that, but not just yet.

"What?" Tilting her head to the side she stared at him. "Why would you ask me that?"

Khalil simply smiled, enjoying the surprise in her voice. "Your skin, it's an unusual shade. You have sort of a burnt orange tint, like Native Americans."

"Hmph. I never thought of that." And she truly hadn't. Her mother and Grammy had the same coloring, so she figured she'd inherited it from them. She thought for a moment. "You know, I once heard Grammy mention Indian heritage when she was talking about her parents, but I didn't ask any questions."

"You should, it's important to know your heritage. That way you can pass it on to your children."

"I guess you're right. I'll have to look into that. Next question."

"Do you want children? I mean, someday, do you want to have a family of your own?" He did. He'd wanted it so badly he'd asked Sonya to marry him even though he'd felt no love for her.

"I think I'd like to have a baby or two sometime in the future. I don't really think about it that much, though."

His brow furred. "Why not?"

"Because you have to have a man to think about having kids, and as I told you yesterday, I don't have a man."

"That's purely by choice, I'm sure."

Reka gave a wry grin. "More by necessity."

"Necessity?"

"Yes, my need to remain sane. Men drive you crazy."

With another question he could have her tell him about her past relationships, about what had gone so wrong that she'd sworn off men, but at that moment he really didn't care what mistakes the other men in her life had made. He only wanted to make things better. "I wouldn't drive you crazy, Reka."

She paused, took a drink of wine. "What would you do, Khalil? If I were your woman, how would you treat me?"

He finally pinpointed what he liked most about her—it was her candor. Most women would have smiled, cooed at him, told him they knew he wasn't like their past mates and so on and so forth, yet she hadn't done that. She wanted to know how he was different, how he would measure up to the men in her past and he admired her for skipping all the bull and getting to the point.

"I'd treat you like a woman is supposed to be treated. I'd cherish you, listen to you, do everything in my power to please you. I'd treat you the way you deserve."

Was it suddenly very hot in here? Or had she drunk too much wine? His words sounded too good to be true. He was too good to be true. He was polished and debonair, looking as if he ate at this type of restaurant at least two or three times a week, while she was struggling to keep that napkin on her lap and the burp in her throat at bay. "If you don't mind, there are a few things about you I'd like to know."

For the second time tonight he realized he'd shocked her. Good, maybe with enough shock she'd realize he was sincere. "Ask me whatever you'd like."

"Where did you go to school?"

"I was raised in Greenwich, Connecticut. I attended private schools there until I went to college. NYU was my choice. That's where I met Keith."

"Oh, you know the judge?" Cienna hadn't told her that.

"Yes, we met in college and have been close ever since. We play ball every weekend. He's a great guy with a wonderful family."

"So that's how you got the IT job?"

Khalil shrugged. "Keith said they were having some computer problems. I volunteered to help."

Reka nodded. "So your parents still live in Connecticut?"

"Yes, our family home is still in Greenwich."

"And you're an only child?"

"I have a younger sister, Danielle. She's been married for four years and has a three-year-old son, Delano."

"Does she work?" For some reason Khalil seemed to be from the type of people that didn't allow their women folk to have jobs of their own.

"Danielle's a CPA. She works at my father's company."

Bingo. "Your father has his own company?"

Khalil could see where she was going with this line of questioning and didn't like it, but he'd said she could ask, so he answered. "My family owns a reputable investment brokerage. It's been passed down from son to son for the last four generations."

"But you're in computers. How does that relate to investments?"

It was clear that she didn't understand. The question was, what didn't she understand? Why he didn't work for his family, or why he'd be stupid enough to turn down such a wonderful opportunity. His parents wanted an answer to that question.

"I like computers. My father likes investments and running the brokerage. It's as simple as that."

"Breaking a family tradition is simple for you?"

Because she was treading on touchy ground, Khalil took another drink. "Not simple, just necessary. I had to become my own man. I wasn't meant to work for the family company. That's something I can't deny."

"Mmmm, interesting." Reka nodded to the waiter who'd come to retrieve their plates. "I'll bet your father's having a hard time accepting that."

"At first it was difficult, but they've come around, for now anyway." Donald and Naomi Franklin thought their son's hobby in computers would soon run its course. Too bad they couldn't see that his decision was permanent.

She was quiet then, seemingly content to simply watch him. He wondered what was going on in that pretty little head of hers but admitted, only to himself, that he was afraid to ask. Reka looked at him as if she could see things nobody else could, just as she'd heard the words he hadn't spoken.

"I'm wondering," she began.

Khalil removed his napkin from his lap and placed it on the table. "You're wondering what?" He was a little tense, not sure what she was going to say next.

"I'm wondering what you'd be like on a dance floor." Reka rubbed her finger absently over her chin, surveying him.

"A dance floor?" Of all the directions this conversation could have gone, Reka had done one spectacular three sixty on him.

"Yeah." She stood, walked around the table to grab his hand. "I know this great club where we can go get our dance on." She was pulling him behind her, stopping only long enough for him to throw a few bills on the table and grab her purse.

Once they picked up their coats and he held hers again so she could slip her arms inside, she turned, moved close enough that she could smell his cologne, almost feel his body heat. "I've seen the professional, serious Khalil. Now I'm interested in the laid back Khalil." She watched him as he eyed her suspiciously. "You game?"

6

Reka turned to face Khalil in the front seat after he'd parked the car. "Now, this is a different type of place than the restaurant, so you need to loosen up a little bit." She reached for his tie and pulled it from his neck. "Take your coat off."

"Reka," he sighed in confusion. "It's about twenty degrees outside."

She released herself from the confines of the seatbelt and leaned over the console, using her palms to push the heavy leather from his shoulders. "I know it's cold outside. You can put the coat back on, but you need to get rid of this suit jacket first."

Khalil shrugged out of his coat, let her assist him in removing his suit jacket—not that he needed the assistance, but her hands were warm on him, spiking his already growing desire.

"Relax. We're going to go inside and get our dance on. Then we'll go home."

She was unbuttoning the first few buttons of his shirt, her fingers skimming his bare chest. He sucked in a gulp of air and counted to ten before releasing it. She seemed really serious about getting him to relax but he doubted she knew just how unrelaxed he was becoming. His sex throbbed between his legs. He slipped his arms back into his leather coat while she pulled a little mirror out of her purse and smeared more lipstick on her lips. It was a simple motion, a task he'd seen performed a million times before. On Reka it added another layer to her complex character. She made a simple act graceful, alluring, enticing. He almost groaned, but instead he opened the door and got out, appreciating the twenty degree coolness a lot more now.

This time Reka knew to stay seated until he opened her door. He seemed to like opening doors for her, and she wasn't about to complain.

When she stepped out, she surveyed him once more, then led the way into the club.

The music was loud and, because it was a Saturday night, the club was crowded. After Khalil paid the cover charge, they checked their coats once again and she grabbed his hand and led him toward the bar. It was dark inside, and blue and silver lights bounced off the indigo walls as they made their way through the crowd to find two seats at the end of the bar.

"We'll have a drink first," she told him, then signaled for the bartender. She ordered a rum and Coke for him and a straight martini for herself before facing him again. He looked absolutely edible. When she'd touched his chest in the car, she'd had to keep an extra tight rein on her emotions. Not only was he broad and buff, but rock hard. When she'd helped to remove his coat, he'd stared at her strangely, as if he'd never had a woman undress him before. A bolt of desire had shot between her legs with a direct hit.

Now he sat stiffly at the bar, as if this were the last place he wanted to be. But turnabout was fair play. Since she'd scrounged enough class to eat at that fancy restaurant without making a fool of herself, he could surely enjoy a few hours of partying. "Don't you like the music?" she yelled over the thumping bass.

He did, but hadn't admitted to liking club music in a really long time. "Yeah, it's great." Though his words seemed forced, it wasn't because he was uncomfortable with the club or the music. He wanted to show her how a woman should be treated on a date but he knew if he were forced to get on that dance floor and hold her closely, all his good intentions would be shot straight to hell. He was having a hard enough time keeping his hands off her as it was. If they danced...

As he felt her touch his shoulder and run her hand down his arm, he closed his eyes. Did she secretly enjoy torturing him?

"You okay?" she inquired.

"I'm cool," he lied, taking a deep breath and chancing a look at her. Her eyes glittered, and her lips were shiny and enticing—God, he wanted to kiss her. "No appletini tonight?" he asked, desperate to think about something else.

When her eyes found his, Reka's heart skidded to a halt—no man had ever looked at her that way before. She licked her lips. "Uh, no, not tonight. When I'm in a party mood, I need all the fuel I can get. The apple tones down the vodka."

He laughed, trying to dismiss the erotic way her tongue had run over her lips before disappearing again.

When their drinks arrived, they both took long sips.

"So this is more your scene, huh?"

Reka nodded, then bobbed to the music. "I like to dance. Tacoma and I usually hit the clubs once a month. We used to go more frequently, but he's really settling down into the couple life with Terry and I—"

"You aren't looking to meet anybody," he finished for her. Coming to a club like this and shaking that fine ass body all over the dance floor would definitely result in her meeting more than her share of men, he realized—and didn't like it one bit. But he was with her tonight, and no other man would get close to her. That was a fact.

She hadn't meant to bring that up again, didn't want to keep harping on her bad luck with men, so she simply shrugged. "Oh, that's my song. C'mon." She slipped off the stool, grabbed his hand and pulled him onto the dance floor. She was really enjoying the feel of his long, strong fingers entwined with her own. She'd been pulling him along all night but he hadn't seemed to mind.

The bass was thumping just the way she liked it and they began to dance. At first, there was about two feet between them but the congestion on the floor changed that quickly.

Crunched between sixty or so other gyrating bodies, Reka watched Khalil to see if the brother had any rhythm. She didn't want to be embarrassed by some stiff-assed man. She gulped. He looked even better in motion, moving his head to the beat, his arms raised in the air and his feet gliding from side to side. One of those strong arms came around her waist, pulling her close to him and she went along willingly, placing an arm around his neck.

Their bodies were pressed together, a natural rhythm developing between them. It was an instant connection, as if they'd been dancing together for years. The music played and he moved. She felt his hard body against hers and she moved. The sixty or so people in the room seemed to disappear, leaving only them and the music.

Her breasts pressed against him and Khalil clenched his teeth. Keeping his eyes focused on her face, he attempted to balance the desire he felt for her with the simple need for them to just be together. It was now an understatement that he liked her, that he wanted her. In an instant it had blossomed into so much more. There was a new need now. A new purpose where she was concerned. She shifted, her hands moving to cup the back of his head, her fingers splaying over his neck, spreading heat like wildfire.

Reka was caught in a dream. The room was dark but there seemed to be a spotlight on Khalil. She heard the music but concentrated more on his touch. He held her possessively, confidently, and she let herself be held. In fact, she liked it. A lot. There was something about this charming, business-like man that she'd never thought would appeal to her. But this evening, what she now admitted was a date,was turning out to be one of the best nights of her life.

His hands moved up and down her back and she pressed closer to him, needing that contact like she needed her next breath. Her center pulsed and she instantly recognized another need. She flattened her palms on his chest and let the feel of thick pectoral muscles meld into her palm. The sensations were overwhelming and she let her head fall back in enjoyment. She wasn't prepared for it to get any better than this—after all, it was just a dance.

But then she felt his tongue hot and thick on her neck and she gasped.

Khalil couldn't resist. She'd all but begged him to taste her, baring her slender neck to him like a willing victim to Dracula's love. He'd assumed the role of the dark, menacing male and dropped his lips directly over the blood-filled vein and suckled. Her fingers clenched, grabbing his shirt, and he stroked and swirled his tongue from her jawbone to the beginning of her cleavage, tasting her sweetness.

She had to see his face, had to decipher what this meant to him. But when her gaze found his, she wasn't prepared for what she saw there—desire—thick and heavy. Then his lips crashed down over hers, demanding that she open her mouth and accept him fully.

Before her eyes closed completely, his tongue was stroking hers, a silky smooth motion that mimicked the now slow movements of their dance. He touched every recess of her mouth, scraping across her teeth, drawing her bottom lip into his mouth to suck even harder. Breathing frantically, Reka was trying like hell to figure out how her idea of relaxing him had brought them to this point. She had planned to go out with him only once and end it there. Yet his mouth promised her so much more.

As her breasts pressed seductively against his chest, he groaned into her open mouth. She was every bit as sweet and firey as he had anticipated, but kissing her in a crowded club, in the middle of the dance floor, was definitely not the best idea. With iron will he pulled a few inches away from her, but held her close enough to feel her erratic heartbeat. Or was it his? He couldn't tell. All he knew was that he needed to get her out of this club and into a bed. A few seconds later, he grabbed her by the hand and headed for the door.

Miraculously the sixty or so people that had seemed absent while they'd danced reappeared and Khalil found himself navigating through the crowd, all the while, his mind racing with purely sexual thoughts about Reka. Every muscle in his body was tense with wanting. When they finally made it off the dance floor, Khalil helped her into her coat, grabbed his and headed towards the door.

Reka followed, her heart hammering in her chest. Only she couldn't seem to figure out if anticipation or dread was causing it. Khalil was moving fast. He made it out the door before her and held it until she was outside, too. He took a few steps, then he stopped, turned and looked at her. A slight breeze had picked up and she welcomed the coolness against her heated face. His gaze was sizzling and she turned away.

Khalil swore, ran a hand down his face and took a deep breath. The valet pulled up to the curb with his car. He walked over to where Reka stood and with a hand lightly on her elbow, led her to the waiting car.

He was quiet as he drove, probably regretting asking her out. In retrospect, Reka thought, her actions could be construed as wanton behavior. She'd dragged him to the club, ordered him a drink, then practically made love to him on the dance floor. Yeah, he was most likely figuring out the best way to tell her they wouldn't be seeing each other again, except in the office. Well, that wasn't her fault. It served him right for asking her out in the first place. Any fool could see how different they were.

"The club's not your scene, huh?" she asked when the silence was too much for her to bear any longer.

Khalil cleared his throat, thankful that she was still speaking to him. After taking such liberties as he had, he had been sure she was going to blast him the moment they were alone in the car. So far, she'd sat close to the door, her eyes trained forward as he drove. He'd kicked himself numerous times already for going too far. He was a grown man, for goodness sake. He should have been able to simply dance with her without taking things to the next level. She wasn't ready for the next level, he'd known that already, yet basic control had escaped him. "I wouldn't say that. Just haven't been to one in a while."

He didn't sound angry. She turned slightly in her seat. "Really? Then what do you do for fun? Besides play ball with the judge."

He thought a second, realized all too quickly that he really didn't do anything for fun. Never had the need to. He worked, attended to the social obligations his mother and sister arranged for him, and slept—that was his life. That was the life he'd anticipated sharing with Sonya, resigning them both to an early death from boredom. "Not much."

Reka tsked. "All work and no play makes Khalil a very dull boy," she said, even though lately she'd been guilty of the same thing. But her situation was different—she did know how to have fun. She was afraid that Khalil needed a little help in that department.

Khalil smiled. "You don't say." Then, as if the proverbial light bulb had at that moment appeared atop his head, he asked, "You could help me with that, couldn't you? You could show me how to relax, to enjoy myself more?"

Reka sat back, gave the question some thought. Well, not that much thought, since she'd already considered offering to do that for him, but he didn't need to know that. "I guess. But I don't know if now's the right time. You have to find out who's sending those emails. I know Cienna wants that taken care of right away."

He remembered his new assignment, the job that had brought this magnificent woman into his life. "I know enough about relaxation to know the first step is to leave work at the office."

Reka smiled. "You're right. You may not need my help at all."

"Oh no, I definitely need your help." Slightly panicked that she might not agree, he pulled the car into a parking spot across the street from her house and turned to face her. She looked up at him and he felt his loins stirring again. Damn, but she was sexy. Despite the dire warnings from his brain, he lifted her hand, rubbed his thumbs over its smoothness. "I'd like you to show me how to relax. I need to enjoy myself more. I think you'd make a fabulous teacher." She'd make a fabulous anything, he was beginning to realize.

As he held her hand, she thought about what had happened on the dance floor. She'd felt like ripping his clothes off and sexing him down, right there in the middle of the club. She had to be some kind of idiot to even consider doing anything with him outside of the workplace, yet she couldn't come up with one plausible excuse. "I guess I can give you a few pointers," she said softly.

"Then it's a deal," he said with a smile.

The interior of his car seemed way too cozy to Reka. He apparently felt the same way because, on the heels of her response, he leaned closer to her.

"We should seal our agreement with something." She was scant inches away, her lips parting for him.

"Something like what?" She knew what, and couldn't wait for it to happen. Reka could kiss for days and never get enough of the sensual contact—when it was done right. And Khalil had already proven that he could tongue her down.

A slow, soft connecting of lips and then he pulled slightly away. "I like kissing you, Reka."

Her eyes fluttered and she leaned into him. "I think I like kissing you, too." And to prove her point she covered his lips this time, moving her mouth sinuously over his.

Khalil grabbed the back of her neck, holding her steady, and opened his mouth to grant her the access she so expertly requested. And as he reveled in the experience, letting her take the lead, allowing her to explore, to tantalize him to her satisfaction, he knew he would never get enough of her.

Khalil closed the door, tossed his keys on the table and headed for his bedroom. He stepped out of his shoes and placed them on the rack at the bottom of his walk-in closet. Grabbing a hanger, he draped his suit jacket neatly over it and placed it on the door handle, then retrieved his tie from the side pocket and carefully strung it over the tie rack. A grin crept across his face as he remembered Reka slipping the silk from around his neck.

The hard-on he'd had for the last two hours throbbed and he groaned. Reaching for his belt buckle, he was headed toward the bathroom, toward a cold shower, or a hot one with plenty of soap, whichever offered the quickest form of relief, when the flashing red light on the answering machine stopped him.

Beep.

He continued to undress while he waited for the first message to play.

Khalil, your father and I do not appreciate being stood up.

As he stepped out of his pants and folded them at the crease, he cursed. He'd completely forgotten about dinner at the country club with his parents.

However, I'm sure you have a good excuse for being rude. I'll expect to hear it tomorrow at brunch. Don't be late.

Khalil pressed the erase button. Sunday brunch at the Franklin house was a ritual he and his sister rarely missed. It was the time the family used to catch up. Their business and social lives were so involved that this was the only time they could carve out for themselves.

Now he'd pissed his mother off. So the normally two hour family conference would now be marred by Naomi Franklin's dismay over her son's thoughtlessness. Oh well, he'd deal with that tomorrow.

He shrugged out of his shirt and prepared himself for the next message. No doubt his mother had called Danielle to question her as to his whereabouts and, since Danielle had no idea where he'd been this evening, she would have called him with a few choice words herself, angry because he'd involved her in this mess.

However, the voice that echoed through his bedroom was not that of his little sister.

Hello, darling. I was just sitting here thinking about you. And you're not at home. I remember the Saturday evenings we used to spend together.

Sonya's sophisticated drawl settled over him and he sighed. For a woman as educated and polished as she was, she had a really hard time understanding that their relationship was over.

I really need to speak with you. Call me whenever you get in.

Silence.

I'll wait up.

Khalil quickly hit delete. "You're going to lose a lot of sleep tonight."

He moved to the bathroom, his thoughts returning to the soft lips he'd kissed, the full breasts he'd felt pressed against his chest, the plush, round bottom he'd gripped only hours ago. Turning the nozzle to the left, he knew cold water would never suffice. Grabbing the bar of soap he let his head fall back as hot water sprayed against his skin and his body demanded release.

7

To: *rlboyd@passolaw.com*
From: *Jack*
Date: *November 29, 2004*
Subject: *Up All Night*

Jill wasn't in the mood this weekend so I went out alone. Imagine my surprise when I saw you. That little black dress was hot, but I think your choice of men is all wrong.

The way you moved on that dance floor had me thinking about you all night. Luckily, Sensuality's latest Masterful Massage Oil was available. With every stroke I imagined it was you, and suddenly Jill disappeared.

Jack

Reka gasped, her eyes quickly closing, then reopening. Was this for real? Had this pervert really been at the club Saturday night?

She focused on her computer screen, then frowned as she noticed only her name and email address in the 'To' line, not the firm's group address.

Instinctively, she picked up her phone to call Khalil. He needed to see this. Then she put the receiver down as she remembered yesterday's resolution.

Khalil Franklin was a co-worker, a co-worker who had kissed her senseless then asked her to do him a personal favor, but a co-worker nonetheless. There wasn't now, nor would there ever be, anything intimate between them.

She had no intention of making a fool out of herself for him, or any other man. Therefore, she would treat him as she treated everybody else at Page & Associates, as if she could do just fine without them. She'd passed his office this morning without considering knocking to say good morning. The door had been closed and she hadn't even wondered if he was in there, at least not until she'd gotten her cup of coffee and had her morning gossip session with Tacoma.

But this email was business. Or was it? Calling him to report this new message wasn't personal, even though the message was directed to her, and not to the company. Maybe she should simply delete it and get on with her work for the day. She drummed her short, polished nails on the desk blotter and considered the matter again.

Glancing back at the screen, she realized deleting the message wouldn't solve anything, nor would hiding out in her office. She'd worked here for seven years and, in that time, she hadn't let anyone intimidate her. She damn sure wasn't going to start now. Besides, they needed to find out who Jack was so they could finally put a stop to his harassment. And maybe with him targeting her email box only, they'd have a better chance of doing just that.

With a click of the mouse she printed the message, saved it to her personal folder then closed it. Paper in hand, she made her way down the hall to Khalil's office.

After the interrogation that was supposed to be brunch yesterday, Khalil had opened a bottle of wine, switched on the football game and immersed himself in the box of emails from the mysterious Jack.

He'd thought of Reka often, but figured he wouldn't pressure her by trying to see her every day. Besides, he knew he'd see her at the office. Surely he could wait.

But now it was after eleven o'clock on Monday morning and he'd neither seen nor heard from her. However, he wouldn't pursue her in the office, wouldn't allow his personal life to interfere with business. He'd promised to do a job for Keith, and no matter how much she tempted him, he wouldn't allow Reka to mess that up.

Still, the thought of her smile, or one of her smart remarks, warmed him, and he momentarily entertained thoughts of heading down the hall. Dragging his hands down his face, he shook his head to clear his mind. He had work to do.

Just when he'd buckled down, punched in a few lines of code and attempted to trace Jack's last message, there was a quick knock on his door before it swung open.

"It seems our friend Jack has a roving eye." Reka closed the door behind her, then moved to his desk and set the paper down before taking a seat across from him.

In those few seconds Khalil took in the form-fitting wool charcoal gray dress, long black leather boots and glossy frost-colored lips. Her perfume—bold and distinctive, fitting her perfectly—aroused him instantly.

"Oh, good morning," he mumbled, dragging his eyes away from her body and picking up the piece of paper she'd deposited in front of him.

Reka looked at her watch to keep from staring at him. "Right, good morning." He wore brown today. A chocolate-colored suit jacket, beige shirt and spice-toned tie. His square jaw, covered with hair she remembered was soft to the touch, clenched for a moment before he looked down at the paper.

"He sent this to you?" Khalil chanced another look at her. She didn't seem the least bit upset but he'd felt a sudden discomfort after reading Jack's words.

"Yes," she nodded. "So now we know he frequents night clubs and likes to dance."

Khalil's eyes narrowed. "But how does he know who you are?" He told himself he was doing his job. Everybody was a suspect until he proved otherwise.

Reka blinked, not sure she liked his tone. "I don't know how he knew it was me. But he was definitely at the club on Saturday, and now it seems I've pushed Jill to the side." She crossed her legs and sat back in the chair. "He's some kind of hard up to be thinking about a stranger while he jerked off."

Her words touched a familiar spot and Khalil quickly looked away from her. Jack had used the Masterful Massage Oil, while he'd settled for more traditional methods.

"Did you respond to this?" he questioned, refusing to look directly at her.

He was acting weird, as if they'd just met, or as if he were a cop. She felt a sting of disappointment. "No, I didn't answer it." Her lip upturned in anger. "What? Did you think I'd hop at the chance for some cyber sex with this nutcase?"

Her words were curt, her neck rigid. He'd upset her. He pinched the bridge of his nose and took a deep breath. "That's not what I meant."

"Well, what did you mean? It seems I'm having a hard time understanding exactly what you want." At first she'd thought he was just trying to date her for some kind of fling. Then he'd asked his favor, and she figured that's what the date thing had been about all along. Then he'd kissed her; now he acted as if none of that had ever happened. This was exactly the type of drama she was trying to avoid.

Khalil's lips tightened as he considered her words. The answer to that question was so easy that he had to fight to keep it from rolling off his lips. He wanted her, but knew she didn't want to hear that, especially not right now.

He didn't like the message from Jack. Didn't like what it said or what it implied. Jack had just made his little joke personal, and Khalil knew all too well what could come of sexual stalking, whether it be online or in person.

"I want what we both want." He spoke slowly, his eyes fixed on hers. "I want to find out who Jack is and put a stop to these messages."

She shifted uncomfortably beneath his heated glare. "Maybe with him mailing me personally you can track him faster." And then we won't have a need for you here. The office had been functioning just fine without an IT supervisor before he came. They'd continue to do just fine after he left.

That was a thought, a good possibility, Khalil reluctantly admitted to himself. Still, he didn't like the idea of some pervert watching her. "Did you save the message?"

"Yes."

"I'll have to use your computer to initiate the trace codes." He stood, walked around the desk, and opened the door.

He was holding it open for her, just as he had on their date, yet things were definitely different now. Reka lifted her chin proudly. She was not hurt by his coldness, nor did she want him to treat her any differently then he did any other co-worker. If this is how it was to be between them now, so be it. She didn't need or want it any other way. At least that's what her mind said. The sharp stabs in her gut symbolized something else. She walked past him, muttering a quick, "Fine."

Two hours later Khalil cursed loudly. He'd been in Reka's office trying desperately to trace that message. But Jack was clever enough to cover his tracks very well.

He'd read the message again, over and over until he could probably recite it from memory. Not only had Jack seen her and commented on her dress, but he'd also seen Khalil and felt it necessary to advise Reka of her poor choice in men. That, he now admitted, bothered him immensely. Who the hell was this joker to tell her who she should and shouldn't go out with? And what was wrong with them being together? Absolutely nothing. His fingers pounded the keyboard with extra force as he fumed. This would only add credence to Reka's belief that they weren't suited for each other, making his job of convincing her otherwise that much harder.

ACCESS DENIED.

The letters flashed brightly for about the billionth time. He sat back in the chair, refusing to mutter another expletive in this office. He rested his elbows on the armrests and steepled his fingers beneath his chin he tried to clear his mind, to focus on the job at hand. Impossible.

The office smelled like her. The James Brown bobblehead perched on top of her monitor reminded him of her feisty nature. Looking around her desk, he didn't see any photos, not even of her family. He thought that was odd, considering how close she, her mother and her grandmother appeared to be. She had appointments scribbled on her desk calendar and he flipped through a few pages, trying to get a peek inside her life. She was going to the hairdresser one day after work, going to court another and going out shopping with Tacoma another day. What was it with those two? he wondered.

He wondered what the court date was about. Was she in some type of trouble? Picking up a pen, he jotted down the date, time and address she'd written on her calendar, then stuck the piece of paper in his pocket. His snooping was brought to a halt when Reka and Tacoma waltzed into her office with bags of Chinese food.

"You're still here?" she asked.

He couldn't tell if she was still mad at him or not. The fact that Tacoma smiled and moved quickly to the desk, talking in his chipper tone, made Khalil a little more comfortable. If Reka were mad at him, Tacoma would be a good buffer.

"Haven't had any luck, huh?" Tacoma set down the bags and began taking out boxes. "Well, you need to take a break. We've got plenty for lunch, just take your pick. I'll go to the lounge and get you a soda. Is Diet Coke okay?" Tacoma asked with a smile.

Khalil's stomach rumbled. He hadn't had anything since his cup of coffee this morning, and that food was smelling good. "Make that a regular Coke; my body can't digest anything diet." He returned Tacoma's smile.

"I'll be back in a jiffy," Tacoma chirped.

Reka rolled her eyes at him as he made his way out the door, then resigned herself to the inevitable. "We've got shrimp fried rice, beef and broccoli, egg foo yung and egg rolls. Help yourself." She pulled out napkins and plastic forks, placing them on the desk. "And don't spill anything, or you're cleaning my desk."

Khalil chuckled. "I'll be extra careful." She was avoiding eye contact with him, and he realized it was because she didn't know how to take him any more than he knew how to take her. He reached out, took her hand just as she was about to pass him a napkin. "I'm sorry about this morning."

"What?" His touch alone scattered her thoughts, even though the sight of him in her office had done enough of that already.

"I was a little harsh with you this morning, and I apologize." She hadn't pulled her hand away; that was a good sign. Those dazzling eyes pinned him, and he wondered what she was thinking.

"Don't worry about it. We all get that way sometimes in this office." He'd apologized; that was something new to her. A man apologizing, and for something as simple as talking to her harshly. She was amazed. Although his coolness had agitated her this morning, she wasn't going to give him the pleasure of mentioning it. Now she didn't need to, he'd taken care of it.

"It won't happen again," he promised.

They were silent, each watching the other, until Tacoma re-entered the room.

"So Khalil, what do you think about evening weddings?" Tacoma put the sodas down and dropped into the chair across from Reka's desk. "I think they're romantic, but Terry thinks we should have something earlier, like a brunch or something." He rolled his eyes skyward before reaching for one of the little white boxes and flipping open the lid.

Khalil was still staring at Reka and had to focus to answer Tacoma's question. He opened his mouth, then closed it quickly. Wait a minute, was Tacoma asking him about wedding plans?

Khalil's scrunched-up face made Reka giggle. "This wedding has consumed Tacoma's life. You'll have to excuse him."

Taking the box of food and napkin she offered him, he sat back in the chair and gave the question a little more thought. He and Sonya had been planning to have an early afternoon wedding. "I like the evening idea."

"See, that's what I'm talking about. I'm thinking candlelight and an elegant dinner," Tacoma continued animatedly.

Reka kept quiet while she scooped noodles into her mouth.

Noticing that she'd given him the spicy beef and broccoli, Khalil nodded in her direction, then took a bite. "That should be nice. Where are you thinking of having the wedding?" He prayed Tacoma didn't say in a church.

"Ms. Thang here is supposed to be venue shopping for me."

Khalil looked to Reka. "Really? What are your thoughts on the perfect wedding, Reka?" Again, any and everything about her intrigued him. He simply couldn't gain enough knowledge where she was concerned.

Reka rolled her eyes at Tacoma, then looked casually at Khalil. "Personally, I don't know why there has to be all that pomp and circumstance. If you're really all that hyped about being together, then a simple ceremony at someone's house should be just fine."

"Is that what you'd have for your wedding?" With his plastic fork he dug into the box, not looking up at her.

She leaned her head to the side in thought. "Seeing as I'm not ever getting married, it really doesn't matter." She knew that would make him look up, and before he could speak she continued, "But if I did, yes. I'd have a small ceremony with only my closest friends. Maybe in a nice restaurant or on a balcony somewhere. But it wouldn't be anything fabulous, just me and my man committing to each other."

Nothing fabulous, he thought. She was right, the fabulous part would be building enough trust for her to even accept a marriage proposal. This gave him even more to think about.

Lunch was over soon enough, and by four o'clock Khalil still hadn't found a connection between the email and the sender. Sitting back in the chair, he let his head loll and closed his eyes. He had to think of possible connections. The person sending these emails was good, very good. He was covering his tracks like a professional. And even a professional could work from inside the network.

The niggling fear that had been circulating in the back of his mind demanded his full attention now. What if Reka had something to do with the messages? It was weird that when Jack finally decided to contact someone personally it was her. Why wasn't it Cienna? Or someone higher up in the firm?

And he'd been at the club. Reka said she and Tacoma used to frequent the clubs on a regular basis. What if Jack was someone she'd met there? What if the general emails had all been a charade to get to her? What if she knew the person sending them and was using this entire scam as some way to get back at the company?

So many questions soared through his mind, none of which he really wanted to acknowledge. She couldn't be involved. Not when he was beginning to feel things for her he'd never felt for anyone else before. This was a sticky situation for him, one he wasn't sure he was prepared to deal with.

"Okay, your time's up. I can't work out there with Tyrese another minute. That girl has serious issues, and one of these days she's going to catch me in a bad mood and then it's on."

Reka came bustling into the office, dropping files on her desk and ranting about their mutual co-worker. Khalil had met Tyrese, and while her long hair and mulatto skin turned some men on, her blatant conceit and selfishness turned him off.

"Then I guess it's a good thing I'm all done in here." He got out of the chair and moved around the desk so she could take a seat.

With her hands to her temples Reka took a deep breath and sighed. "I'm sorry. I shouldn't have bothered you with all that. She just gets on my last nerve."

"Don't worry about it, I understand."

"So did you have any luck?"

"No, actually I didn't. But I'm thinking that if Jack saw you at the club and emailed you here, there's a possibility that he may contact you at home. You know, on your home email."

"You think he'll go that far?" Reka crossed her arms, trying to ward off the chill that had run up her back.

"It's possible. I mean, it couldn't hurt to put up an extra firewall. That way if he tries to hack in, I'll have a better chance of tracing him."

She thought about what he was saying. She did work a lot from home and she often emailed stuff to the office, so there was definitely a possibility. "Yeah, I guess you're right."

Khalil moved to the door.

"Um."

Her voice stopped him. He turned to face her, saw her struggling with her words. "Yes?"

This wasn't personal. It wasn't because she'd liked being with him on Saturday and had actually been disappointed when he hadn't called her on Sunday. It was business. "If you don't have other plans, you could come home with me this afternoon and work on my computer." Folding her arms behind her back, she prayed that sounded professional. He tilted his head, a hint of a smile playing at his lips, and she felt her heart skid to a halt in her chest. Damn, he was sexy.

"I don't have any other plans." He licked his lips because he knew she was staring at them. "And if I did, I'd readily break them at the prospect of going home with you, Reka."

With that, he was gone and Reka sank back into her chair. She was sinking fast, and no matter how many attempts she made at keeping herself afloat, Khalil and his soft-spoken charisma increased their hold on her.

8

Khalil answered the phone with major irritation since he'd been on his way out the door to meet Reka at the elevator. "Khalil Franklin."

"Hello, darling. You sure have been hard to catch up with lately."

Khalil frowned as Sonya's voice vibrated through the receiver. "I'm not real sure why you're trying to catch up with me in the first place."

Ignoring his curt tone, Sonya continued, "I was thinking we could go to that steak place you like so much tonight. I've had a horrendous day and am in dire need of a drink and a massage."

He looked at the receiver with an astonished expression. "I'm sorry to hear about your day, but there's really nothing I can do about that. As for the steak and the massage, I suggest you find someone else to cater to those needs as my tenure in that department is over."

She was silent for a moment. "Khalil, this separation has gone on long enough. We are perfect for each other, and you know that. Neither your parents nor mine are happy about this little stunt you've pulled."

Pinching the bridge of his nose, Khalil tried not to raise his voice. That was not in his character. "Neither your parents nor mine have to live my life. I broke the engagement because I don't love you and marriage would be foolish." Taking a deep, exasperated breath, he finished, "Sonya, I have to go. Please don't call me at work anymore. In fact, there's really nothing else we need to talk about." Hanging up on her hadn't felt half as rude as he thought it would. In fact, it felt rather good. He closed and locked his office door and walked down the hall towards the lobby.

"I'm home, Grammy," Reka yelled as she walked through the door. She dropped her keys on the table and hung her coat on the rack.

From the spot on the sofa that she was quickly getting used to, Grammy yelled, "I took that ground beef out of the freezer. I feel like spaghetti tonight."

Reka turned at the sound of the door closing behind her. "That sounds good, Grammy."

"I thought she was going back to Sunny Days?" Khalil whispered.

Reka rolled her eyes. "So did I."

"Is that Mr. Handsome?" Grammy called.

"Hi, Mrs. Grant." Khalil gave his coat to Reka and made his way inside, kissing Grammy on the cheek.

"You can call me, Grammy. We'll be family soon enough."

Reka ignored her grandmother's foolish remark and grabbed the remote, quickly changing the channel.

"Hey, I was watching that," Grammy complained.

"You don't know anything about Jerry Springer."

"I know them down low brothas were looking kind of good." She winked at Khalil, who tried to hide his grin.

"Whatever. Watch the news or something. Khalil, the computer's over there. If you look in the top right hand drawer you'll see the passwords. I'm going to go change and start dinner."

"I can cook my own dinner. Why don't you two go out?" Grammy suggested.

Khalil moved towards the computer. "Not tonight, Grammy. I've got work to do."

Ignoring the sound of Khalil calling her grandmother by that name, and the sight of him comfortably moving through her apartment, Reka hurried to her bedroom. "I'll be right back."

Stripping out of her dress and boots, she chastised herself. So what if Grammy had taken a liking to him and he seemed pretty comfortable with her? So what if she happened to like the way it felt for him to come home with her and go to the computer to work while she prepared dinner? She was not the settling down type; that fact had been made painfully clear to her over the years.

Still, she couldn't deny her reaction to him. If there was one thing that was always definite with her, it was her attraction to a man. If he made her nipples tingle and her thighs clasp together tightly to soothe the aching inside, then she wanted him, and there was no doubt about that. Khalil had done all that and then some. That kiss the other night had her nipples so taut she thought they'd cut through her dress and her coat. When she'd gotten into the house, in the privacy of her own bedroom, she'd peeled her panties away only to find them moist and clinging.

Being in the same room with him caused great breathing difficulty that she'd unsuccessfully tried to ignore. And when he talked to her, just casually held a conversation, she felt as if she were the only woman in the world, the only woman he was interested in speaking to. It was foolish, she knew, and she rolled her eyes at her reflection as she passed the mirror to grab some sweat pants from her closet. Whatever this chemistry was between them, it would pass, hopefully before she made a fool of herself and pounced on the poor man.

Until then, all she had to do was keep a clear head. He was a business associate and a friend, if that's what you wanted to call someone you'd agreed to help relax. He was not a prospective boyfriend, nor a candidate for the hot sex she was in dire need of. Pulling a t-shirt over her head, she fluffed her hair, then made her way back out towards the kitchen. Fixing dinner would keep her mind off the man invading her personal space.

Grammy had switched that television right back to Jerry Springer and was kicking up her feet in fits of laughter as two drag queens swung at one pitiful looking woman while the crowd roared hysterically. Reka kept right on moving. Grammy was a lost cause. Out of the corner of her eye she glimpsed Khalil hunched over her computer, already deep in concentration. He'd shed his suit jacket and his dress shirt stretched over that broad back. Momentarily her fingers clenched as she imagined them scraping along that rock hard surface. Then she took a deep breath and made her way into the kitchen.

She needed a drink. A strong one.

Forty-five minutes later she was removing a loaf of Italian bread from the oven and switching off the spaghetti. She opened the cabinet to get plates and found herself picking up three without hesitation. She actually hummed as she got out three glasses and three sets of silverware. Making her way out of the small kitchen into the corner she called a dining room, she set the table.

Grammy was watching something else on the television now—Reka swore that was all the woman knew how to do anymore—while Khalil was still at the desk punching furiously on her keyboard.

"Dinner's ready," she said in a voice that sounded way too homey.

Grammy jumped right up. "Good. My stomach's been growling so loud I thought it was talking to me with all the time I've been waiting."

Reka wanted to tell her that if she were back at Sunny Days she would have had two complete meals and a multitude of snacks by now, but she didn't.

Going back into the kitchen, she retrieved the pot of spaghetti and brought it into the dining room, setting it on top of a dishtowel to keep from scorching her table. "Khalil, you're welcome to join us." She made a point to say that as she was making another trip into the kitchen. She didn't want it to seem that she was trying to keep him here longer, although he didn't look as if he were trying to go home anytime soon.

Returning to the dining room with a basket of hot bread in one hand and a container of parmesan cheese in the other, she noticed that Khalil hadn't budged.

"That boy works too hard," Grammy said as she reached for the basket of bread.

"Wait until we've said grace," Reka scolded while walking towards the desk and Khalil.

His fingers raced over the keyboard, and his eyes were glued to the screen. "Khalil?" she called to him.

He didn't answer.

Touching a hand to his back, she held back a sigh of bliss. His back was warm and rigid, just as she'd imagined, warm and rigid. "Khalil?"

He jumped, turned and looked at her with wide eyes. "Hmm?"

"I fixed some dinner. Take a break and join us."

His forehead was knotted into neat little rows that she felt a sudden urge to rub away. His eyes searched her face, but she got the distinct impression that he really wasn't seeing her. Reaching down, she took his hand and guided him out of the chair. "Come on, it's time you came up for air anyway." She pulled him along behind her, wondering if this was what he was like when he went home to his own apartment. Most computer guys probably were, so why should he be any different? Still, in her mind she thought it was a shame.

Khalil followed her without a hint of resistance. His gaze fell to the gentle sway of her hips, noticeable even through the bulky fabric of her sweat pants. He'd been at that computer trying to work himself into a coma to keep from thinking of how close she was or how right this entire scenario felt. He was working, she was cooking and Grammy, well, Grammy was doing her thing. He was comfortable here. That surprised him since his upbringing was so dramatically different from this quaint setting. His mother did not cook. And all of the Franklins were rarely free at the same time to sit down to a meal together.

When she'd interrupted him a moment ago, he'd made the mistake of turning immediately to face her, not preparing himself for the fact that since he was sitting he'd be at eye level with her breasts. So when he turned, Wham!. Those luscious globes had all but smacked him in the face and his throat had instantly gone dry. She was forever leaving him speechless.

Now he sat across the table from her and her grandmother, about to partake in a meal that smelled wonderful. When Grammy grabbed his hand and Reka scooped up the other one, he was at a loss. Then he watched the two of them bow their heads and mimicked their motions. The prayer was silent but he gave thanks nonetheless. While the Franklins didn't do intimate family meals, they had plenty of dinner parties around the six foot cherrywood dining table and antique china dishes. But they never gave way to a blessing.

"You know, at that psych ward you and your mother put me in they served the sauce with the noodles separate. Now ain't that stupid?" Grammy scooped spaghetti onto her plate, talking as she went along.

"That's how some people serve it, Grammy."

"Hmph. It's stupid, if you ask me. You end up mixin' it all together anyway."

Reka sent Khalil an apologetic look. Her grandmother was a pistol, a sour grape that needed years and years to get used to, but Khalil didn't seem to mind. In fact, he was smiling.

"It's good. So you're fine *and* can cook." He twirled the noodles around his fork before looking at her again. "I'm baffled as to why you're still single."

She didn't want to blush. Had he called her fine? Yeah, so what? Plenty of guys noticed that about her. "My single status is my choice, as I've told you before."

"And that's a stupid choice, if you ask me." Grammy grabbed a piece of bread. "Why a woman would choose to be alone all the time when they could have a nice strapping man in bed with 'em every night has always been a mystery to me."

Reka rolled her eyes. "Sex is not everything." But she sure could go for some right about now, she thought as she inhaled Khalil's scent and squeezed her thighs tighter together.

Grammy almost choked on her food. Khalil was instantly patting her back and lifting her right arm into the air. "Mmmm, excuse me," Grammy groaned. "I know you done bumped your head. Ain't nothing like good sex and when you get it, believe me, it *is* everything."

It was Khalil's turn to cough now as Reka shook her head. There was nothing that Grammy and her mother didn't say. That was probably where she got her candor from. She wasn't surprised at Grammy's remark, but she did feel sorry for Khalil's sensitive ears. "Okay, let's not talk about sex while we're eating."

"Hmph, that's the best kind of sex, if you can get it right."

Khalil kept his head down and Reka kicked Grammy under the table. "That's enough, Grammy. Maybe I'll call the cable man tomorrow and have him take away all those extra channels you like watching so much."

"There ain't no need to get sassy now. Besides, Mr. Handsome surely ain't no virgin, and we both know you're not fresh as the driven snow."

Oh goodness, this was really too much. "Grammy!"

Khalil touched a hand to her arm. "It's okay. I'm not a virgin and I'm not against talking about sex."

"But at the dinner table?" Reka asked in surprise.

"I'll admit that's different, but I'm simply the guest. If that's the topic of discussion, then so be it." He shrugged.

Reka didn't take it as lightly. She did not want to talk about sex with him, and especially not with him and her grandmother. "No, it's not the topic of discussion." Cutting Grammy a dangerous glare, she silently informed the old woman that she wasn't joking about making that call to the cable company.

For the duration of their meal they talked about the weather and the Knicks.

Grammy was going to bed early, which was music to Reka's ears. She was going to have a serious discussion with her mother first thing tomorrow morning. Either Grammy was moving in with Janell or she was going back to Sunny Days. She liked her solitude and was tired of having it disturbed by the rantings of a horny old woman.

Khalil helped her clean the kitchen and was about to make his way back to the computer when her words stopped him mid stride.

"That's enough work for the night, don't you think?"

She was leaning against the doorjamb of the kitchen. He turned, slipping his hands into his pockets and giving her another one of those killer grins. "That's what I came here for. Besides, the firewall's already installed. I'm just running a few tests. It won't take me that long, then I'll be out of your hair." He was enjoying his time with her but hadn't expected her to reciprocate the feelings.

"Oh, I'm not putting you out. I just thought we could watch a movie or something. You know, relax a little. You did want me to show you how to relax." She'd thought of the movie during dinner after she allowed herself to accept that she really liked being around him.

"Yeah, you did say you'd help me...ah...relax." He was having a hell of a time grasping the idea of relaxing when creamy mounds peeked at him from the rim of her t-shirt. Luckily his hands were already in his pockets, else the tent in his pants from his arousal would have been embarrassing. "I'll just set up the test runs and then I'll join you for the movie."

"Great." She pushed away from her leaning position and moved to the television and the cabinet beneath it where she kept her DVDs. "What are you in the mood for? I've got some action, some suspense, some sci-fi."

And they all would probably give him insight into the vivacious woman he was already coming to adore. But what he really wanted to see was her soft side, her passionate side, because he knew without a doubt that she had one. And he suspected that was the better side of Reka Boyd. "Why don't you pick your favorite and we'll watch it."

Reka looked over at him, uncertainty clear in her eyes. "Are you sure you want to trust me to make the choice?"

Looking up from the computer screen, Khalil considered his decision. Judging from her expression, again he'd managed to surprise her. That was good; he liked keeping her on her toes. "Positive."

She shrugged and slid her favorite DVD from the cabinet and put it into the machine. "Okay," she called to him and patted the pillows on the couch next to her, "we're all set."

Punching the last few lines of code in, Khalil left the computer to do its thing without him and joined her. He had to admit that a part of him was a little uncertain at giving her the go ahead to pick the movie. But how bad could it be? He got his answer the moment the perky music began and a silly cartoon drawing popped up on the screen. "What's this?" he asked as soon as a tiny mailbox appeared with the now familiar saying, 'You've got mail,' echoing from the speakers.

He turned to her. "You're kidding, right?"

"Nope." She grinned. "You said I could pick my favorite, and this is my favorite."

"Tom Hanks and Meg Ryan?" He gave her a perplexed look. "I would have figured you for *Ocean's 11* or *The Italian Job* or something like that."

"Why? Do I look like a thief?" She nudged his shoulder.

His arm instantly warmed. A thief? Maybe, since she was making a good attempt at stealing his heart. "No, because they're packed with action and danger. I'd think those things would appeal to you."

"And a romantic comedy wouldn't?" She didn't know if she should be offended or not.

"You haven't given any signs of being a romantic."

She began to rise from the chair, now deciding on being offended. "Then I'll turn it off."

Khalil grabbed her arm, pulled her back down until she was almost on his lap. "Don't. I like romances too."

She glared at him over her shoulder. "Liar."

"I'm not lying. Any man with a brain knows that these movies are the key to pleasing all women. So I watch all of them and take notes."

She smiled. "I knew you were a smart guy." Settling back, she watched the beginning of the movie, wondering if knowing that he was a romantic was a good or bad thing. She'd never known a guy that liked chick flicks before. She started to compare him to Donovan or one of her other disasters but quickly decided against it. There was no comparison, so why waste her time?

They watched the movie in virtual silence with Khalil taking note of each time she sighed, each time she smiled and each time she made a wry comment. He watched her watch the movie more than he actually watched it himself. In the span of an hour and fifty-seven minutes he learned a great deal more about her, and was quite pleased with that fact. So much so that when the movie was over he was the one to get up and turn the television off. He was the one who came back to the couch and pulled her closer again. "Thank you for helping me relax tonight," he said, nuzzling her neck.

Reka melted at his touch, wondering why she'd never experienced these sensations before. "You're welcome. But I've got to get you more used to it. I shouldn't have to remind you to relax, it should just come natural."

"Speaking of natural." With a finger to her chin he turned her face to his and lightly grazed her lips.

Reka puckered in response, let her hands fall on his chest. "This does feel natural, doesn't it?" She questioned herself more than him.

"Very," he said, brushing over her supple lips again. Then out of sheer curiosity his tongue snaked out, traced the beauty mark at the base of her lip and he felt his entire body quake as she moaned in response.

Boldly Reka let her own tongue repeat the action on his lips. His thin mustache tickled but in a good, arousing sort of way. His lips were soft and after she'd traced their outline, opened, ready for the assault. Slowly she slipped inside, invading his warm mouth, and her hands came up behind his head and pulled him closer.

She controlled the kiss, and did a damn fine job of it, too. Khalil kept his raging hormones to himself and let her lead him. She was used to leading. So was he. Somebody had to give, and this time it would be him. Her mouth slanted over his, taking the kiss deeper even as his hands roamed up and down her body until his thumbs were brushing past the engorged mounds of her breasts.

Her mind was fuzzy as the need to devour him crept slowly throughout her body. What was she doing? This was a mistake. Wasn't it? She pulled away, then stared into his half closed hazy eyes. It didn't feel like a mistake. It felt like…his thumb found her nipple. It felt damn good. That's what it felt like. On a ragged moan she took his mouth again as he toyed with her breasts, making her center moist with anticipation.

She was kissing him like a woman ready to take the plunge. This was what he wanted, right? He wanted her in bed, he wanted to be inside her, a part of her. He wanted that so badly. Yet his mind screamed that he wanted so much more. So he was the one to pull away this time, dropping tiny noncommittal kisses on her lips because he couldn't quite break the connection. "You're a really good kisser."

She smiled. "What can I say? I like to kiss."

"I don't think I've ever appreciated kissing as much as I do now."

Reka didn't know what else to say. She didn't know what she was feeling. Khalil wasn't the man for her. She'd sworn off men, anyway. So why was she debating taking him into her bedroom and straddling him for the duration of the night? He looked at her as if he wanted the same thing, but that was most likely all he wanted. "What are we doing, Khalil?"

Khalil had learned a long time ago that most women were smarter than most men, so lying was usually a waste of time. Reka was no exception. "We're kissing each other because we're very attracted to one another."

"But we know that this attraction can only lead to heartache," she said breathily.

"I don't know that." His hands moved through her hair. "Do you? I mean, do you honestly believe that I would hurt you?"

As badly as she wanted to say no, she had been down that road entirely too many times. "I honestly believe that this attraction is dangerous and that we should both give it a lot more thought before going any further." She loved the way he massaged her scalp while his eyes searched her face, as if he were trying to memorize every feature.

He chuckled lightly. "I think about you so much now I think I'm going crazy. But you're absolutely right. We need to take this slow because what I have in store for you is serious. I want you to make sure you can handle it."

Pulling her head back slightly and blinking quickly, Reka looked him up and down. "Handle what? You?" She was about to tell him that he should be the one worrying, but his seriousness stopped her.

"Yes, me. Can you handle a real man, Reka?" Her mouth was poised and open, he knew to tell him a thing or two in that brash way of hers, but he quickly put a finger to her lips to stop her. "I'm not playing and I'm not asking if you can handle me sexing you like crazy. I'm asking if you can handle how a real man treats his woman. And how a woman should be with her man. Think about that, Reka, because that's what I'm coming to the table with." He stood to leave then because he wanted so badly to carry her into that bedroom and simply show her all he had inside for her. But that's what she was expecting. So with every ounce of strength he had, he grabbed his suit jacket and coat and headed for the door.

She was still sitting on the couch, probably stunned at what he'd said to her. Good, that would give her something to chew on for the rest of the night. He opened the door, then turned back to her momentarily. "Shut your computer down completely before you go to bed."

And just like that he was gone.

Reka released the breath that had lodged in her chest the moment he touched his finger to her lips. He wasn't simply talking about sex, that she knew for sure. And while she also knew how good she was in bed, she sensed that Khalil was even better. But that wasn't what had her trembling, her heart going at an exuberant rate. It was his words, the fierce intensity of that undeniable question: "Can you handle a real man?"

So now he'd not only kissed her but he'd touched her. He'd felt those supple breasts straining beneath thin cotton and longed for the flesh even more.

Sighing, he turned the key, letting himself into his apartment. He was not a teenager, and sex had come to him fast and steady since his sixteenth birthday. There was no logical reason why just the thought of her, the smell of her perfume, the tilt of her head when she spoke had him horny and hot as a thirty-year-old virgin!

Stripping down to his boxers and t-shirt, he went to his desk and contemplated tonight's events while waiting for the computer to boot up. If he'd stayed she'd be naked by now. His tongue would be flicking across her hardened nipples while she stroked him to ecstasy. She'd moan as he slipped his fingers between her velvety folds. His heart beat faster, stronger and his erection poked boldly through the slit in his shorts.

All he could think about was getting his hands on her, but he knew that was wrong. That wasn't what she needed and it wasn't the only thing he wanted to give her. He wanted her to experience stability and commitment. He wanted to prove to her that men could be trusted, that he could be trusted. Jumping her bones at the first opportunity wasn't going to achieve that.

The telephone rang, startling him. His hand instinctively covered his crotch as if the person on the other end of the phone could see him.

"Hello?" The edge in his tone was completely audible.

"Working late?"

Kahlil sighed at the sound of Keith's voice. "Shouldn't you be entertaining your wife?"

"I would if she'd stop hacking me about the emails and what you're doing about them."

"I've only been on the job a week."

"And yet you've managed to fall for one of my paralegals."

"We're supposed to be talking business." Khalil frowned and punched in the codes to his computer.

"Then get to it."

"It's somebody close to Page & Associates."

Keith was quiet a moment then asked, "How do you know?"

"Reka received a direct email today. I couldn't trace it, but she invited me to her place to look at her home PC."

A low whistle signified Keith was thinking along the personal lines again. "Her *home* PC, huh?"

"It's late, try to focus," Khalil shot back.

"Is that what you were doing? Focusing?" Keith laughed.

Lines of code appeared on Khalil's computer screen. "He mentioned seeing her at a club on Saturday night. So he knows who she is."

Keith was quiet again.

Reading Keith's silence, Khalil sighed. "I thought the same thing. That's why I dropped hints until she invited me to see her home computer." He typed in her password.

"Reka's not like that," Keith sighed.

"I know, but she has a lot of shady characters in her past."

"I presume you're already looking into that."

Reka's email box appeared. "I'll have reports first thing tomorrow morning."

"Keep me posted."

Khalil nodded, scrolled down her list of received messages. "Will do."

"One more thing."

"What's that?"

"Don't sleep with her if she's a part of the investigation."

Khalil's fingers paused over the keys. "I know what I'm doing."

"All right. Explain it to me after you catch this creep."

On instinct Khalil switched screens, pulling up his own personal email. "Will do."

Replacing the phone in its cradle, Khalil typed her address in the 'To' spot. Acting on impulse and remembering Tom Hank's success in the movie they'd just watched, he typed: "Thoughts of You" in the subject line.

9

On one side of the glossy brown table Jonathan Peterson, the CEO of Sensuality, Inc., sat with his sloe-eyed son, Barkley. On the other side Reka and Cienna sat, the epitome of professionalism.

They'd had an eight-thirty appointment and it was now ten-forty-five. They'd discussed everything from the launch party to the possible liability of underage models used in the latest catalog. Now they were discussing Jonathan's will and the changes brought on by his nasty divorce from former model Eleanor DePalma Peterson.

Reka drew lazy circles on her yellow legal pad while they talked. She probably should be paying attention, but Jonathan Peterson was a selfish whiner if she ever saw one. He didn't want to give his wife one dime, even after she'd had the pleasure of interrupting him while he humped their twenty-year-old maid in the laundry room. He looked at Cienna as if he wanted her to be next in line, but wisely held back after he was reminded of her stand on sexual harassment. Reka definitely didn't like the man or the lecherous look in his eyes.

Now his son, that was another matter entirely.

Barkley was about twenty-five, probably six feet tall, with a smooth raisin complexion and gray bedroom eyes. His voice was silky, like fine wine, his smile mind-blowing. Reka sighed. But his rap was weak. She'd heard his tired lines too many times before and was far from impressed. He flirted openly with her and any other woman with a pulse. The one thing he did have going for him was a huge inheritance he would collect upon his father's death or his thirtieth birthday, whichever came first. That was enough to both spoil Barkley and entice women into his bed.

It was a good thing she was into making her own money and planning for her own future, else she'd have to give those skanks a run for their money. Still, sitting across from him didn't amuse her as it usually did. This morning she'd been preoccupied. Thoughts of last night, and Khalil's parting words, still danced in her mind.

"So we're clear that any models appearing at the launch party need to be over twenty-one? The press will be there and they'll be hungry for news. You can't afford another lawsuit right now, especially not with Eleanor on you about money." Cienna began to gather her papers.

"Barkley will ensure that all the models are legal." Jonathan shot his son an eerie look.

Barkley nodded. "Legal and fine." Licking his lips, he looked towards Reka.

He was such an immature goof; she smiled in response. "No doubt." Then made a point of licking her lips in return.

He shifted in his seat uncomfortably. Reka grinned. Just as she thought. Barkley couldn't handle her.

"Then I think we're done here. I'll call Eleanor's attorney, then get back to you." Cienna spoke quickly as she stood.

Reka followed her lead, watching out of the corner of her eye as Barkley's eyes roamed the length of her suit.

Jonathan rose, extending his hand to Cienna. "It's always a pleasure doing business with you, Cienna."

A clearly fake smile spreading across her face, Cienna shook his hand. "Likewise, Jonathan."

They were out of the conference room when Reka heard an intake of breath from behind.

"Is it sexual harassment if I tell you how hot your legs make me?" Barkley all but hissed.

When she turned abruptly, he stumbled, putting his hands up to keep their bodies from clashing. With a hand on her hip and in a gesture that she knew pulled her blouse tightly over her breasts, she stared him right in his sultry eyes. "It is, and I won't hesitate to prosecute to the fullest extent of the law."

"Mmmm, I'm scared of you," he chimed.

"You should be." She rolled her eyes and left him standing there.

Reka was hungry. The early meeting had caused her to miss her daily bagel and coffee, and her stomach was about to start a rebellion. So when she passed the reception desk and Clare, the receptionist, called her name, she almost yelled at the poor older woman. Instead, she took a deep breath and turned.

"Yes, Clare?"

"There's someone waiting over there for you."

Reka followed the woman's gaze to the tiny alcove just off the main lobby. There, in all his tall, fine-ass black man glory, was Donovan Jackson.

From across the room he gave her that smirk that never failed to make her panties wet. She frowned. She must really be hungry and frustrated, because all she felt now was irritation. "Thanks, Clare," she said as she walked past the desk.

His body language said 'come and get it.' His thick lips and bald head said he knew just how she liked it. But her keen memory and her desire not to catch a charge for ramming her fist down his throat ruled. "We don't do criminal work," she said with all the attitude she felt.

Donovan chuckled. "That's cool. I'm not looking for a lawyer."

He still smelled good and his gear was tight, a complete Sean Jean denim hookup with navy blue Tims at his feet. She was so caught up in the sight of him here in the office that she slipped up. "Then what are you looking for?"

He smoothed a hand over his clean-shaven chin. "I'm looking for an assistant," his hand moved down over his chest before falling to his side, "to assist me."

Mmph. Nine months ago she would have bent over backwards to do just that. Luckily she'd grown a hell of a lot in nine months. "Look, Donovan, this is my place of employment. You have to take your games elsewhere."

"I'm not running a game this time. Can't I just take you to lunch?"

"You could if I wanted to go, but I don't. As a matter of fact, I thought we'd decided not to see each other anymore."

Donovan took a step closer. "You decided that and I let it go for a minute, but now I'm having second thoughts."

He reached out, touched one of the curls falling from her udo while he talked. She swiped his hand away. "Well, check this. Your thoughts no longer concern me. What we had is over and done with. Buying me lunch won't change that."

"Damn, girl. Why are you giving me such a hard time?"

"I'm not giving you half of what you deserve, that's what you should be thinking about." She took a deep breath, realizing her voice was elevating and that she was quickly reverting back to the street savvy girl from the club. She didn't like it one bit. "Look, it's just over between us. I don't think lunch, or any other shared meal, is a good idea. So do me a favor and leave for good this time."

She turned to walk away but he grabbed her arm. "I'll leave, but it's not over. Not by a long shot."

With quick strides, a frown on her face and a bag of chips in hand, Reka finally made it to her office and slammed the door behind her. Plopping into the chair, she banged her palm against the mouse and waited for the computer screen to wake from its sleep mode.

Her head began to throb, and her stomach rumbled in protest. She yanked the bag of chips open and hastily stuck two into her mouth. While crunching on the salty snack, she touched the mouse again, dragging the arrow down the list of new emails. Deciding there were no pressing work messages, she switched screens and her personal email account came up. A few jokes, a daily horoscope and a message from a vendor she was checking for Tacoma's wedding showed up in her inbox. Just as she was about to click out of that screen, she spotted a message that made her stomach churn, this time from shock.

To: *sexyreka1@escape.net*
From: *franklinkj@lll.net*
Subject: *Thoughts of You*

If I could stop thinking about you for just one minute of the day I'd probably get a lot more work done. But since meeting you that's been impossible. I cannot begin to erase the past or the heartache that you've endured, but I can promise you one thing, I will be the best man that you never had.

KJF

P.S. Open your top right drawer. Someone's dying to meet you.

Slowly she swallowed, her eyes roaming over the message again. The background was of lively pink roses, the font a pretty script that put her in mind of romance. His signature, simply his initials, gave the impression that he was the only one in her life who would send her a message like this, which incidentally was true. As if the words had just sunk in, she sat up in her chair to pull the desk drawer open.

Inside was a green box with a lovely gold ribbon. Her heart fluttered and her eyes almost watered. Shaking herself free of romanticizing, she tugged at the bow and cracked open the box. Whatever it was had been wrapped in a mess of tissue paper that Reka none-too-gently tore away.

"Oh," she gasped when the lightweight crystal figurine settled in the palm of her hand.

Now her heart all but stopped as she blinked furiously. How had he known? She hadn't told anybody of her collection.

He must have seen them in her apartment, in the curio cabinet on the wall near the door. Damn, he'd paid that much attention.

The painted white face was sad, the red mouth downturned, one lone tear inching down the cheek. Big red pants, a wide yellow shirt, colorful bowtie and huge shiny black shoes, a form she'd grown to love. The delicate crystal and the tag noting the store in which it had been purchased gave her a clue as to the price.

But that really didn't matter to Reka. What seemed abundantly clear was that a lot of thought had gone into this gift. Thoughts of her, just as his message had stated. He had been thinking of her.

Her heart found an unsteady rhythm as an idea formed in her mind. Khalil was definitely different from any man she'd ever known. His leaving her hanging last night and this extremely thoughtful gift were evidence of that.

So what was her reason for not pursuing things with him again?

Age? No, he wasn't simply older than her by seven years; he was more mature, more comfortable with his manhood than the boys she was used to.

And that, she decided, could be a good thing, a very good thing.

Reka was in meetings all morning. He had been behind closed doors with Cienna and Keith all afternoon. By the time he made it back to his office and called her, she was already gone for the day. Unable to quite describe the emptiness inside him, Khalil packed up his things and headed home himself.

Entering his apartment, he performed his usual ritual. He switched on the computer and began to undress. The only place he really let himself go was within the confines of his own home. Slipping into an old pair of basketball shorts and leaving his sleeveless undershirt on, he walked in his socks back into his home office and prepared to work on breaking into the Page & Associates network. If he could figure out how the network had been accessed, hopefully that would narrow down his list of suspects.

After working nonstop for about an hour, exhaustion began creeping into his bones. Glancing at the clock, he noticed it was almost seven. He'd work until eight, pop a TV dinner into the microwave and then be done for the night. Then the doorbell interrupted him.

Reka had left the office an hour early. Taking a trip to the nearest department store, she headed straight for the lingerie department and found herself once again immersed in the products of Sensuality, Inc. It took close to an hour before she selected the right combination and headed towards the subway and home.

"Hot date with Mr. Handsome, huh?" Grammy chirped from her favorite spot on the couch.

Yes, she was still here and truth be told, Reka didn't really see her returning to Sunny Days. But she'd have to deal with that dilemma later. Right now she had another objective. After thirty minutes in the tub, she moistened every inch of her bronze skin, paying close attention to the troublesome areas like the heels of her feet and elbows. She didn't know about anybody else, but she wouldn't want to be all up on a guy and then feel his ashy heels or elbows. That was an instant turn off.

The lingerie lay against her like cool wisps of silk, in an awesome burnt orange hue that almost clashed with her skin tone. Even though it was November, stockings were not going to work with this outfit, and neither were garters. She'd simply go barefoot with her spiky heeled sandals, she thought as she slipped her legs into the form-fitting black bodysuit. Clasping a gold chain belt at her waist, she turned from side to side to survey the results. "Go get him, girl." She winked and gave herself one last pep talk.

Wisely, she'd taken her trench coat into her room with her so Grammy wouldn't see the outfit she was going out in. That would take another half hour of explaining, and she didn't have time for that. "Don't wait up, Grammy," she chimed as she closed the door behind her.

Her heels clicked along the sidewalk as she walked the few blocks to Khalil's condo complex. With each step her heart beat a little faster, and her center pulsated a little more persistently. She'd made up her mind; she was moving forward with Khalil tonight. And whatever happened afterwards would simply happen. But tonight she was going to have that man. She needed to have a taste of him.

She pressed the bell and debated whether to untie her coat and give him a sneak peek right off the bat or keep it closed and let his suspense build. He answered so quickly the decision was made for her.

"Hi." His surprised expression instantly alerted her.

"Hi." Her voice wavered slightly. "Am I disturbing you?" She hadn't really thought far enough into her plan to consider whether he might have company.

"Ah, no. No, you're not disturbing me." When his heart found its rhythm again, Khalil stepped to the side to let her in. "I'm a little surprised to see you here, though."

She walked past him, her perfume following behind her like a dog on a leash. He closed his eyes and willed himself to close the door and follow her into the living room.

"I didn't feel like staying in tonight." Reka stood in the middle of his living room and looked around. Plain furniture, expensive but bland, with straight lines and not a lot of character. "Thought I'd come over and give you another lesson in relaxation." In a few weeks she'd school him on decorating, but first things first.

Her back was to him. Then she turned slightly, her head sort of peeking at him over her shoulder. Her hair was loose, her eyes glittering, her lips shiny and beckoning. He swallowed deeply. "Relaxation. That sounds like a good idea." He took a step closer to take her coat.

He was a gentleman. He'd want to take her coat, to hang it up for her. Reka slowly undid the belt, then slipped the material from her shoulders. He stopped in his tracks, his eyes moving from her head to her feet. She almost purred in pleasure. "Can you hang up my coat?"

Swallowing hard wasn't helping. Taking deep breaths wasn't helping. His groin pulsated, growing with each sweep of her body. Whatever it was she wore, it wasn't enough. The material was like a second skin, making her look like a sultry silhouette instead of a flesh and blood woman in his living room. Again, he had to remind himself that he wasn't a horny teenager. "Ah, sure. Sure. Let me take that for you." He reached for the coat, making sure not to touch her hand as he did. "Make yourself at home," he yelled as he made his way to the closet.

"Go right to my bedroom," he wanted to say, but caught himself. What was she trying to do to him? When he returned to the living room she was sitting on the couch, her legs crossed, painted toenails glittering at him. "So," he wiped his palms down his thighs before sitting down a couple of inches away from her, "I didn't get a chance to see you at work today. Was everything okay?"

Reka shifted on the sofa so that she was now facing him, one leg bent on the cushions, the other still resting on the floor. "Well, it started out horrendously. Then I received this note that sort of made that all better." She smiled at him.

He smiled in return. "Really? A note from who?"

Resting her head on a propped up hand, Reka continued to stare at him. He was so handsome. She could look at him for hours and hours and not get tired of his chiseled features. "I don't really know; he signed it with only his initials. But he gave me a gift." She paused as her emotions threatened to take over. "A really thoughtful gift that I will cherish forever."

Her normally strong, authoritative voice had changed to a soft, almost vulnerable whisper, and despite his better judgment he moved closer to her. "You should be cherished forever." With a palm he cupped her cheek, then lowered his head to kiss her softly on the lips.

"How did you know about the clowns?" she asked, not quite ready to get hot and heavy with him, despite her earlier plans.

Khalil pulled back but couldn't stop touching her. His thumb traced the line of her jaw, then ran down her neck to her exposed collarbone. "I saw them at your apartment and figured you liked them a lot from the way you kept them off by themselves. You do like them, don't you?"

She nodded. "I've always had this thing about clowns. You see, they could always make me smile. No matter what I was going through personally, they never failed to brighten up my day."

"But the one I gave you had a sad face." He frowned.

Reka shook her head. "It doesn't matter. That's his job. Sometimes they act that way only to show you how easy it is to smile. So the outcome is still the same." His touch was making her dizzy.

"Next time I'll buy you one that's smiling."

"You don't have to buy me things. I'm not like that." The last thing she wanted him to think was that she was a gold digger or something.

He'd offended her. "I don't think you're like that. I like seeing you smile and seeing you happy. And if buying a clown makes that possible, then that's what I'll be doing."

She smiled at his words, hoping there was at least some small thread of truth in them. "You're really kind."

Khalil chuckled. "I've never had a woman call me kind before."

"I know it probably sounds weird, but you are. I don't know a lot of kind guys."

Khalil saw the moment her mind reverted to all the bad men in her life and wanted to erase those thoughts as quickly as possible, so he leaned in and kissed her again, this time teasing her with a taste of his tongue. "It sounds wonderful coming from you."

Reka felt calm again. Hell, she was getting hotter with each kiss he carefully distributed. It was time to get this show on the road. Coming up on her knees, she continued to face him. "So, like I said, I came over to help you with that relaxation that you have such a problem with."

Her breasts were scant inches away from his face and Khalil had substantial difficulty keeping his gaze focused. "Okay, so what did you have in mind?" He prayed she didn't want to go out dressed like that. He was barely surviving alone with her in his apartment. If they were out and other men were looking at her, which they undoubtedly would be, he would definitely be visiting the city jail tonight.

In one smooth motion Reka straddled him, clasping her hands behind his neck. His thighs were thick, muscled and provided a stern cushion for her bottom. He looked stunned for a moment. Then his eyes darkened, falling to her lips.

"And you call this relaxation?" Khalil's hands instantly went to her hips, his thumbs grazing over the juncture of her legs while his fingers splayed against soft pliable skin.

Reka inhaled deeply. She hadn't been prepared for the myriad sensations rippling through her. Sure, she'd known she was attracted to him, but every fiber of her being was now on alert. Every sweep of his eyes, the powerful hold of his hands, the intoxicating scent of his lingering cologne had her center moistening in response.

"I know it seems a little stimulating now," she began breathlessly. "But the end result promises you'll be more tranquil than ever." She shifted, bringing her throbbing core closer to his now rigid erection. To her utter delight, those gym shorts did nothing to hide his arousal.

Gritting his teeth, Khalil tried like hell to remain objective, but she wasn't making it easy. His hands moved up her back, buried themselves in her hair, even as he pulled her partially open mouth down to his. The kiss was rough, filled with the sexual energy surging between them. Lips, teeth, tongue, moaning, groping and intense pleasure cocooned them and without any warning Khalil lifted her, turning them so that she now lay on the sofa beneath him. "I'm not feeling tranquil right now, Reka," he growled.

Reka clasped her legs around his waist and arched her neck so his wandering mouth could find that spot just beneath her ear that simply made her weak. "No? What are you?"

Nipping her earlobe, he moved his kisses further downward until they were on the inviting cleavage peeking from her outfit. Like a man possessed, he pulled the material from her shoulders and down her arms, until her breasts sprang free. Raising slightly, he noticed the colorful material and how it barely covered her darkening nipple. All the blood rushed from his head to his center and for emphasis, he ground into her with a ferocious need. "I'm about to explode."

Clearly inebriated by his brazen desire, Reka grabbed the back of his head, pulling him down towards the heavy globes now tingling in anticipation. "Oh no, baby, not just yet," she whispered.

Again Khalil felt his strength slipping. He'd given her control of the kiss the night before and she'd taken him to heights he had never been. Now it seemed she'd taken control again and he was sinking fast. His mouth closed over her right breast even as he deftly slid the material of her bra down, grasping the complete roundness.

Reka sucked in a breath, her eyes fluttering before closing completely. Her center throbbed and no amount of undulating against his erection was helping. She needed him inside her, now! "Khalil." She whispered his name in invitation.

Her voice echoed throughout his brain even as his tongue slid over to lavish her other breast.

Don't sleep with her if she's a part of this investigation.

The words rang in his ears.

Reka slid her hand down inside the rim of his shorts and felt her heart stutter when she discovered that he wore no boxers or briefs. Anxiously her fingers wrapped around his hot length. She dragged her hands up and down, feeling him pulsate with each movement. "Khalil, please," she practically begged.

I promise to be the best man you never had.

Funny thing, those words had him halting instantly.

Staring down into eyes glazed with passion, breasts bared, a body ready for the taking, Khalil took a deep breath. His throbbing erection was now at war with his brain as he slowly pulled on the underwire of her bra until her breasts were covered once more by the bright material.

"What's the matter?"

Her voice was a wounded plea and he avoided her eyes as his fingers brought the sleeves back onto her shoulders and he eased off her.

Suddenly chilled, Reka pulled herself to an upright position, staring at the now retreating body of the man she'd thought was about to make love to her. "Khalil?"

He kept walking towards the bedroom. "Get your coat on, Reka."

Deflated, dejected and thoroughly pissed off, Reka thrust her arms into her coat and was prepared to walk out the door never to speak to Khalil Franklin again when his hand on her arm stopped her.

Pulling her back with one hand and slamming the open door with the other, Khalil looked down into her confused face. "When I take you, it won't be on a couch and it won't be because you're trying to help me relax or it's your way of thanking me for a gift. It has to mean much more than that." He gritted his teeth. "It *will* mean much more than that." He kissed her then, his lips bearing down on hers with all the pent up frustration he was now feeling.

Reka tried to pull away, unwilling to hear his words and too angry to accept his kiss. But when his arms embraced her gently and he dragged his lips over hers in a soft caress, she heard herself moan. Her arms snaked around his neck and she drifted into the safe haven she now considered him to be.

No, she didn't understand him not wanting to sleep with her for a second time. She didn't understand what was going on in that head of his. But what she did understand was the building need to get to know this man better, to open her heart to him as well as her body, to give him the chance to prove that he was the man for her.

And as his tongue dueled with hers, she prayed that he was the right one.

10

"So what's going on with you?" Cienna punched the buttons to set the treadmill and took a swig of water while keeping up with the moderate pace.

Reka shrugged, setting her pace just a little faster. She had a lot of frustration to walk off. "What makes you think something's wrong?"

Chuckling, Cienna tossed her friend a knowing look. "Because for the last hour you've been trying to kill yourself on the weights and now you're acting like you're training for a marathon." Reka remained quiet. "Your forehead's all knotted and you grit on everyone that even makes an attempt at pleasant conversation. Something's going on."

Expelling a deep breath and concentrating on unknotting her forehead, Reka decided it was best to go ahead and tell her. Cienna was absolutely ruthless when it came to weeding out her problems. Outside of that, she and Cienna had become really good friends. And while they were two totally different types of woman, she found herself admiring all that Cienna had built out of her life. Keith Page was not a bad catch at all. They both had successful careers, a beautiful home, the cutest daughter ever seen and they loved each other to death. A part of Reka wished she could have just a fraction of that happiness.

"It's a man," she groaned.

Cienna rolled her eyes. "Good Lord, not again, Reka. What man? And what did the creep do this time?"

This was exactly the reaction Reka had hoped to avoid. Everybody seemed to know her track record with men and they all shared the same view, that she had no taste when it came to picking a mate. Well, this time she hadn't actually picked him, he'd sort of dropped the ball in her court and was now content to watch it bounce around. With a small measure of triumph, because she knew this was the last man Cienna would ever expect her to be involved with, she raised a brow and looked over at the toned woman taking even strides on the machine. "It's Khalil, the computer guy."

Cienna did a double take, opening and closing her mouth a couple of times before finally huffing like she was out of breath. "You're kidding, right? The computer guy? Keith's friend?"

"No. Yes. And yes. We've sort of been seeing each other since he started working at the firm. Outside of the office, of course."

"That's, ah, surprising."

"Why? Because he's the polished, socialite, career-type and I'm one step above ghetto-fabulous?" Although she really didn't mean it, Reka heard the irritated sound in her voice.

Leveling her a surprised look, Cienna simply replied, "No." She took a few more steps, then resumed speaking. "It's surprising because he seems so studious, while you're outgoing and vivacious. I just never would have paired you two up, that's all." Leaning her head to the side Cienna looked at herself in the wall-length mirror for a moment. "But I can see where the attraction would come in. You're both from oppo-site worlds. It's only natural that you'd be curious."

Reka shrugged. "Well, this curiosity is quickly growing."

Cienna's head snapped. "Did you sleep with him?"

Sighing, Reka let her head loll back and closed her eyes. All the while her legs were beginning to burn. "No. But that's not for lack of trying on my part."

"Wait." Cienna held up a hand, giggling. "You're trying to sleep with him and he hasn't jumped your bones yet? That's a first."

"You can hold up on those kinds of remarks, Cienna," Reka said in a mild tone. "It's not like I'm throwing myself at the guy. Whenever we're together there's this thing, something that happens between us. It like draws us closer until I can't help touching him or he can't help kissing me." Reka sighed at the memory. "He kisses me a lot."

Cienna resumed a straight face. "Okay, he likes kissing you. That's a good sign, right?"

"I thought it was, but every time we get a little beyond kissing he puts on the brakes so fast my head spins. I don't understand him at all."

At that moment Cienna could tell her friend was serious. Seriously into Khalil. Never in the years she'd known Reka Boyd had she seen her like this over any man. "Maybe this is about more than sex."

Reka looked over at Cienna, then at her reflection in the mirror, then at Cienna again. "He says he wants it to be more than that."

"And what do you want?"

"I don't want to be hurt again," Reka said without hesitation.

"Nobody wants to be hurt, Reka. Just like nobody wants to be mugged or hit by a car. But they don't barricade themselves in their house afraid to come out either. Tell me this: Do you like him?"

With a wistful sigh Reka gave in. "Yes, I think I like him a lot. He's so different from anybody I've ever met. He's thoughtful and kind and so damn sexy in those expensive-ass suits. I never thought a man dressed to the T every day could move me like that. But man, I almost look forward to seeing his hookup every morning."

Cienna laughed. Reka and Tacoma were obsessed with clothes. "But you see something beyond his looks, and it sounds like he sees something in you beyond your body. I'd say this is a prelude to your first mature relationship. You think you can handle that?"

With burning thighs and sweat pouring from her forehead, Reka jumped off the treadmill. "What I can't handle is another minute of this tortuous workout. I'm heading to the steam bath."

Avoidance. Cienna recognized it and felt sorry for her co-worker. Avoiding the inevitable would not last long. As strong as Reka could be, she was nevertheless putting her money on Khalil to wear her down. Stepping down from her own machine, she followed Reka into the steam bath, thinking over all the things the girl had been through. She deserved some happiness. And for years Cienna had been telling her to leave those clubbing guys and hood rats alone. Maybe Khalil was the one to finally make her see that she needed a real man in her life. After stopping in the locker room to strip and wrap the thick towel around her body, Cienna slowly stepped into the blistering steam.

Thoughts of talking to Keith about his friend the moment she got home crept into her mind.

Maybe Reka and Khalil needed a little push.

It was Friday. Reka hadn't spoken to Khalil at all yesterday. After Clare informed her that he was in meetings, the thought that he was avoiding her quickly faded from her mind. Yet she felt a pang of something every time she thought about him. Dropping her head onto her desk, she sighed. She missed him.

Pulling up her personal email account, she found the message he'd sent her the other day and hit the reply button. Since he was nowhere to be found in the office, she'd communicate with him this way.

Unable to avoid her another minute, Khalil walked into Gramercy Tavern, where Naomi Franklin had made reservations for them to have lunch. He'd talked to his sister Danielle earlier this morning and she'd relayed the information that their mother was very concerned about his love life. So with dragging steps, Khalil made his way to the table, knowing that this would be the longest hour of his life.

"Hello, Mother." Bending forward, he kissed the smooth coffee-toned cheek of the always elegantly dressed Naomi Franklin.

Naomi raised her cheek to his kiss and patted her son on the shoulder. "It's so wonderful of you to give me a little of your time."

Taking the seat across from her, Khalil hastily picked up his menu. The sooner they got on with this confrontation the better. "I told you I had a new assignment and it's been keeping me very busy."

Ignoring his comment, Naomi signaled for the waiter. "Your father is having some difficulties with the computer systems at the firm. He'd love for you to take a look at them."

The waiter approached.

Without so much as glancing at the thin man, Naomi rattled off her order. "I'll have the grilled chicken with pasta and a glass of Chardonnay."

The waiter smiled and nodded, then looked to Khalil.

"Filet mignon, well done, with the potato purée, hold the relish. And a Coke."

"Steak is better rare and needs a nice red wine to truly complement its taste," Naomi commented.

Khalil looked at the waiter, whose gaze was shifting from him to his mother. "Well done and a Coke. Thanks."

With a flick of her wrist, Naomi gave the waiter her menu and waited while he walked away. "I see you're in a defiant mood this afternoon."

A four and a half karat diamond sparkled on her ring finger and smaller diamonds glittered at her ears. Her perfectly colored hair was curled meticulously. Khalil sat back in his chair, making a big show of unfolding his napkin and placing it in his lap. "A grown man has the right to select his own food and drink. I really don't see that as being defiant."

"Don't get flippant, Khalil. I'm still the mother."

He smiled. "That you are. Now tell me, what's the urgency? When you called you acted as if you wouldn't see me this weekend."

Naomi unfolded her own napkin. "Since your no-show at our last dinner party, I'm not sure when I'll see you."

That was a low blow, one that Khalil decided immediately to ignore. There was really no sense in arguing with his mother. "Okay."

"I've talked with Sonya."

Inwardly he groaned, but outwardly he fixed his lips into a thin line and waited for his mother to proceed.

"This separation is ridiculous. If we start now we can still have a grand summer wedding planned. I can call the papers and officially announce the engagement just as I was about to do before you momentarily lost your good sense. Our families can make this mutually beneficial connection."

"Lamar Davenport is already one of Dad's biggest clients. Marrying his daughter is not going to make him invest any more money with the company."

"But a merger of the companies would be phenomenal."

So that's what the ultimate goal was, to merge Franklin Investments with LDS Trading. He knew his father always looked to the bottom line of a financial sheet, but up until now he hadn't been quite convinced that his mother was the same way. Obviously, he'd been wrong. "I am not marrying Sonya."

Their food arrived, as well as another guest.

"Did I hear my name?"

Five feet, eleven and a half inches of toned ivory-colored skin stood between Khalil and his mother. She wore a red Chanel suit, with a long straight skirt and a jacket with an almost indiscreet plunge in the neckline. Her hair was cut in a short, shiny black bob grazing the line of her jaw. Cool brown eyes rested on him as pert lips shimmered with too much red lipstick.

"Sonya." Khalil stood in a mannerly fashion directing her to a chair. "I can't really say I'm surprised to see you here." Casting his mother a deliberate gaze, he returned to his seat.

Before sitting, Sonya air kissed Naomi on the cheek then turned her gaze back to Khalil. "You're looking well. It's been a few weeks since I've seen you."

"As I mentioned the last time I spoke with you, there's really no need in us seeing each other."

"Khalil, I want you to stop this foolishness. You and Sonya were the perfect couple. And I'm not getting up from this table until you've changed your mind about this separation."

Khalil slowly picked up his silverware and began to slice his steak. "I sincerely doubt the management will allow you to sit here forever, Mother."

Naomi gasped.

Sonya frowned.

Khalil stuffed a perfectly well done slice of steak into his mouth.

He was back at the office after a grueling hour and a half lunch with his mother and ex-fiancée. He closed his office door and sat down heavily in his chair. How many times would he have to tell them that it wasn't going to happen? He was not now, or ever, going to marry Sonya Davenport and he could care less about a merger between her father and his father's company. If the two men wanted to merge, then they could damn well work the deal out amongst themselves. He would not sacrifice his personal happiness for the sake of business.

But that steak had been good, and the potatoes nice and smooth, with just a hint of garlic. His stomach now full, he was ready to concentrate once again on his job. But first he'd check his personal email box. He was waiting for a message from his friend at the criminal court in response to the check he was running on a few of Reka's old beaus.

To his surprise, he came across a message from Reka.

To: *franklinkj@lll.net*
From: *sexyreka1@escape.net*
Subject: *Mixed Signals*

I would assume you aren't interested in me if it weren't for the mixed signals. First, you want a date, then you want me to help you relax, then you kiss me like you can't wait to rip my clothes off, then you send me home. It would be an understatement to say I'm confused, but intrigued. I've mentioned how different you are from the other men in my life and you continuously prove me right. So if you want to play the game of seduction, I'm up for the challenge.

RB

A smile spread across his face. She was a challenge all right, one he was looking forward to accepting. He'd thought of her constantly since that night at his apartment and continued to kick himself for turning her away. But deep down inside, he knew that had been the right thing to do. Sleeping with her too soon would destroy any trust he'd gained with her so far. Reka needed to be courted, the old-fashioned way, and he planned to do just that.

Lifting the phone he placed an order, then hit the reply button to her message.

To: *sexyreka1@escape.net*
From: *franklinkj@lll.net*
Subject: *Accepting the Challenge*

Let the games begin!

KJF

After the disappointing lunch experience that afternoon Sonya was happily looking forward to her meeting tonight. She'd needed a change of scenery so a friend had recommended a sort of support group. For the last three years she'd been a part of these support groups but didn't like to stay with one for too long. After a while the same people started to grate on her nerves.

This was exactly what she needed tonight, new people, new experiences. She'd come home to her apartment after the lunch date, a margarita, her favorite drink, and taken a long, hot bath in preparation for tonight. A year ago her life had been right on track. She had been going to marry well, extremely well. Her father would be proud of her and she'd finally feel a part of his life. As it stood now, Lamar Davenport barely knew his daughter was alive. It was her fault, she supposed, for not being born a son. She'd done everything humanly possible to get his attention, but becoming involved with Khalil Franklin had been the only thing to work.

The day Khalil came to her apartment and announced that he didn't love her enough to marry her had been a body blow, but she'd taken it with all the courage and strength she'd inherited from her father. Love didn't have jack to do with them being perfect for each other. Hell, she'd been cheating on him the entire time they'd been seeing each other and she doubted she could ever love a man as dry and stuffy as Khalil. But that didn't change the facts: Marrying Khalil would ensure their families' businesses merging , and her father would be forever grateful to her for that.

Khalil's love cop-out wasn't about to work. She'd get him back; it was simply a matter of time. Since lunch she'd been trying unsuccessfully to think of something she could do to force the issue. The ringing phone interrupted her thoughts.

"I've got some information for you," the voice on the other end announced.

Sonya's mood instantly perked up. "What is it?"

"How much are you willing to pay for it?"

Poor people always had money on the brain. "That depends how valuable it is to me."

"Oh, it's very valuable. In fact, I think this throws a monkey wrench in your crusade to get Khalil Franklin back."

"Just tell me and then I'll decide how much I'm going to pay." Her heart thumped loudly in her chest as she anticipated the news.

"You must think you're dealing with an amateur," the voice chuckled. "Remember, you contacted me with your little problem. I only agreed to help because of the obvious financial gain. Now, I think this information is worth about fifty grand. Get a pen so you can take down my account number. I want it deposited before this conversation goes any further."

The person on the phone talked to her as if she didn't know who she was. Sonya fumed. Fifty grand wasn't a large sum of money to her but without knowing what she was paying for, it seemed like a fortune. "Your information needs to be confirmed first. I still don't know that it's that valuable."

With a smile in her voice the person on the phone spoke slowly. "You can't marry a man who's involved with another woman."

Raking her hands through her hair, Sonya paced the floor. Another woman? That was impossible. She and Khalil had broken up less than three months ago. How could he be involved so fast? "He's welcome to appease his sexual appetite where he chooses if that's what you're hinting at." Sex with Khalil had been less than adequate for her, so if he kept a mistress, discreetly, she wasn't terribly upset over that. After all, she had her needs taken care of by someone else as well.

"Last time I checked you don't send flowers to a good lay. Now here's the account number. As soon as the money hits my bank, I'll call you back with the name of the woman and the specifics of the relationship. Deal?"

Sonya stared out the window of her apartment. The view of Central Park was dismal, at best, but this was all she could afford until Daddy released her trust fund money, which he wouldn't be doing until she married. Her patience was wearing thin but this person knew Khalil and was definitely in a position to know what was going on with him. She'd simply have to pull some strings to get the payment. "Fine. I want to hear from you before seven tonight."

"Hmph, it's almost three now. You'd better get moving on making that transfer."

The line went dead and Sonya tossed the phone across the room.

"Hey man, I need you to do me a huge favor tonight."

Donavan puffed on his cigarette again as he listened to Blade, his lifelong running buddy. "What favor? And why do you *need* me to do it?"

"You know about the parties I be throwing?"

"Yeah," Donovan nodded. Blade was an entrepreneur not solely limiting himself to street pharmaceuticals.

"I got two of them tonight and one of my other dudes can't make it so I need a fill in."

"How much?" In Donovan's world everything boiled down to money.

"Five grand."

Donovan's gloomy mood instantly lifted. He'd been thinking about his run in with Reka. She'd really messed him up. The time he'd been with her had been so different from being with any other woman. And when she walked away from him he'd been devastated. But years on the streets had taught him how to mask his emotions, so he'd simply let her walk, believing that in time she'd come back. But she hadn't.

Finally he'd had no choice but to go to her. Funny thing was, Reka didn't seem affected by him anymore. He remembered a time when all he had to do was touch her and she'd be like putty in his hands. He'd had her any and every way he wanted. She had been the ultimate relationship for him, and he wanted it back. She'd changed since then, he noticed. Her clothes were different, even her hair and the way she talked were different. Maybe working in that business world was changing her into a snob. Nah, Reka could never be that. But he had to admit she looked like she was making a pretty good amount of money at that big fancy law firm. So maybe he needed to step up his game with her. Maybe he needed to show her he had money too.

"All I gotta do is show up and I get paid?" Donovan asked, still thinking of Reka.

"Nah, man, you gotta participate too. But I'm telling you, you're going to love it. I'm thinking about expanding so if you go tonight and you're really feeling it, maybe the next location could be yours to run.

I pull in about fifteen grand a week for one or two parties. And it's a lot more legit then cutting and dividing out the goods."

Donovan thought his words over for a minute. Fifteen grand a week was definitely more than he was used to bringing in, and he could still keep his hustling on the side. Nodding his head, he put the cigarette out. "Yeah, give me the address. I'll do it."

From outside it looked like all the other brownstones on the West Side, but once he stepped through the vestibule and into the foyer, Donovan quickly thought differently. He wasn't accustomed to this type of fancy setup, but didn't allow his ignorance to show. The walls were painted deep green, the thick carpet cushioning his steps a darker hue of the same color. Thick pieces of furniture that looked really old and really expensive were strategically placed. As he approached the living room, his eyes continued to roam.

In here the walls were burgundy, the carpet the same green as in the foyer. Floor to ceiling curtains with some fancy burgundy and green design hung from the windows, casting the room in a gloomy dimness. Candles were alight throughout the room and he inhaled a scent similar to the incense he had at home. On one wall was a long sectional sofa, burgundy velvet with big green and burgundy pillows. In the center of the floor was a black rug, furry, like some kind of animal or something. The only other furniture was a black leather recliner and as his gaze rested there, he noticed it was already occupied.

A man, dressed casually from what he could see, sat in the chair. A woman with flaming red hair that hung past her hips was sprawled on top of him. Donovan was instantly aroused. The woman's skirt was hiked up so that the man's dark hands on the pearly skin of her bottom were clearly visible. The woman moaned even as the man's tongue thrust deeply into her mouth again and again. Then one of the man's hands moved to her hair, pulling her head back as he traced his tongue down her neck to the swells of her breasts.

Donavan shifted as his erection strained against his zipper. Lifting a fist to his mouth, he faked a cough and waited for the couple to notice he was there.

The woman turned, casting him a sultry glare. Then the man hustled up out of the chair, but not before giving the woman a playful swat on her voluptuous rear end.

"Hey, man. You must be Donovan. Blade told me you were filling in for Mike tonight." The man held an outstretched hand to Donovan.

With a shrug Donovan shook his hand. "That's right. I thought there'd be more people here than this." His eyes found the woman again. She was now sitting on the recliner, her legs spread wide, her breasts almost falling out of her blouse.

"Oh yeah. They're on their way. Jeanie and I were a bit early. I'm Larry."

"Okay, Larry. So what do I do now?" Donovan had never done a party like this before, but from the looks of that redhead he was sure he could get into it quickly.

"Just chill til the others get here. Then we'll get started."

With another shrug, Donovan started toward the couch, but was stopped by Larry.

"Why don't you go on over and get to know Imani before the others get here. Imani loves to party and usually by the time all the guests arrive, she's too busy to give personal attention."

Imani had one finger in her mouth, licking its tip, then sinking its length inside. Donovan groaned, casting Larry a glance.

"Trust me, you want Imani's personal attention," Larry said as his hand went to massage his own throbbing groin.

Donovan didn't need any further convincing.

11

Sonya arrived five minutes late, as usual. She didn't like to seem too anxious about these types of things. Letting herself into the house, she first took in the gaudy décor and almost turned around to leave. But she'd had a horrendous day and needed this release like an addict needs a fix.

She'd gotten that return phone call at fifteen minutes to five and, while she'd hated being told what to do by such a no-class commoner, she had to admit the information she received was valuable. Khalil was seeing another woman and from the hundred dollar flowers he'd sent her today, it was serious. After fuming for another hour, Sonya finally decided on a way to get her man back. Though Khalil had always been adamant about not sharing his women, she blatantly disregarded that little rule of his, sure if he'd only known about her outside escapades it would have driven him wild with jealousy.

As she sashayed into the living room, a devious smile stretched across her face. It was past time to drive Khalil wild.

Donovan saw her the moment she walked in, and while he was presently indulging in the D cup breasts of Imani he couldn't seem to tear his eyes away from the pretty tall woman. Easing his mouth away from Imani's magnificent breasts, he continued to palm them as he took in the full appearance of this Nubian goddess. She looked like money from her designer shoes to the slinky red dress he knew had cost a small fortune. Diamonds glittered at her ears, her hair was styled perfectly, and her lips were not too thick, but just right. Imani gripped his penis and was about to lower her mouth on him when the goddess's gaze locked on him.

He was darker than any man she'd ever been with. His clean-shaven head glistened in the candlelight. His eyes were dark, filled with a passion that matched her own. His lips—hanging slightly open—begged to be kissed. Instinctively her nipples hardened and she didn't hesitate to lift a hand to massage them.

His eyes grew to mere slits as his tongue traced his lips. She knew that he watched her, thought of her, even as his hands were on that fat tramp. Knowing she had an audience and loving every minute of it, Sonya slipped the thin straps down off her shoulders, holding the dress on simply by keeping her arms planted firmly at her sides. With a little maneuvering, her fingers managed to hike up the side of her skirt until all her leg was exposed and the thin strap of her thong was on display.

Like a moth to a flame, the ebony hunk rose from his seat on the couch, leaving a befuddled woman in his wake. Sonya didn't hesitate as he crossed to her. She knew what she needed tonight, what would make this horrendous day worthwhile. Her eyes fell to his crotch, to the exposed length of his manhood and she smiled, her tongue snaking out to moisten her now dry lips.

"I'm Donovan," he said as his hand reached out to grab one partially exposed breast.

"Donovan?" What a coincidence, she thought. The woman Khalil was seeing had an ex-boyfriend named Donovan pay her a visit on the job yesterday. "What a peculiar name. Tell me, Donovan," she leaned over and thrust her tongue into his mouth, then quickly pulled it away, "what's your last name?"

Donovan's hand had quickly moved from her breasts to beneath her skirt, slipping past the brief barrier of her thong. "Jackson," he whispered as his finger slipped inside her already wet center and he leaned forward to take her mouth again.

Her day had made a three hundred and sixty degree turn. Sonya's legs trembled as Donovan slipped another finger inside of her. Imagine the good fortune of searching for a way to make Khalil jealous and running into the ex-boyfriend of Khalil's new woman. And by the way he was working his fingers inside her and his tongue in her mouth, Donovan was going to be quite good in bed as well. Hot damn, she'd hit the jackpot tonight! She'd have to thank her friend for referring her to this new party.

Khalil was still anxious. Each time he knew he was going to see Reka his pulse quickened. The anticipation of being with her again filled him. What was it about this woman that made him feel this way? There were so many answers to that question. He could say her smile. Or he could say her confidence. Her wit, her savvy, her professionalism. The list went on and on.

He knocked and waited with anything but patience for her to answer.

"Hi," she said with a smile when she opened the door.

"Hi."

They stood for a few moments, like teenagers on their first date.

"The flowers were beautiful. Thank you." Reka had sworn not to throw herself at him anymore, well, at least not for a while, but she couldn't help wrapping her arms around his neck and holding him tightly. The large bouquet of yellow roses had brought tears to her eyes when they were delivered to her office yesterday afternoon. She'd known instantly who they were from and couldn't stop smiling. Unfortunately, Tacoma had been in the office with her. Actually, he'd been the one to retrieve the bouquet from the front desk, bringing it and a mouthful of questions into her office.

"A beautiful woman deserves beautiful things," Khalil whispered into her hair.

Reluctantly pulling away, she folded her hands in front of her and smiled up at him. "You're going to spoil me."

Tweaking her nose, Khalil resisted the urge to pull her close again. "That's my intention." Actually his intention was to make her fall in love with him, but for now he'd settle for baby steps.

"C'mon and sit down. We've already had dinner but I could fix you something if you want." Escorting him to the couch, Reka chatted amiably.

"No. That's okay. I just wanted to spend a little time with you."

They sat close, thigh to thigh. Reka didn't know what to say next. In truth, she didn't really want to say anything. She wanted him to kiss her, then take her into her bedroom, no, wait a minute. Grammy was in her room, lying down. She was going to have to do something about her grandmother's living arrangements soon.

Khalil broke the silence. "Actually, I wanted to ask you something."

"What?" At this moment he could ask her just about anything and she'd happily oblige. In the weeks she'd known him she'd discovered that she not only liked him, she really liked him. That wasn't new for her, though. She'd really liked a lot of men in her life. But this didn't feel the same. She thought about him constantly, about what he was wearing, what he smelled like, how his hands felt on her, how his lips felt. It was a wonder she could still do her job with all the Khalil thoughts running rampant through her mind.

"Thanksgiving is Thursday."

"I know." Reka waved a hand. "Don't even start talking about it. Grammy's talking about going out to shoot her own turkey and my mother's claiming she doesn't eat pork all of a sudden. Shopping for food is going to be a task this year."

"Oh. You're cooking dinner?"

He sounded disappointed. "I usually do the cooking for me, Mama and Grammy. We have our little meal, and then we sit and watch movies for the rest of the day. How does your family celebrate the holiday?"

"That's kind of what I was going to ask you. I wanted you to spend Thanksgiving with me at my parents' house."

Reka's mouth opened, then closed, then opened again. "Your parents? The ones that live in Greenwich?"

Khalil chuckled. "I only have one set of parents, Reka. But it's cool if you already have plans. Maybe I'll come by here for dessert."

"She don't have no plans. She'll be happy to go meet your parents." The crotchety voice came from the direction of the stairs, signaling Grammy's entrance.

Khalil immediately stood, going to help Grammy down the remaining stairs. "Hi, Grammy. How are you this evening?"

"I'm just fine, handsome, just fine indeed. Now you don't pay my grandbaby no mind." Grammy continued to talk as Khalil helped her into another chair. "You go on and meet his parents, chile. It'll be fun."

Khalil returned to his seat beside Reka. Reka cut Grammy an evil glare that the old woman paid no attention to. "Then what are you and Mama going to eat? She can't cook, and you'd probably burn my house down."

Grammy rolled her eyes and tucked a wayward strand of gray streaked hair behind her ear. "I'm the one that taught you how to cook, young lady. Plus, I might go down to Sunny Days."

"You're going home?" Reka sounded hopeful.

"That ain't my home. But this fella, Cletus, he called me yesterday, said they were having a bingo marathon on Thursday after that taste-less holiday meal they serve." Grammy crossed her heavy ankles and sat back in the chair, patting her hands together. "Cletus knows how I love me some bingo."

Khalil suspected Grammy also loved her some Cletus. "So are you gonna come?"

Reka readily admitted to herself that she was nervous. Meeting Khalil's parents, the people that brought him into this world, the rich folk that he'd been raised by, was something she hadn't thought about. But he looked so hopeful, how could she turn him down? "Sure, I'll go."

The telephone rang, effectively ending that conversation and Reka thankfully got up to answer it.

"Listen, handsome." Grammy leaned over towards Khalil and whispered, "You're moving way too slow. Now the gifts are a good touch 'cause ain't no man ever bought her stuff like that before. But it's time you put forth a little more effort to woo my grandbaby."

Intrigued by the woman's candor, Khalil leaned over to hear her better. "What do you suggest, Grammy?"

Without a moment's hesitation, those wine-colored eyes focused on him. "I suggest you and her get busy."

Khalil's widened with her words. "Come again?"

"You heard me. Mount her, put that old-fashioned whip appeal on her. That's how you keep a woman like Reka. She's a good girl, she's smart and she has plans for her life. But God bless her soul, she's just like me and her momma. We needs some good lovin' and we needs it all the time."

Khalil couldn't contain his laughter a moment longer and only ceased when Grammy smacked him on the knee. "Now stop that foolishness. You take her to meet your parents Thursday, and then you take her back to your place and you lay it on her. I guarantee it'll do you both some good."

"You guarantee, huh?" Khalil didn't know whether to take Grammy seriously or to remind himself that she was an aging old woman. Either way, her idea had some merit to it.

"Grammy, Cletus is on the phone for you," Reka announced.

Grammy struggled to get out of the deep cushioned chair. Khalil rose to help her. "See, Cletus got a taste of my good lovin' and that's why he keeps a-callin'. Take my advice, handsome, and make your move."

Khalil stared at her questioningly as she wobbled to the other end of the room to answer the phone.

"What was she rambling about?" Reka asked.

He turned to her, looked at those luscious lips and that curvy little body, and felt all the blood in his body rush immediately to his groin. "Oh, nothing," he lied even as he hurried to take his seat again before she saw his arousal.

He was going to have to give Grammy's words some serious thought.

To: mail@passoclaw.com
From: Jack
Subject: The Naughty and Nice Collection

I've finally hit the jackpot! Jill was just as sweet as I'd thought. Forget the Tantalizing Thong Collection, it's all thanks to the Long Lasting Lickin' Lingerie. Kudos to the firm for offering Sensuality, Inc. all that good advice.

I've made it past first base and I owe it all to you!

If anybody needs some pointers, please don't hesitate to contact me!

Jack

At 10:45 A.M. the email hit every computer at Page & Associates. At 11:00 A.M. Khalil was reading it for the third time. He was having zero luck tracing this guy, and that frustrated him. Not only that, his mother had called and left a message about Thanksgiving dinner and the possibility of him inviting Sonya. Add that to the fact that he wasn't sure if he was getting to Reka or not, and he was more than frustrated.

His mind reeled with computer code, interfering family and a woman who drove him mad with desire. No wonder he hadn't yet found out who Jack was. There was just too much other stuff going on in his mind. His temples throbbed as he downed the last drops of his now-cold coffee. Rubbing his eyes one more time, he resigned himself to the job at hand. He needed to find out who was sending these emails, and he needed to do it quickly. Once he had that part figured out—once Reka or one of her friends was excluded from the list of suspects—he could move forward. Keith would have someone to prosecute and he could concentrate all his attention on Reka. Maybe even take Grammy's advice.

That advice had been uppermost in his mind since last night, and coming in the office this morning to a message hinting at Jack's oral pleasure was not helping. As he read the message for the fifth time, he found himself growing more irritated.

A brief knock on his door almost had him yelling for whoever was on the other side to go away. Instead he took a deep, steadying breath and answered gruffly, "Come in."

"Good morning. I thought I'd bring you another cup of coffee."

Khalil looked up to see Tyrese, her long blond-streaked hair hanging well past her shoulders. Her facial features, inherited from the Caucasian side of her family, were more prominent as she smiled. "Ah, thanks, Tyrese. You really didn't have to do that." And that was the truth. Since she was the firm's accountant, there was really no reason why she should be bringing him coffee.

Tyrese took a seat and crossed her legs. "It was no problem. I wanted to talk to you anyway."

His brows raised in question, Khalil slid the cup of hot coffee out of his immediate reach. When he worked he had a tendency to push his keyboard around and he didn't want the task of cleaning spilled coffee to be added to his already stressful day. "What did you want to talk to me about?" He focused on her instead of what he really wanted to be concentrating on—that message from Jack. She was a pretty enough woman, a little too conceited for his tastes. Although she was attractive, her heavy breasts were clearly meant for a thicker person and made her slim build a bit awkward. He had noticed that her blouses were always left unbuttoned, displaying a good amount of cleavage. That was probably meant to turn somebody on, but it wasn't him.

"I noticed you stay to yourself a lot, and was wondering why."

He shrugged. "I was hired to do a job, that's what I'm doing."

A slender hand lifted, rested at the hollow of her neck, then slipped down the opening in her blouse. "Did you read this morning's message?"

Khalil didn't miss the gesture, but kept his eyes carefully trained on hers. "Yes. That's what I was working on before you came in."

"Really?" Tyrese licked her lips. "So what do you think? I've got to tell you I'm tempted to head over to Sak's and pick me up a couple pieces from that Long Lasting Lickin' Lingerie. What colors do you think would look good with my complexion?" With a flick of her wrist, the next button came undone, revealing her black lace bra.

Suddenly his little office was ten times smaller. Khalil took a deep, steadying breath. After all, he was a man. Creamy, ivory-toned mounds scarcely covered by black lace were there for his perusal. Was there anything more sexy than black lace?

"I think that Jack is losing sight of the fact that this is an office and that his messages are more than inappropriate here."

Uncrossing her legs, Tyrese let them gap a little, just enough to provide a hint of what was beneath her skirt. The tip of a finger traced one puckered nipple just before she stood and moved around his desk.

Khalil turned in his seat, shifting so that his arousal wouldn't be apparent, but now facing her as she came closer.

"And what about the rest?? What color do you think would look good on me? On these?"

Her blouse came completely open, her heavy breasts jutting towards his face. If he but sat up, leaned forward and opened his mouth, she'd gladly breastfeed him. Khalil's mouth watered. Then his eyes went to her face again and he realized it wasn't the face of the person whose breasts he'd like to feed from. She looked down at him with clear implications, her hands lifting the globes for him to indulge. Abruptly he stood, grabbing the ends of her blouse and pulling them closed.

"Tyrese, I don't have to tell you how inappropriate your behavior is, do I?" He spoke sternly as he pushed her back and out of his way, moving towards the door. "Cienna has a stiff policy about sexual harassment. Do I need to file a report?"

Tyrese frowned as she hastily buttoned her shirt. "No!" she almost shouted at him. "You don't have to file a report. Although I would suggest seeing a doctor for your obvious ailment." With her clothes back to normal Tyrese approached him at the door, standing toe to toe with him, still flaunting her goodies.

"I don't have an ailment. But I'm wondering if you don't have some issues of your own."

Tyrese smiled, moved in a little closer until just the tip of her breasts rubbed against his chest. He could tell Cienna whatever he liked. She wasn't staying at this dead end job too much longer, anyway. She was being paid well to deliver information, and she'd be out of here soon enough. With a long red painted fingernail, she traced the line of his jaw, heard the crackle of his light beard beneath her ministrations. "I don't have any issues that can't be resolved by a real man. It's not my fault if you're not what I thought you were." Licking her lips again, she let her nail linger just beside his mouth. "But it is a pity."

Repulsed by such a blatant come-on, Khalil grabbed her wrist, pulling her hand away from his face, then opened his office door and forcibly pushed her out. "Don't make the mistake again," he growled. She'd just lost all his respect.

Reka had seen the message and talked to Tacoma for about twenty minutes about it. Walking from the copy room back to her office, she found herself still thinking about it. She didn't consider herself a freak, sexually uninhibited maybe, but not a freak. And normally erotic words or insinuations had little effect on her, but this morning as she'd re-read the message for the second time in her own office, she'd felt the telltale tightening in her lower belly and had to squeeze her thighs together tightly to keep from wanting to pleasure herself.

It was crazy, she knew, and most likely due to all the kissing and rubbing she and Khalil had done last night on her couch. Lord, she didn't know how much longer she was going to be able to stand him stopping their progress just as it was getting good. Last night she'd taken a lukewarm shower—'cause that cold water was for the birds— and rubbed her tightened clit until a release of some sort had taken over.

In the morning, however, she realized that Khalil was being just what he'd told her he was: a good man. He desired her, she was sure of that point, but he wouldn't push things. It dawned on her then that she wanted so much more beyond the physical with Khalil. Something that she had been afraid to ever want from a man. She'd been through enough relationships, enough heartache, enough disappointments in her life to know that wishing didn't always make your dreams come true. But with Khalil there was hope.

She wore a long flowing skirt this morning with a button up blouse and matching vest. So while she stood at the copier thinking of Khalil, and not Jack's message referring to Jill's sweetness, feelings beyond the physical need for him began to take root and she shivered at their intensity. She looked at her watch. It was 11:45. In another fifteen minutes she'd take her lunch break. She'd go outside and partake of the crisp fall air and attempt to clear her mind. Now, more than ever, she needed to focus where Khalil was concerned.

She'd just passed Conference Room C, the smallest one on this floor and the one usually used for storing closed files instead of actual meetings because of its size, when something akin to a moan echoed in her ears. For a minute she thought she'd actually moaned aloud. She looked around to make sure nobody had seen her. But this part of the office was deserted as the attorneys and their assistants were lined on the opposite side. Just as she took another step, the moan sounded again.

Now she knew it wasn't her this time. She stopped, looked around again and saw nothing. When she backtracked a few steps, the moaning increased in volume and in speed. On impulse she leaned an ear against the conference room door.

"Yes, baby. Bite my nipples. Oh yes!" she heard a male voice say.

The moaning increased and Reka flattened her ear completely against the door. She wished she had a glass or something to improve the sound. But when she heard the next voice she was glad she didn't.

"Yeah, suck it harder. That's right, just like that."

She had to cover her mouth to keep from screaming. It was Tacoma! He was in that conference room with somebody telling them to suck it harder. She'd know his voice anywhere. She wanted to turn that knob and barge in there. She liked Terry, and they were planning a wedding. No way was Tacoma in there cheating on his fiancé.

"Mmmmm, Terry. Terry. Terry," Tacoma chanted.

Reka's anger turned to giggles as she clamped her hand down even tighter over her mouth. Lord have mercy, Tacoma and Terry were getting it on in the conference room. Out of respect for her friend and because, quite frankly, she didn't think she could stand hearing any more from the two of them, she eased away from the door and hurried back to her office.

When her office door was securely closed behind her, she quickly picked up the phone and paged into that conference room. It beeped several times. Then she hung up and did it again. Tacoma still didn't pick up.

"So he wants to play like he's not in there. Okay, I've got something for his ass." Reka beeped into the office again, but this time she spoke into the receiver, knowing that the phone system they had would instantly switch into intercom mode and her voice could be heard throughout the room. "I know you're in there and if you value your job, you'll finish up quickly and take the rest of the day off."

She heard their gasps, then the shuffling of the phone as Tacoma finally picked up.

"Reka?"

"You're damned lucky it is me, fool! What are you thinking? You know you can get fired for what you're doing!" she screamed at him.

Out of breath and sweating, Tacoma tried to speak. "I know. I know. But girl, that message got me all worked up. I just had to call Terry."

"And invite him down to the office for a quickie. That is sick and dangerous, Tacoma. Now I suggest you and Terry fumigate that conference room and get the hell out of there before somebody catches you."

In the background she heard Terry's voice. "Yeah. Yeah. Tell him I said hi. I can't believe you two." She shook her head and hung up the phone.

Shaking her head, she reached for the folder that held the list of suggested models for Sensuality, Inc.'s launch party on Saturday. She'd been working on it since last week and had most of the women's ages confirmed. She'd have to be at the event on Saturday and for a moment wondered if she should ask Khalil to be her escort.

That's all it took, that one work-related thought of him. Coming on the heels of Tacoma's sexual escapade, the thought of Khalil had her nipples tightening again. She'd never craved a man like this before in her life. Was it because he incited something in her mentally as well? Whatever the case, he was on her mind more and more lately.

It must have been mental telepathy because not two seconds after she had the thought Khalil knocked and entered her office, closing the door behind him.

12

"Good morning," Reka mumbled. Khalil looked different this morning. His dark suit and brooding expression made him look almost sinister. His light skin seemed flushed and she saw the muscle in his jaw twitch as he approached the desk.

"Is it a good morning, Reka?"

Even his voice sounded different, rough, as if he'd just awakened. "Are you upset about the email? Everybody's talking about it. You wouldn't believe what I just witnessed a few minutes ago." She was babbling, she knew, but she couldn't help it. He was different, and that difference alarmed her.

"No. I can't seem to keep my mind on that email, or work, or anything else for that matter," he admitted before taking a seat across from her.

Reka licked her lips nervously. "Then what's on your mind?" She was almost afraid to ask. She didn't know what was going on with Khalil but her heart now hammered in her chest with a sense of dread.

"You." Khalil took a deep breath. "You're always on my mind."

"Is that a good or bad thing?" she asked tentatively.

Khalil smiled, then visibly relaxed. "Only you would ask that question. Of course, it's a good thing. I'm trying to tell you how much you've come to mean to me, Reka."

Her heart settled into a smooth little rhythm and she gave a huge smile. She'd thought for a minute that she'd done something wrong, or that maybe he'd realized that pursuing a relationship with her was a bad idea. "Really? Then proceed." With a wave of her hand she sat back in her chair, enjoying his handsome features and his strong aura.

Khalil commanded respect. She saw it when they were in the restaurant and in the way the majority of the staff treated him at the office.

He was all business when he needed to be and yet all man at the same time. It was no wonder she'd fallen for him.

Khalil studied her. There she was, all professional and yet sexy, sitting behind that desk daring him to come and take her. Daring him to rescue her at the same time. There was a vulnerability to Ms. Reka Boyd that she didn't want anyone to see. But he'd seen it. When she was at home mothering Grammy or when she was with Tacoma being the friend that he needed. These were sides that the tough-as-nails Reka didn't want anybody to see, or if they did see, she dared them to mention it. These were the sides of her that endeared her to him even more.

"You are a very special woman. Has anybody ever told you that?"

"No." She cleared her voice. "I don't think they have."

She kept her eyes level with his but he knew his directness was making her uncomfortable. "They should have. I've never met anyone like you and I can't help feeling that I've been missing something great all these years. There is so much I want to do for you."

Reka stood then and moved around the desk. "I don't need you to do anything for me, Khalil. I'm capable of taking care of myself."

Khalil realized the error in his wording, then stood, taking both her hands in his. "No, baby, don't misunderstand me. I know you're independent and I know that you can handle yourself and anybody else that comes along." His thumbs rubbed the soft skin of her hands as he spoke. "But you've had to do that all your life. For once, I want you to be able to sit back and know that there is somebody that will take care of you. I want you to let go and allow yourself to be loved."

At those words Reka tried to pull her hands free. "No. I can't do that."

Khalil held on to her. "Why?"

"Because that's how you get hurt. You depend on people and people let you down. They disappoint you and then you're left to deal with all those emotions and situations that you weren't prepared for." She'd been looking away from him as she spoke but now she stared up into his warm eyes. She could fall in love with those eyes. She could easily wake up every morning and happily smile into them. But she lived in the real world, where happy endings weren't easy to come by. "I take care of myself, at all times," she said solemnly.

Khalil released her, lifted his hands to cup her face and smiled. "It's time to learn a new song, Reka." He caressed her smooth skin, then bent down and kissed her softly on the lips. "I'm going to teach you how to trust." He kissed her again, lingering over the softness of her lips. "How to let go." His tongue stroked her bottom lip, nipping and drawing it into his mouth. "How to love."

Reka was used to his kisses, used to his touch by now. But this she hadn't expected. Maybe it was his words, or maybe it was the deep sincerity with which he'd said them. Whatever the case, her senses froze, her lungs stalled, her heart seemed to stop. Then his tongue lovingly stroked hers and she melted. Right there in her office, with her bottom pushed against her desk, Khalil's large body looming over hers, his hands cupping her face ever so gently. She felt his steadiness, his protection, his vow to be the man she needed.

And then it shifted.

His hands moved around her waist pulling her closer; his head angled to take the kiss deeper. And his pledge to her changed to something more primal, more absorbing than anything she'd ever felt before. His lips moved on hers in a compelling, but not demanding, way. He sipped and suckled her lips, stroked his tongue deeply inside her mouth. His hands moved over her back, caressing her, kneading her, convincing her.

She kissed him back, wrapping her arms around his neck and pulling him closer. Pleasure, hot and wet, a combination of lips and tongues and, she now admitted readily, emotions. Emotions swept through her, lifting her from the defensive perch she'd been on these last few years. She went willingly, letting him lead the kiss but giving as good as she got. She was letting go, giving him what he asked of her. And she was enjoying it.

When he lifted his head it was with a reluctance she knew they shared. Her arms remained around his neck as her heart thumped loudly in her ears. She stared straight ahead, at his chest instead of into his face. She wasn't sure what to say after that, what to do.

With a finger to her chin Khalil lifted her face. "Don't think about it, just let it be."

"You seem so certain." And she was so scared.

"I learned a long time ago to trust my gut instinct. And the moment I met you I knew I needed you. It'll be good between us, I promise you."

Reka drew in a shaky breath and decided to take him up on his promise. "I'm going to hold you to that," she said jokingly. But she'd taken his words seriously. She was taking a risk. She was giving him a part of herself she had decided never to give again. And he'd better be worth it.

"Please do."

She arched a brow, then tried to move out of his grasp. "But right now we are in the office. Cienna has very strict rules about personal relationships in the office."

Khalil knew about those rules. Keith had already warned him. "You're right," he said with much regret. Then he pulled her to him one last time, for one last embrace that would need to last him the rest of the day. "I'll let you get back to work."

Reka smiled as he released her, feeling the giddiness of a young girl. It was just a simple hug, but it moved her almost as much as the kiss had. "Yeah, and you need to get on that email situation. I think it provoked an all time low in the office this morning."

"Really? What happened?"

Reka shook her head. "I'll tell you about it on our personal time."

He warmed inside at the sound of 'our personal time.' "Okay. Lunch or dinner?"

He had opened the door and was now standing half in and half out of her office. Reka sat back in her chair, unable to stop the incessant smiling. He made her feel so good. "Both."

Tacoma's face was scrunched up as he listened to Reka.

"I mean, he just seems too good to be true. After that kiss, the rest of my day was shot right to hell." Reka snapped peas at Tacoma's kitchen sink. It was the day before Thanksgiving, and she'd gone over to his apartment after their three-hour-early release from work. He and Terry felt no shame for their office antics. Both of them grinned from ear to ear when Reka walked in fussing about their office rendezvous.

"Don't make that face," Reka warned. "The least you can do is listen to my sickeningly sweet moment after I had to listen to you and Terry in the conference room."

"True." Tacoma put four fingers to his lips to still a smile. "Okay, so he's a great guy, a gentleman and a good kisser. Now what?"

"You make the answer sound obvious. I don't know why I even told you." Because that's what she was used to doing, she thought to herself. For as long as she could remember Tacoma had been her sounding board. Cienna was a good listener too, but given office policy, she would have been a fool to run and tell her boss.

"Well, that's the bottom line. My question is, why are you here instead of at his place finishing up your business? I've never known you to be shy about sleeping with a man."

For some reason that made her sound like some sort of hussy, and Reka was positive she didn't like that. "Thanks a lot." She snapped one pod a little too hard and the peas flew out of the bowl.

Tacoma sighed and picked them up. "We'd like to have some left for dinner, if you don't mind."

"But that's just it, sex was easy with those other guys because there was hardly ever any real emotion tied to it. I can say that now, because I know I've never felt what I feel for Khalil with anyone else," she sighed, ignoring his smart retort. " I mean, take Donovan for instance…"

"Woo girl, don't even mention Donovan and his fine ole chocolate self." Tacoma fanned his face. "If I didn't have Terry and you weren't my girl, mmm, mmm, mmm. Something definitely would have popped off there."

Reka rolled her eyes. "In your dreams. Donovan is as straight as that lamp pole over there. Besides, I was just using the relationship between me and Donovan as an example. Donovan and I had good sex, but I think that's all we had."

"And you and Khalil have what?" Tacoma could see that she was serious, so he'd let the jokes rest for a minute. "You really like him, don't you?"

Nodding, Reka let that little revelation sink in. She really did like him. So what was she going to do about it? "I'm just wondering why he seems to like me so much."

Tacoma nudged her until she almost fell in the floor. "Don't ask stupid questions. You know you've got it going on."

"No. I mean, yes, I know I'm a good person and that I'm not a bad looking woman."

"If I wasn't happily in love with my man I'd be trying to get with you," Tacoma added with a smile.

Reka cast him a teasing glare. "And I'd be running like hell." She giggled.

Tacoma snapped the pod open and let his peas roll into the bowl with much attitude. "Not funny."

"Seriously, though, I just don't know what he sees in me. I mean, he's educated and sophisticated and from a wealthy family. And I'm just me, with my community college degree and my looney tunes grandmother walking around my apartment in pieces of the Sensual Safari Collection."

Tacoma threw his head back, laughing. "You didn't tell me Grammy still buys lingerie."

"She didn't buy it. You know I get samples of all Sensuality, Inc.'s new stuff because Cienna likes to keep her guard up with lawsuits against the company. Well, I thought I had all that stuff carefully hidden away until I got home the other day and she was modeling some of it for her friend Cletus from the nursing home."

"Lawd, I'll bet that was a sight." He was holding his stomach laughing now.

"No, the sight was seeing Cletus' shriveled old erection as Grammy pranced around in front of him. And then neither one of them having any shame when I walked in. Can you believe she had the audacity to complain about not having any privacy? In my house! If my mother doesn't come and get her soon I'm going to lose my mind."

"Girl, you know Janell ain't hardly worried about you and Grammy, so you might as well get used to the roommate."

Reka sighed and went back to snapping the peas, her mind still on the situation with her and Khalil. She really didn't know why he liked her. The one thing she was sure of was that she wanted the chance to pursue things with him, to try to be the woman he believed she was. She just wasn't sure how.

"Look." Tacoma grabbed her by the shoulders and turned her to face him. "Stop worrying about that foolishness. He likes you because you're smart and you've got ambition and because you're a great person. With the best cheekbones I've ever seen," Tacoma ended with a smile.

Reka smiled. There were times when Tacoma was her biggest fan and champion supporter. That was why she loved him so. "Yeah, I guess you're right."

"Oh, you know I'm right. Now you're going to dinner at his parents' house tomorrow. What are you going to wear? You know first impressions are everything, especially with the rich."

"I was thinking about a pantsuit."

Tacoma nodded his head. "Good move. Wear the silver one with the lame shell and matching shoes. It's an excellent cut and looks amazing on you. And pull your hair up, that's elegant."

"Khalil likes my hair down."

"Honey, you've already impressed Khalil. Now you've got to impress his mama. Do as I say and you'll be just fine."

For the next hour Tacoma told her what to do and what to say tomorrow at dinner. Then they moved on to wedding preparations. And for the first time, while she twisted netting into wedding favors, Reka began to think that matrimonial bliss might be somewhere in her future.

"I just wanted to give you a heads-up about tomorrow," Khalil spoke into the telephone as he lounged on his couch.

"So you're bringing your new girlfriend home to meet the family. Good luck," Danielle said with a sigh.

Danielle was younger than him by three years, but she'd one-upped him by getting married five years ago and giving their parents the first grandchild, Lance. She didn't subscribe to the same book of rules his parents did but she tended to stay on their side since both she and her husband worked for the family company.

"I'm not going to need luck. Reka is a wonderful woman. You're going to love her."

"It doesn't matter what I think. You know whose vote counts."

"Mother just has to get over it. I'm not marrying Sonya."

Danielle sighed. She'd heard all this before and personally wasn't at all bothered by her brother's refusal to marry the catty woman. "So what's this woman like? Does she work?"

"She's a paralegal at this firm I'm working at. She lives a couple blocks away from me with her grandmother."

"Is that all the family she has?" Danielle shifted on the stool in her kitchen.

"Well, I've met her mother, and I think she said she has a brother, but he's in jail."

"You might want to leave that tidbit of information out when you introduce her to Mother."

Khalil laughed. He had been thinking about how this dinner was going to work out. Reka was important to him. And he knew that whatever the outcome, he was going to continue to see her, regardless of what his parents thought. But he still had reservations about how this would all play out. Naomi Franklin could be vicious when provoked, and as much as he loved his mother, he knew that he'd side with Reka should it really come down to it.

"Just try to make her comfortable, will you? I need somebody on my side for a change."

Danielle smiled. If he only knew. She was always on his side because she'd always envied his independence, his determination to be what he wanted despite what was expected of him. She didn't have any of that, and while she was happy with her life, her husband and her son, she often wondered what would have happened had she pursued her acting. "I've got your back, big brother, don't worry about it."

"Thanks, Danielle."

He wanted to call Reka. It was after eight o'clock and he hadn't heard her voice for more than five hours. This morning in her office had been a milestone for them. He wanted her and she wanted him. They'd already discovered that much. But something else had happened in that tiny room. Something had passed between them, something beyond just physical desire.

That was probably crazy, considering he'd known her for all of six weeks. Still, he knew what he felt and he trusted those feelings. Would she fit in with his family? Well, he wasn't blind, he could see the obvious differences, her upbringing, her outlook on life, her candor. But those were all the things that made her who she was, and that was the woman he was falling in love with.

Khalil was scheduled to pick Reka up at two. It would take about an hour to get to his parents' house in Greenwich, Connecticut. He planned to take the scenic route, because he knew she was nervous.

Reka was wearing the silver pantsuit and matching pumps with a lamé clasp at her ankle. She'd decided against her long leather coat and instead had gone with the fur-collared black wool. She felt classy and mature as she stepped into Khalil's car. Against Tacoma's advice she'd flat ironed her hair and let it hang around her shoulders. The moment he saw her, Khalil had run his fingers through it, saying she was beautiful. She'd call Tacoma the moment she got home to tell him.

While they drove, they chatted amiably about this and that and nothing. It was a comfortable ride and Reka found herself relaxing. "You know, I recall I was supposed to be helping you relax, but these last couple of days you've seemed more laid back than ever. I guess you didn't need my help at all." She glanced out at the thick trees and huge houses lining the streets.

For a minute he felt guilty for the pretense he'd used to get closer to her. "It's because of you. I think by simply being around you I've become a new person."

Reka turned her lips up in disbelief. "I didn't change you. If you're different it's because that was the real you all along."

"You think so?"

"Yes, I do. Sometimes I think people are raised to be a certain way, but that's not the person they are on the inside."

She'd hit the nail right on the head and Khalil cast her a serious look. She'd summed his entire life up in one neat sentence and she probably didn't even know it.

"Do you think your parents will like me?"

Because she sounded vulnerable, her voice going very low, he was concerned. Was this a good idea bringing her out here? "They'll like you, and even if they don't, they'll respect you and the role you play in my life."

"And what role is that? I mean, what are we doing, really?" She'd lain in her bed last night pondering their relationship. He'd said he was going to show her how to love. Had he been serious?

Khalil thought about her question and, while he readily knew the answer, he wanted to phrase it so that she wouldn't be afraid or discouraged. "We're dating. And moving towards a meaningful relationship, I hope."

"Oh."

"What did you think we were doing?"

"I wasn't entirely sure. That's why I asked. I mean, we've been out and we've shared meals and we've, ah, kissed." Although their kissing seemed a lot more significant than the average, she couldn't think of a way to say that to him without embarrassing herself.

"That we have," he said wistfully.

She nodded at the sound of his voice because it mimicked just how she felt when she thought of their kissing. "So I was a little mixed up as to what exactly you would call us."

"Let me make it simple for you. You're my woman, which means I'd better not even hear whispers of you being with someone else." He pulled into the driveway and put the car in park before turning to face her. "And I'm your man." With a finger beneath her chin, he lifted her face so that she stared at him.

"Which means if I even hear whispers of you being with someone else I have permission to cut her and make your life a living hell," she whispered.

Khalil smiled. "That's it exactly."

Reka wasn't really sure what she expected, but it certainly wasn't the large foyer—the size of her living room, dining room and kitchen put together—with marble floors and a huge crystal chandelier. The walls were stark white, the floor covered in a white woven rug with an intricate gray design. On one wall was a large picture, a countryside scene. On another wall a picture with swirling muted colors. She had no idea what it was supposed to represent. A woman who looked to be in her mid-thirties and was dressed in a gray uniform, complete with white bib and hat, came to take their coats. She looked to be Hispanic.

"Good afternoon, Marla," Khalil said as he shrugged out of his coat, then reached to help Reka take hers off.

"Mr. Khalil, it's always good to see you. But you're a little on the thin side."

Reka looked at the maid as she surveyed Khalil.

"That's okay, I've fixed enough food today to fatten you right up. And who is this pretty little thing?" Marla looked at Reka now.

Khalil placed an arm around her shoulder, pulling her closer. "This is my girlfriend, Reka Boyd."

There was no turning back now. He'd introduced her as his girlfriend. Taking a deep breath, Reka extended her hand, not sure if she was supposed to shake hands with the help, and frankly not caring. "It's nice to meet you, Marla."

Marla swatted her hand away and whisked Reka into a tight hug. "You like family now," she said, patting Reka's back. Then she turned to Khalil and hugged him. "It's good you get back out there and start again."

Reka wondered at her words. Khalil had told her that he hadn't found the right woman to settle down with but she'd never questioned him about any of his past relationships.

"Is Danielle here yet?"

"Ms. Danielle is in the den with the little one and your parents. Go on in, they're all expecting you."

Marla cast Reka another smile and Reka smiled in return. She liked Marla and hoped the rest of his family would be as receptive as she was.

Taking her hand, Khalil escorted Reka down a long hallway, passing a room she could see was the living room and a formal dining room with the table set with china, fine crystal and silverware. Reka could hear voices and the tiny laughter of a young child as they approached a room at the end of the hall. She immediately tensed.

Sensing her dismay, Khalil rubbed his thumb over her hand, tightening his grip, then looked down at her and smiled. "You're beautiful, and they are going to like you as much as I do."

Because his warm gaze held hers, because her hand felt comfortable being swallowed by his, and because with his very closeness he made her feel safe and protected, she calmed and walked into the room with a smile in place.

"Khalil! It's about time you got here." Danielle jumped up from her seat on the cushiony couch and ran to her brother, hugging him close. "And this must be Reka." Turning her attention to the petite woman beside him, Danielle made a quick assessment. She was definitely attractive; her eyes, the highlight of her round face, were an amazing hue. Her hair was lovely and her taste in clothes almost comparable with her own. Yes, she nodded, Khalil had done well with this one. Extending her hand, she offered a sincere smile. "Hi, I'm Danielle, Khalil's sister. He's told me a lot about you."

Amazed that Khalil had talked about her to his family but not wanting to show it, Reka extended her hand and returned the smile of the tall woman in front of her. She had Khalil's coloring, but her eyes were wider, lighter than his. Her hair was swooped up into a fancy French roll, showing off the not-too-small diamond studs in her ears. Tacoma would be happy to hear he was right about something. "It's very nice to meet you, Danielle. I'm afraid Khalil hasn't told me much about his family."

Danielle took Reka's arm, tucking it in the crook of her own, and moved away from Khalil. "Men can be so secretive at times," she whispered to her. "Now come, let's get this over with."

Reka followed her lead as they moved further into the room. A very tall, very studious man with a wide mouth and deep set green eyes was first to come forward. "Andre Miller, Danielle's husband and this little one's father," he said jovially, lifting a plump, cherub-faced little boy into his arms.

Danielle reached out and pinched a chubby little cheek. "This is Lance, he's two."

"Andre." Reka nodded to the man. "And hello, Lance." On impulse she took a step closer to the little boy and touched his curly hair. "Aren't you a handsome little man." He giggled. "And you know it, don't you?"

Lance gurgled and raised his arms for Reka to take him. She looked to his parents, who didn't seem to mind, before reaching out to take the toddler in her arms. The first thing she noticed was how sweet he smelled. The second how soft and cuddly he was. The third was how right holding a baby in her arms felt. It wasn't as if she never got the chance to hold a baby. Cienna and Keith had a little girl, Tiana, and she spent lots of time with her whenever Cienna brought her into her office and over the summer when she'd go to Cienna and Keith's for cookouts. But she'd never given much thought to having her own. Today, with Khalil by her side and her feelings for him so fresh and new, she thought it might just be possible.

"He's drooling on your jacket," a cool voice announced.

Reka was so caught up in making cooing sounds and bouncing the happy baby in her arms that she barely glanced down before saying, "It's okay, that's a problem for the dry cleaner."

"You're quite right, but you should take better care. Appearances are everything when you're a guest."

The frosty tone settled over Reka and she turned to see from where it came. Garbed in a mauve-colored skirt and matching jacket with a diamond brooch stood the woman Reka knew would be her biggest hurdle. From the perfect hair to the excessive yet elegantly made up face, Naomi Franklin looked like the socialite Reka suspected her to be.

"It's not a big deal, Mother." Danielle moved to Reka's side. "But I'll take him and get him cleaned up a bit."

Reka quickly gave Lance over to his mother, then smoothed down her jacket and faced Khalil's mother once more. "Mrs. Franklin, it's a pleasure to meet you."

Naomi neither took a step closer to Reka nor made any attempt to shake her hand. Luckily Reka hadn't extended hers, so she didn't feel too foolish.

"I must say I'm surprised my son would pick a holiday meal to introduce you to us. It's rather presumptuous of him to think we'd simply roll out the red carpet."

Was she serious? Reka didn't know whether to curse her out or simply leave. Khalil cast her an apologetic glance and she squared her shoulders, taking a step forward instead. "I don't need any special treatment. It's simply nice to meet Khalil's family, since he's already met mine."

A man who looked so much like Khalil that he had to be his father joined them then. "Reka, is it? That's a different name," he said, then seemed to dismiss the thought. "We're glad you could make it this afternoon. Unlike Danielle, Khalil hasn't told us much about you. Come, have a seat so we can get to know each other."

Relieved that she didn't have to fight a double battle, Reka followed the man's direction, with Khalil coming to sit next to her on the couch. Donald Franklin led his wife to a chair, seated her, then moved to another chair himself.

"So how long have you and Khalil been dating?" Donald asked.

"Not very long, I'm certain," Naomi chimed.

"We've been seeing each other for about six weeks now. The law firm I'm working at is where Reka works as a paralegal."

"Oh, you're in law. That's a growing field and a good living." Donald pulled a cigar from his suit jacket and prepared to light it.

"Yes, I've been in law for a few years now. I enjoy it," Reka added.

"I'm sure you do."

That was Naomi again. In a minute Reka feared she was going to ask the old battleax what her problem was. Khalil rested his palm on her knee, silently advising her not to go that route. She wondered what the odds were that Naomi would skip the meal and take her angry behind upstairs for the duration of her time here.

Slim to none, she deduced.

Dinner was scrumptious, with Reka consuming things with names she couldn't even pronounce. Conversation had been cordial, but that was mostly due to Danielle and her husband. They were very talkative and very much in love. Reka couldn't help envying them.

They were having drinks in the living room when Khalil sensed that Reka was ready to go. But before he could announce his departure, the doorbell rang and Naomi seemed to perk up. Khalil was instantly concerned, but held his tongue and waited until Marla came in to announce who was at the door.

In a few minutes Marla entered the living room with their new guest right on her heels.

"Happy Thanksgiving," Sonya crooned.

Naomi was up and out of her chair instantly, going to capture Sonya in an overzealous embrace.

Danielle looked to Khalil.

Reka looked from the impeccably dressed young lady to the mean woman she'd just endured a meal with, to the sister that she'd found likable, then finally to Khalil, who looked as if he'd just witnessed a murder.

Khalil looked at his mother with annoyance. He didn't look at Sonya at all.

13

"Isn't this a lovely surprise?" Walking forward arm in arm with Sonya, Naomi came to stand in the center of the room.

"It's a surprise, all right," Danielle said blandly, not bothering to mask her disapproval.

Naomi disregarded her daughter's comment, as if she'd said nothing at all. "Khalil, aren't you going to say hello to Sonya?"

Reka watched as Khalil's jaw clenched and he hesitated. Oh yeah, this woman was definitely somebody from his past. Somebody his mother happened to like a lot from the way Naomi Franklin was now smiling at her son. If she were in the club she'd simply move to Khalil's side and claim her territory. But since she was out here in richville with these so-called classy people, she'd have to re-group. Taking a step in front of Khalil only seconds before Naomi and the woman named Sonya reached him, Reka extended her hand.

"I'm Reka Boyd. Sonya, is it? It's a pleasure to meet you."

For endless seconds the room was totally quiet. Reka could swear she heard Naomi's intake of breath while they waited. Sonya, however, remained cool. With dark shifting eyes, she looked Reka up and down with what could only be described as amusement. Then she shocked everyone by extending her hand with a quick smile. "Sonya Davenport, Khalil's fiancée."

Reka's hand stiffened as Sonya held on a few seconds longer than necessary. She wanted to spin around and slap Khalil, but then that would be giving Naomi what she wanted. She'd deal with Khalil later. "Really? Then you've got to be asking yourself why your fiancé would bring another woman to his family's Thanksgiving dinner. I know I would."

Danielle muffled a giggle. Andre quickly moved to her side, sensing fireworks about to begin. Donald, who was watching the events unfold, finally stood and took control.

"Khalil and Sonya were engaged, but broke up a few months ago. It's always nice to see you, Sonya, but I have to admit I'm a bit shocked by your arrival, just as I'm sure the rest of the family is." Donald cast a warning gaze at Naomi.

As if he'd finally been snapped out of his trance, Khalil stepped closer to Reka, putting a protective arm around her shoulders. "Reka and I were just leaving."

Sonya grinned up at Khalil. "Please don't leave on my account. I came especially to see you." She wanted to get closer to him, to wrap her arms around him and convince him that being with this other person was below him and that they were so much better suited, but she refrained. "Can we talk for a minute? Alone?" She tossed Reka an ominous glare.

Reka was not one to be played with. If she was his ex, then she definitely wanted him back. Reka didn't fight over any man, but she wasn't up to being embarrassed by a cover girl reject either. "That sounds like a wonderful idea. Why don't you walk with Khalil to retrieve my coat, and you can talk then." Giving Sonya the sweetest smile she could muster, she waited for the woman's response.

This could go one or two ways: Either Sonya was woman enough to accept her limitations with Khalil here today or, like any other jealous female, she would jump on the opportunity to go one-on-one with Reka. Either way, Reka was ready for her.

"Splendid idea." Sonya smiled happily, grabbed Khalil's arm and pulled him behind her as she headed out of the room.

Khalil looked over his shoulder at Reka but she glanced away. When Khalil and Sonya were out of the room, Reka moved towards Danielle and her husband. "Danielle, Andre, it was truly a pleasure spending this day with you and I look forward to seeing you again."

Danielle pulled Reka into a hug, whispering in her ear, "Great job."

Andre hugged her as well. Then she turned to Mr. Franklin. "Mr. Franklin, I enjoyed today. Marla prepared an excellent meal."

Donald shook the young woman's hand, uncertain what was coming next.

Then Reka turned to Naomi. The woman held her head up high, disdain for Reka clear in the way she looked down on her. Reka could cuss her ten ways from Sunday and it probably wouldn't ruffle one silky gray hair on her head. *Kill 'em with kindness*, Grammy always said. "Mrs. Franklin, you've been a gracious host. I'm sure Khalil and I will be visiting more often." She didn't bother to extend her hand to be shaken because she knew the frigid old hag wouldn't accept it. She simply smiled and turned to leave the room. Let her chew on that for a minute or two.

With confident strides she headed towards the hallway where she knew their coats were hung. As she drew closer she could hear angry whispers coming from Khalil and not so modest pleading from Sonya. They were definitely broken up, but Miss Thang couldn't seem to accept it. She'd have no choice, though, when Reka got finished with her. Approaching them quickly, Reka put a hand on Khalil's arm. "Baby, why don't you go and get the car warmed up? I want to speak with Sonya a moment."

"That's not necessary. We're leaving," Khalil said through clenched teeth.

Reka took her coat from his arm and gave him a cool stare. "Oh it's definitely necessary."

"Actually, I'd like to talk to her, woman to woman. I'm sure she'll understand what's going on here." Sonya folded her arms over her chest.

Khalil looked from one woman to the other.

"I won't bite her, Khalil," Sonya said.

Reka chuckled. "This won't take long," she assured him.

Reluctantly, Khalil walked away. "I'll be back in a minute."

"Take your time," Sonya called.

Reka casually slipped her arms into her coat. "You know there is nothing more pitiful than a woman chasing a man who obviously doesn't want her."

Sonya gave a cold chuckle. "Sure there is. A woman with a man she knows is out of her league."

Because Reka had been wrestling with that very thought the words stung for a minute. "Whether he's in my league or not, he's with me now."

"That'll be over soon enough."

"Maybe so, but it'll be fun while it lasts." Reka buttoned her coat. "So you go on back in there with your partner in crime and have night-caps or whatever it is you people do instead of communicating with each other. Khalil and I have a wonderful evening planned. I'd invite you to tag along but you might not like what you see."

"You're vulgar and common, and the sooner Khalil finds that out the sooner he'll come running back to me."

"My leftovers usually aren't much, but if and when that happens, you're welcome to him." With that Reka turned, leaving her standing there to stare after her.

Khalil was just about to come back into the house when Reka opened the door and stepped out. "What happened?" he asked.

"Take me home." She didn't look at him, simply walked straight to the car.

For the first twenty minutes they drove in silence. Khalil kept his eyes on the road while his mind replayed the events at his parents' house. It was obviously a mistake to take Reka there. He'd thought his mother would at least behave herself for one day. Inviting Sonya over was low, even for her. He'd sensed the moment Reka turned against him. What he couldn't figure out was the exact reason she was mad with him. Did she think he'd planned it this way? Could she possibly believe that he still wanted Sonya? There was only one way to find out.

"We should talk," he began.

"About what?" she asked stiffly.

"About what just happened."

Reka turned slightly in her seat so that she was facing him. "What? Your ex-fiancée showing up, or the fact that you neglected to tell me you even had an ex-fiancée."

Khalil inhaled a deep breath and exhaled it slowly. "I had no idea Sonya was coming today."

"But you did know that you had an ex-fiancé. You simply forgot to give me that tidbit of information."

"I've had past relationships just like you have, Reka."

"Oh no, it's not the same. I was never engaged and I never tried to hide any of my past relationships from you. Tell me, Khalil, what was the big secret? Is it prohibited information for the rebound girl?"

He sent her a quick look mixed with hurt and anger. "You're not the rebound girl. Sonya and I had been over for more than a month when I met you."

"Over for a couple is different from over for an engagement. You were going to marry her. What happened? Did you get cold feet?" She couldn't look at him anymore. The thought of him loving another woman enough to propose to her hurt more than she was willing to admit. She turned her head to stare out the window.

Khalil drummed his fingers on the steering wheel, debating what he should say next. He should simply tell her the truth. But would she understand? There was only one way to find out. "Sonya and I dated for nine months. In that time we went to all the social functions and business dinners required of us. To the outside world we appeared to be the perfect couple. But I sensed something was wrong. We weren't intimate."

"So you broke up with her because she wouldn't give you some?" she spat.

His lips going into a tight line, he tried not to overreact to her hurtful statement. "No. We had sex, but there was no connection. My feelings for her never went beyond a general liking. The proposal was more of an assumption than anything else. But it wasn't long after the assumption was made that I called it off. I simply could not marry a woman I didn't love." Reka was silent. "I pictured a future with Sonya and I didn't like what I saw. I didn't like the person I was when I was with her."

Reka heard his words and, unfortunately, could relate to them. While she was with Donovan she'd felt incomplete, as if anything else they did beyond sex wasn't real or fulfilling. "You weren't relaxed then, were you?"

Her voice had changed. That open hostility was no longer there. "No. I wasn't relaxed. I felt like I was walking in my father's footsteps and I wasn't happy with that. I don't want to live like them. I don't want the cold, non-emotional relationship that he and my mother have. I want to love my woman with all my heart and I want to know that she loves me just the same. Can you understand that?"

Reka shook her head, speaking around the newly formed lump in her throat. "No. I can't. I've never been in love like that."

The rest of the drive was completed in silence. Khalil left her to her thoughts even as he made up his own mind. He pulled into the parking garage of his building. She looked at him in question but he didn't respond. After parking the car, he simply got out and went to the passenger side door to let her out. She stepped out of the car and he took her by the hand, leading her towards the elevators.

She didn't speak and neither did he. He knew what it was he wanted, and planned to get it. If she couldn't understand what it was to love and be loved, then he'd have to show her.

Letting them into the apartment, he took her coat, hanging it with his in the closet. She didn't walk further into the house but stood right there by the closet with him.

"Now what?"

She looked up at him with questions clear in her eyes. He could sit her down and explain it to her. He could admit all that he'd been feeling for the last few weeks and then some. But it wouldn't have the same effect. With Reka, actions spoke louder than words. So he'd give her the words later, after the action.

Cupping her face in his hands, he brought his lips down on hers, taking her surprised mouth with a fierce passion. His lips spread over hers and he slid his tongue inside the warm contours of her mouth.

She didn't resist him, she couldn't. She should be mad at him. She should have demanded to go home but something in his eyes, something in the way he looked at her, kept her quiet.

She grasped the back of his head, and he thrust his tongue more deeply into her mouth, claiming its warmth, creating an erotic rhythm, a rhythm that played specifically for her.

Reluctantly, Khalil pulled away. "Now I'll show you how it feels to be really loved." Bending over, he scooped her up, cradling her in his arms as he walked towards the back of the apartment, towards his bedroom.

Because she was experiencing a flurry of emotions at this point, Reka simply lowered her head to his shoulder and allowed herself to be carried away. His bedroom was dark until he placed her on the bed and switched on a bedside lamp. She surveyed the room of the man she was with. It was decorated in shades of brown with big heavy pieces of furniture and bare walls that signified a man lived here. The soft feel of chocolate-colored silk beneath her head said that this was no ordinary man.

And she was in his bed waiting for him to come to her. This moment had been building since that first day in Cienna's office. With each time they'd been together they'd laid another brick in the foundation of their relationship. She would be the first to admit she didn't have a clue where they would go from here. But she'd also admit that at this moment she didn't really care. He was in the room, looking at her as if she were the only woman in the world. No, at this moment bricks and rules and ex-girlfriends came in a distant second.

He went to his knees in front of her, lifting her feet to remove her shoes. Reka watched him as he unclasped and slipped away each shoe, then massaged the arch of her feet. His hands felt heavenly, so when he reached up to unbutton her jacket she didn't say a word. Slowly he peeled her clothes away until only her bra and panties were left.

She propped herself up on the pillows as he stood and began to remove his own clothes. His body was gorgeous, and that one word didn't really seem to do it justice. The taut muscles she'd felt numerous times through his shirt were revealed. Bulging, smooth, sinewy biceps gave way to rigid pectorals and a lean stomach. When his fingers went to the buckle of his pants, her eyes followed.

Stepping out of his shoes he let his pants fall to the floor. His erection was prominent, even through his boxers. Toned thighs led to muscled legs and she licked her lips in anticipation. His skin seemed to glow in the dim light, and her fingers itched to touch him.

From his view at the bottom of the bed she looked wanton and enticing. The curvaceous body he'd seen up until this point only through her clothes was now almost bare to him. Heavy breasts sat perched and ready for consumption, while a tiny wisp of material covered the place he longed to explore. Climbing on the bed slowly, he made his way to her feet, stopping to kiss the arches he'd just massaged. His tongue swirled around her ankles, up her calves to the backs of her knees.

Reka sucked in her breath as his tongue slowly tortured her.

Without hesitation he spread her legs apart, kissing along her inner thighs until she was shaking beneath him. When he kissed her mound, still covered by her panties, her hands went to his shoulders. "Don't touch me," he said in a ragged voice. "Not yet."

Momentarily startled, she pulled her hands away, planting them on the silk comforter beneath her.

With maddening slowness Khalil pulled her panties down her legs and off her feet. With both his hands he lifted her at the backs of her knees, spreading her wide like a buffet before him. Reka bucked beneath him, her fingers clenching into the spread, biting her bottom lip. All her senses were caught in the flames he ignited and fanned with each caress. He grasped her thighs tightly and touched her center with his tongue, licked her slick folds until her bones went limp and she sank into the mattress, willing this madness to stop but lifting her hips for more. His mouth came down on her, hot and sizzling, his tongue devouring her.

Then when she thought she could take no more of his assault, he slowed his pace, gently lathing her nether lips with his hot tongue. He moaned and oohed and aahed as his head moved up and down and side to side. "So sweet, baby. You are so sweet."

Reka couldn't think, couldn't see her own hand in front of her face. That's how good his lovin' was. Her insides trembled, her nerves standing on end waiting, wanting, knowing that pleasure was on its way.

Khalil knew women and he especially knew this woman. He sensed her needs and felt his own clawing viciously at him. But they had time. He had all night to show her what it was to be cherished and wanted and adored. He pulled away, remaining close enough so that his breath still whispered over her. Then, because he couldn't hold back the urge, he stroked her moistened center with a finger. She moaned. He reveled in the sound she made, then slipped two fingers inside her. Her back arched in response and he knew another level of ecstasy. She was beautiful, her arousal intoxicating. He continued to stroke her.

She screamed and he rose above her, the rhythm of his fingers slowing. "It's okay, baby. Scream all you want." His pace quickened and her breathing hitched. He kissed her neck, her chin, then finally her lips a second after another scream broke free.

Her muscles clamped down around his fingers and he moaned as he imagined thrusting his manhood inside of her. "Damn, Reka. You're killing me."

Through clouded eyes she watched him remove his hand from between her legs, bringing each finger to his mouth and tasting her yet again. Then she sat up, grabbed his wrist and put one of those damp fingers into her own mouth.

The sensations swirling through him instantly made him dizzy as she pushed his boxers down his hips and grabbed his throbbing manhood with both hands. He moved his finger in and out of her mouth as she moved her hands up and down his rod, her eyes riveted on his.

He was supposed to be loving her. Yet he was lost in the warm sensations her hand on his penis created. She stroked him long and slow and he trembled with fear of exploding in her hand at any moment. "Enough," he murmured when he thought his eyes would cross from the pleasure. Grabbing her by the shoulders he laid her back on the bed, then leaned over to the nightstand and retrieved a condom. "Put it on," he said through clenched teeth. "And hurry."

He was above her, big and dominant, yet her protector also. Her heart hammered in her chest. She wanted this part of him because it was real, it was tangible. Her fingers had never moved so fast as they did when she smoothed the latex over his engorged length.

It didn't quite fit, but Khalil didn't care. Pushing her down into the mattress, he covered her, spreading her legs wide with his knees. "Know that I want only you, Reka. No one else but you." He kissed her lips softly and entered her.

Inch by mesmerizing inch he sank into her as she slowly but surely gave herself completely to him. He wanted only her and there was no doubt she needed only him. She spread her hands over his back, feeling the hard planes flex as he moved deeply inside her.

Moving slowly at first until he thought she had acclimated herself to him, Khalil continued to shower her face and neck with kisses. When he was up to the hilt inside of her, he pulled almost all the way out, then pumped her fiercely, giving her all the pent up frustration she'd built in him since their very first meeting.

Reka wanted to scream, then she wanted to cry, but at last she simply moaned as pleasure unlike any she'd ever known before took over her body. Wrapping her arms and legs securely around Khalil, she rocked her hips along with him, wondering if he were made especially for her.

As the sensations built inside, with her release near and well earned, she felt something else. The something different she'd noticed about him from the very beginning as she struggled to name that feeling, he kissed her again, pulling her back into the cyclone of their loving. Closing her eyes, she gave way to the need. He slid one hand down, over her hip and around to cup her bottom, anchoring her at just the right angle before thrusting into her again and again.

She moaned, bit his shoulder to keep from screaming again. Her mind was a haze, a lust-filled cloud hovering over her body. Holding him close to her she could feel the heightened pace of his heart against her own. He gave her everything she needed, everything she wanted while taking all he wanted in return.

He pushed her faster and faster and she strained to meet him in return. She pulled back from the kiss and struggled to breathe. He held her hips down, thrust into her harder and harder, with quick thrusts full of emotion and desire.

"Look at me," he demanded.

She did and in his eyes she saw what he'd been trying to tell her all these weeks. "Khalil."

"Yes," he whispered, then pumped into her with power fueled by passion and desire and a longing that went deep for both of them.

Her release came fast, along with a realization and an admission.

She felt so complete. He was her completion. He was a good man, just like he'd told her he was. He hadn't lied to her about Sonya. Even though he hadn't told her beforehand, if he didn't love Sonya then there was nothing else she needed to know. He'd said he would respect her, that he would treat her like no man had ever done before, and with each deep stroke he'd vowed it anew. "Khalil," she breathed into his ear.

"Yes, baby," he whispered right back in hers.

"I love you."

Khalil froze on top of her, his eyes searching hers, desperately wanting, needing her words to be true. "What did you say?"

In that moment Reka knew that the other times she'd made this declaration she'd really had no clue what it meant. This time, however, with this man, she was sure she did. Cupping his face in her palms she pulled him close, kissed his lips, then told him again. "I love you."

Wrapping his arms securely around her, Khalil flipped them over so that she was now on top. With a huge grin he looked up at her. "It's about damn time."

"What?" Reka slapped playfully at his chest.

He responded by grabbing each globe of her bottom and squeezing. "I said it's about damn time. Since that day I saw you in Cienna's office I've wanted nothing more than to hear you say those words."

She wanted to cry from the sweet sound of his voice alone, but instead she rotated her hips until his erection was deeper than it had been before. "Is that all you wanted when you first saw me?" she asked teasingly.

"Mmmmm," he groaned. "You know that's not all I wanted."

Sitting up straight, she adjusted herself so that he was perfectly embedded inside her. With her palms flat on his chest she lifted slightly, then slid down sinuously. "What else did you want?"

Khalil's eyes rolled in the back of his head as his fingers sank further into the soft skin of her behind. "Ooooohhhh, I wanted you. Just like this."

Reka circled her hips, then moved up and down on him over and over until he was biting his bottom lip. "Is this all you wanted, baby?" she asked breathily. "Am I giving you what you want?"

"Damn! You sure are!" he growled, grabbing hold of her hips, adding a little speed to her motions. "And I love it! I love all that you're giving me!"

Her breasts bounced as Khalil orchestrated her movements. Her head fell back, her hair brushing against her shoulders. She had something else to say but for the life of her she couldn't think of it right now. He was pumping frantically, moving her the way he wanted her to move and she didn't give a damn! At this point it was his show; she was simply enjoying the ride.

Khalil watched her with bated breath. She looked wild and savage as her face contorted with the first pangs of release, her hair flying around her face, and those magnificent breasts circling, teasing. He couldn't think straight anymore. His mind had one focus and one focus only. She was his now, he knew that without a doubt. He would never let her go, not without a fight.

As their bodies thrashed together the world around them seemed to still. Somewhere in the distance he could hear her moans, her cries of pleasure, but he was blinded by his own impending release. Her muscles clenched around his manhood, preparing to pull his release straight from him at any minute now. Holding her hips perfectly still, he slammed up into her one final time, the lower half of his body rigid as stone as something more than just his release was pulled from him.

Reka collapsed on top of him, her cheek pressed firmly against his rock hard chest and fluttering heartbeat.

When some of the smoke had cleared from his mind, Khalil moved his hands up and down her back, holding her tightly in an embrace that he'd dreamed of for weeks now. "Reka?"

"Mmmmm," she moaned half asleep.

"I love you."

She smiled but couldn't manage to lift up. Instead she kissed his chest. "I love you, too."

14

Reka awoke the morning after Thanksgiving, Black Friday, in her own bed, her thighs sore from hours of Khalil's loving. She had no idea what time it was but the minute she cracked her eyes open to the sunlight streaming through the window, the telephone began ringing. Groaning, she rolled over, pulling a pillow over her head.

The ringing persisted.

With a few choice expletives ready and waiting, she reached for the phone and stuck it under the pillow to her ear. "Hello?"

"You were supposed to call me when you got in last night and you didn't. I expected you to call bright and early this morning but you didn't. It's almost eight and we should really have been in the stores an hour ago but we're not. What the hell is up with you?"

"Dammit, Tacoma, I was trying to get some rest," she complained. He was rattling in her ear with way too much energy for her taste this morning.

"You're still asleep?" Tacoma sounded surprised. "Why? Are you sick? Did they do something to you out there in GrenRich? I'll be right over."

Abruptly Reka sat up, knocking the pillow to the floor. "No!" Slapping a hand to her forehead she closed her eyes and lowered her voice. "I mean, there's no need for that. Nothing happened yesterday that I couldn't handle."

"Mmm-hmm, but something did happen?"

Lying to Tacoma was useless. He'd eventually get it out of her, if he had to come to her apartment to do so. "Yes, something happened."

"What? Did they say something to you? 'Cause we can go out there. I've got my knife right here," Tacoma said seriously.

Shaking her head, Reka couldn't help grinning. "Put your knife away, Rambo."

"Oh please," he clucked. "Sly's got nothing on me. And all that sweat and dirt, uh uh, that's not attractive at all."

"We were talking about me and the Franklins, not how attractive or unattractive Sylvester Stallone is."

"Definitely unattractive as Rambo. Now Samuel L. Jackson as Shaft, that's another story entirely."

"Tacoma!"

"What?"

"Can we stay focused here?" Crossing her legs Indian style, Reka sat in the middle of her bed and glanced at the clock. They really should have been at the mall by now.

"All right. You're the one taking forever to get to your point."

With a deep sigh Reka switched the phone to her other ear and told Tacoma about Sonya and Naomi. She told him about the rest of the Franklin family and the house in general as well, but, of course, Sonya and Naomi took precedence.

"You mean some skinny heifer had the audacity to show up uninvited? She must be whipped."

"More like mentally disturbed to me." Reka picked at a hangnail. "Anyway, Khalil and I talked about it on the drive home and she's not an issue, although I don't think she's gotten that message yet."

"We can make sure she gets it," Tacoma suggested.

"Hush, these are not those types of people. If we bumrush this woman, she'll have us locked up so quick the judge will get called out of his sleep to come get us."

"We don't have to do it ourselves."

Reka grinned. "Nah, I'm going to handle her personally the very next time she crosses the line. I kind of liked the war of words instead of my normal smack first and ask questions later."

"My, my, my, we sure have changed."

"Whatever. Are we going shopping or what? I need some new lingerie." Her feet dangled from the edge of the bed now as she was closer to getting up for the day.

"Lingerie? What do you need? Oh no, you didn't!" Tacoma exclaimed.

Reka laughed, picturing his bony honey brown legs pacing the kitchen with his black kimono skimming his thighs. "Meet me at the subway in an hour."

"You better not hang up!"

"Come on, Tacoma, if I tell you everything now what'll we have to talk about at lunch?" Besides, she did not want to talk in the apartment about what she and Khalil had done last night, Grammy was liable to be on the other line listening at this very minute. She really had to do something about her living arrangements.

"All right, hurry up. And I'm not waiting until lunch either. You're telling me on the train."

"Whatever." Reka laughed as she hung the phone up. Standing, she stretched until she thought her bones would break before meandering on into the shower. Fifteen minutes later she was slipping into jeans and a t-shirt. As she pulled a NYU sweatshirt over that, she glanced at the phone and wondered if she should call Khalil.

Deciding against it, she went to her dresser and put on sterling silver studs, then pulled her hair back into a ponytail. "No makeup today," she said as she wiped moisturizer onto her face. It was now eight-thirty and she was just walking into the living room when the doorbell rang. A cursory glance around the room told her Grammy wasn't in here, and for a moment she wondered if she'd stayed at Sunny Days with Cletus. Wouldn't it be a blessing if Cletus and his shriveled up penis could get her to go back for good?

Reka smiled at that thought as she answered the door. That smile quickly faded.

"Mornin', beautiful." Donovan leaned over and kissed her cheek before waltzing right past her into her apartment.

He smelled good and he looked good but he had no business in her house at this time of morning or at any other time, for that matter. Still holding the door open, she turned to him. "I think you must have the wrong apartment," she said icily.

"C'mon girl, don't start that again. You told me not to come to your job so I didn't." He plopped down on her couch.

"Actually I told you it was over between us so seeing each other again was pointless."

Donovan scrunched up his face as if he were trying to remember. "I don't recall you saying all that."

Waving an impatient hand, she quieted him. "All right, there's no need to go over exactly what I did or did not say. I'll say it again, one last time. We are no longer a couple. I've moved on, as I'm sure you have. Therefore, there is no reason for us to see each other, at my house, at my job or anywhere else for that matter. Is that clear enough for you?" She hadn't closed the door and now made a motion with her arm telling him to leave.

Instead, Donovan stood, walked over to her and stood very close. "Can you really say that you don't want to see me again?" He took another step forward, making her breasts rub against his chest. He cupped the back of her neck and pulled her to him even as he lowered his head to kiss her.

Instinctively Reka turned her head and his kiss landed on her cheek. But Donavan didn't seem to mind. He kissed her jaw, her neck and was steadily moving downward until she pushed at him with all her might. He stumbled backward with a questioning look on his face.

"What's up, Reka? Why you actin' like you don't remember what we had?"

This time she slammed the door closed because she had no desire for her neighbors to know all her business. "Oh, I remember what we had, Donavan. We had a lot of hot nights. Yes, the sex was truly off the chain with you and me." Taking a step closer to him, she pointed her finger as she spoke. "I also recall that you were so proud of your sexual prowess that you felt the need to share it with anything with a split between the legs." She continued jabbing at his chest until Donovan had taken so many steps back he was now up against the wall. "I also remember getting pulled over in your car because of the false tags. And I also remember finding some of your stash in my nightstand drawer. Shall I go on with the memories?"

Donavan sighed. "It's not like that anymore. I've got this new business, so I won't be hustlin' no more."

"I don't give a damn what you have now. Like I said, we're finished." She turned to walk away from him but he grabbed her by the waist, pulling her back roughly against his chest.

"Oh, it's not over. You think 'cause you hangin' with that pretty boy now you can just kick me to the curb?"

He kept one arm firmly around her waist while the other hand went to her breast. "Mmmm, you remember how I used to suck on these?" he whispered in her ear.

Reka tried to pull away, repulsed by his touch. "Any boy can suck a breast, Donovan. That doesn't make you my man."

"You know I did more to you than that. And you did much more to me in return." The more she squirmed, the more aroused he became. He'd come to see her this morning because he'd missed her, and even the wild night he'd shared with Sonya didn't begin to measure up to being with Reka. He could sleep with a million women and not get that same feeling. He needed her back.

When he moved his hand down to rub between her legs, she elbowed him hard in the ribs, then spun around and sent one powerful punch to his groin. Donovan leaned forward, mouth open, eyes bulging, quiet pain soaring through his body. Reka hurried to the door and swung it open. "I don't give a damn what we did in the past. It's over now! You can either leave on your own or I'll call the police to escort you out!"

Staggering, Donovan made his way to the door but found enough breath to look up at her one last time. "You're gonna be beggin' me to take you back," he gasped. "Soon."

"In your dreams," she said as she shoved him through the door and slammed it.

Putting the phone down for the third time since ten o'clock this morning, Khalil looked out onto his busy street, wondering where she was. It was close to one now and he hadn't spoken to Reka since he'd left her at her door at about two this morning.

He'd wanted her to stay the night, to wake up in his arms this morning, to share breakfast and conversation with him. But she'd declined.

"This is the first time I've actually been in love and I don't want to mess it up by moving too fast. I have a feeling we'll be spending lots of nights together soon, so this one isn't a big deal." She'd stood on tiptoe and kissed him as she said this in the shower.

He'd obliged. Whatever made her happy he was willing to do. Still, he'd wanted to spend the day with her, maybe go shopping since he knew she loved to do that. And, no, he wasn't going to try and buy her; he simply wanted to be with her. But she wasn't there.

Holding her in his arms last night had been beyond anything he ever imagined. She was so different from what he was used to, so pleasantly unexpected. He loved her sharp wit, her energetic spirit and her loyalty. She was loyal and devoted to Cienna and Keith for the roles they'd played in her life, for their believing in her. She was strangely loyal to Tacoma and the friendship they shared, the friendship he was just a little bit jealous of from time to time. Tacoma knew her in a way that Khalil was afraid he'd never be able to understand. Yet they shared their own closeness, their new bond forged last night in his bed.

He wasn't going to crowd her, wasn't going to push. A woman like Reka needed her space. But dammit, he wanted to see her or at least hear her voice. Leaving the window, he headed towards his room to shower and dress. He was going to stop by her apartment and if she wasn't there, he'd ask Grammy where she was. They were a couple now, and spending time together was imperative, or at least he told himself it was.

The ringing phone stopped him before he progressed any further. Hoping it was Reka, he lunged for the receiver, snatching it up before its second ring. "Hello."

"Well, hello. Did I interrupt you?" Sonya asked.

Not bothering to mask his disappointment, Khalil sighed heavily. "All your phone calls and all your appearances interrupt my life. Now what do you want?"

"Are you still angry about yesterday?"

"No. I'm not angry. I'm disappointed in you and in my mother. I thought you were a mature woman, one who could walk away when things were over and done with. I see I was wrong."

"That's just it, Khalil, I don't believe things are over and done with, as you put it. Just because you are sleeping with that woman now doesn't mean a thing to me."

He laughed incredulously. "Then you're worse off than I thought. If I'm sleeping with another woman that means I'm involved with her, I'm committed to her. I don't sleep around meaninglessly, Sonya."

"But apparently you did with me," she said.

"No." Pinching the bridge of his nose, he tried to remain calm. "What we had was not meaningless; it just wasn't going in the direction everybody assumed it was. I wasn't in love with you, not the way a man should be when he marries a woman. I thought you'd appreciate me being candid with you about that."

"Please, Khalil, we both know the best marriages don't have an ounce of love in them. The union between you and me will be for profit, a stable merger of our families. It would make our parents extremely happy."

"It would make me miserable."

"And that little hottie you've got won't?" Sonya chuckled. "What do you really know about her, Khalil? She doesn't run in our circles, so why is she so appealing to you? Is it the sex?"

This conversation was quickly getting on his nerves. "That's none of your business."

"Then it must be the sex. That's explainable. I've heard she's quite good."

Taken aback, Khalil looked at the phone, then asked, "What are you talking about?"

"Oh, I didn't tell you I knew Reka, did I? Or I guess I should say know of her?"

"I'm too old for games, Sonya. This conversation is over." But before he could hang up her words stopped him.

"Ask her about Donovan Jackson, her ex. Or should I say her ex-ex, since they seem to have rekindled their affair."

He did hang up then, not only because the sound of her voice was grating on his nerves but because the name Donovan Jackson was familiar to him. He'd gone to court with Reka that day last week that she'd had marked on her calendar. Actually, he'd followed her because she never mentioned the court date to him.

Donovan Jackson was named as the owner of the car she was arrested in and, while all the charges against her were dropped, he'd sensed there was a connection between her and this Jackson person. So calling back to his office, his real office, he'd asked an assistant to run a check on the name. The report had come over his personal email on Wednesday, but he'd pushed it to the side. After Tyrese had left his office and he'd gone to see Reka, his attention had been focused solely on finding the source of those emails so he wouldn't feel that he was betraying Keith and Cienna by being involved with Reka.

Khalil moved into the bathroom, thinking his day now had a new focus. Instead of going to see Reka he would be visiting the offices of Page & Associates, where there was a file on his desk he needed to read.

Reka had spent the entire day yesterday with Tacoma while thinking about Khalil. He hadn't been home when she'd called and, just as she'd thought about stopping by his apartment later that evening, Grammy and Janell had come in and she'd been coerced into going to the movies with them.

She'd dreamed of him all night, though, of his touch, his kiss, his whispers in her ear, and couldn't wait another minute to hear his voice. Rolling over in her bed, she picked up the phone. Before dialing his number she glanced at the clock. It was a little after ten; that wasn't too early to call.

"Hello?" he answered gruffly.

"Mornin' baby. I missed you so much yesterday I had to call you before I even got out of bed this morning."

Khalil had gone through a really hectic day. The Friday he'd imagined that he and Reka would spend together, followed by making love that night, had vanished the moment Sonya called. He'd gone to the office and read the report on Donovan Jackson. Then he'd called his office to get clarification on some points. And all the while in the back of his mind he'd willed himself to believe that Sonya was wrong. Just how she knew Donovan or of Donovan's past relationship with Reka, he wasn't quite sure. After his initial doubts and urges to question Reka he'd finally resolved himself to the fact that she had a past and that past had nothing to do with them now.

He'd fallen asleep believing without a shadow of a doubt that he was in love with Reka Boyd and that she was in love with him. And he'd awakened, thankfully, to her voice.

"Hey you, I missed you too." Settling back against his pillows, he tucked one arm behind his head and relaxed. She was his woman now, and that was all that mattered.

"I take it you had as busy a day as I did yesterday since I didn't hear from you."

He thought about his day again. "Yeah, you could say that. So are you ready for tonight?" Determined not to think about Donovan Jackson or Sonya anymore, he changed the subject.

"Hmph. I'm as ready as can be. But I have to say I'm not looking forward to it." Twirling a strand of hair between her fingers, she thought about Sensuality, Inc.'s launch party tonight.

"Why not? I hear Mr. Peterson throws a great party. I know that Cienna and Keith are looking forward to it."

"That's because Cienna wants to hurry up and get it over with. And I don't blame her. Maybe with the release out of the way those emails will stop."

At the mention of the emails and the infamous Jack another thought worried Khalil. "You haven't gotten any more personal emails, have you?"

Reka heard the concern in his voice and instantly warmed. She had a man who cared about her and sexed her like crazy—she'd hit the jackpot this time! "Only if you count the ones I received from KJF." She smiled as she remembered his last message.

Khalil couldn't help feeling good. She liked his attention as much as he liked giving it. "You know I'm not talking about his messages."

"I know, but they're the ones I look forward to."

"Really? And why is that?"

She cuddled under the warmth of her blankets, wishing he were lying beside her. "I don't know. It's just this feeling I get when I see his name in my Inbox."

"A feeling, huh?" Her voice had lowered and came through the phone like a sultry melody. "Explain this feeling."

"Mmmm, I don't know if I can." She wasn't sure about explaining it but she was feeling it right now, the warmth spreading throughout her body, the tingling of her skin in anticipation of his touch.

"Try. I'm really interested in hearing it." Bare-chested, Khalil adjusted the sheet at his midsection, spreading his legs to accommodate his growing arousal.

His voice had grown husky and Reka sensed he was interested in hearing something else. Biting on her lower lip she wondered if she should do it. With anybody else she wouldn't hesitate, but how would

Khalil perceive her if she did? Hell, he was practically begging her to do it. Besides, they were in love now. Anything goes when you're in love!

"I get all warm inside," she began in a soft whisper. "I start to smile even as visions of him appear in my mind. I instantly remember his last kiss, his last touch and I hurry to open to the message to see what he has to say this time."

"Go on," Khalil insisted, his eyes closing to the sweet sound of her voice.

"I read the message as if he's right there speaking to me, his voice whispering in my ear, sending tingles down my spine. I read it again because it makes me feel closer to him. Then I rub my fingers over the keys on my keyboard, wishing they were moving over his strong arms instead." Because she was really getting into this, Reka liked her lips, and rolled onto her side with the phone cuddled between the pillow and her ear.

"As I type my response I think of how badly I want to see him again. I need not only to hear his voice in person but to look into his warm eyes, to rub my hands over his beard, then brush my lips softly over his. I want him to open his mouth, as he always does when I do this, and let me give him just the tip of my tongue."

"Just the tip?" Khalil asks in a tortured voice.

She smiled. "We both like to lead, so if I start off giving him a little bit, he responds by taking it all. In no time we're kissing, making love with our mouths, feeling every reachable part of each other through our clothes."

His hand on the taut muscles of his abdomen, Khalil groaned. "Clothes are such bothersome things, aren't they?"

"Tell me about it," Reka agreed, her nightgown already beginning to stick to her flushed body. "I wonder what he's thinking while we kiss. I know that I'm feeling more aroused by the minute. The way his tongue strokes mine is heavenly and all I can think about is how I don't want him to stop."

"I love her lips, of that there is no doubt, especially the bottom one. Sometimes when she's just talking she runs her tongue over it and

I have to catch my breath. And she has this pretty little beauty mark just at the corner of her mouth that turns me on too. There are so many things about her that arouse me I can't begin to name them all." He could but he was afraid that he was dangerously close to making a mess on his silk sheets.

"The funny thing about arousal is that once it begins you're almost forced to do something about it." Her nipples puckered beneath her nightgown, and her knees clamped together like a virgin's in the boys' locker room.

Unable to resist another minute, Khalil slipped his hands beneath his sheet, beneath the band of his underwear, sighing as he stroked his lengthened manhood. "You know, they don't live that far apart."

Biting on her bottom lip until she was sure she'd taste blood at any minute, Reka sighed. "That's convenient, don't you think?"

"He could be in her bed, inside of her in less than fifteen minutes." A man could always hope.

For a split second Reka wanted to say that the clock was ticking, but then she remembered her houseguest and moaned. "Ever heard of the houseguest from hell?"

Khalil chuckled. "He'd give her twenty minutes if she promised to leave right this minute."

She'd already thrown the covers off and was rolling out of the bed as he spoke. "She'll be there in eighteen if he's at the door hard and waiting."

"Eighteen and counting," he whispered.

She quickly hung up the phone.

15

Reka had never been inside the acclaimed Waldorf Astoria, unless she counted the scenes from *Coming To America* when Akeem's father came over from Zomunda. But one would never have guessed it from the way she contained her excitement as Khalil, dressed in Armani's best looking black tuxedo, escorted her through the rotunda and into the Starlight Room where Sensuality, Inc.'s launch party had just gotten under way.

Khalil held her hand when he really wanted nothing more than to put her back on that elevator and get her back to his apartment, back to his bed as quickly as possible. This morning had been mind-blowing. She'd showed up at his door in seventeen minutes, clad in her black trench coat and nothing else. For his part, he'd been waiting at the door, looking through the peephole in anticipation of her arrival, hard and waiting as she'd requested.

It was well after noon when he finally walked her home and deposited her on her doorstep without daring to walk her inside. Had he done that, they would have never made it to this eight o'clock party on time. He and Grammy had an understanding, so he doubted very seriously that she'd have any problems with him entering Reka's bedroom.

The room buzzed with executives and their wives, along with an ample supply of press vultures. Khalil used this moment to scan the room. When he'd returned to his apartment alone, it was to emails in response to numerous background checks he'd ordered on Sensuality, Inc. employees. He was positive that the infamous Jack either worked for Page & Associates or Sensuality, Inc. That narrowed the field down some, but not much. Tonight he was specifically looking for any familiar face from the evening he and Reka had spent at that club. That was the evening Jack had seen her, the evening about which he'd decided to email her personally.

"I see you two finally made it." Keith and Cienna approached them after they'd been there for about fifteen minutes.

Reka looked at Cienna, nodding her head in approval. "I told you red was your color. You look chic and festive."

Cienna smiled, modeling her backless red creation that she'd been hesitant about wearing. Since she was the head of a prestigious law firm now, and the wife of a circuit court judge, she had an image to maintain. But in her husband's words, she also had a man to please, and from the way his hands continuously roamed over her bare back and arms, he was definitely pleased. "I decided to throw caution to the wind." She smiled at Reka. "And that dress is fabulous. Tacoma picked it out, didn't he?"

Looking down at the gold sheath gracing her own limbs, Reka smiled. "You know it. I swear, I don't know where he got his eye for fashion but he's always on the money."

Khalil looked her up and down again, appreciating the garment in all its glory. "I'm going to have to give him his due this time. He made an excellent choice."

Keith sipped from his glass of champagne, smiling at his friend over its rim. "Be careful about giving Tacoma his due. It'll go to his head."

As if he'd heard his name being spoken, Tacoma and Terry appeared, both dressed in matching cream-colored tuxedos with peach vests. "Good evening. I see we all showed up prepared to dine and dazzle," Tacoma said in his sing-song voice.

Reka shook her head. Never had she seen two people more suited for each other. The two, Tacoma with his honey brown complexion, close-cut hair and clean shaven face next to Terry with his cappuccino skin, bald head and infectious smile, looked good tonight. They were happy and ready to commit to spending the rest of their lives together. Suddenly she envied them. "Peaches and cream," Reka cooed. "I like. I like a lot." Nodding in approval, she let Terry take her hands as she leaned over to kiss his cheek.

"You look wonderful as always, Reka." Ending the embrace, Terry reached for Khalil's hand. "Glad to see you're still around, man."

Khalil accepted the shake and offered a smile in Terry's direction. "Yeah, for the long haul, I hope."

Reka didn't miss his words, even though she was now hugging Tacoma, who whispered in her ear, "You two are practically glowing."

"Shut up," she shushed him before pulling away.

"So where's the Page & Associates table?" Tacoma asked Cienna.

"We're up there, right across from Peterson and his family table." With a nod she directed their attention towards the front of the room.

"Oh goodness, please tell me Mrs. Peterson isn't going to make an appearance," Reka groaned.

"With that stock her attorney all but demanded, she'll be here all right, with bells on. But the settlement is almost done so, that's one less headache. I guess we should get up there."

Keith took his wife's arm, leading her towards the table. Khalil and Reka followed behind them, with Tacoma and Terry pulling up the rear. They were the only ones from the office invited to the party. They were all at the table just about to take their seats when the first round of models came out.

It was hard to believe it was twenty-seven degrees outside. The models were not only built like brick houses but they walked with attitude, tossing their hair and flaunting their stuff with such blatant sexuality that Reka felt as if she were at a strip show. Cienna must have been thinking the same thing she was because she turned to look at her with a look of pure disgust on her face. Reka shrugged. "He sells lingerie. What could we expect?"

Stepping between Keith and one of the models who was vivaciously flaunting her leopard-striped thong and bra set a few inches from him, Cienna struck a pose of her own. "I expected some class," she said while giving the model a deadly glare. Ever the man, Keith followed the woman with his eyes as she walked away until Cienna's elbow to his ribs had him grinning and taking his seat.

Reka looked over at Khalil, who had suspiciously just turned towards her as well. "Hmph, it's a pitiful shame men are so predictable. Say what you want about his tactics," she said while taking her seat, "but Peterson knows how to make his money."

Tacoma, who was already seated, rolled his eyes. "Please, this trash doesn't know the first thing about modeling. They've got some nice pieces but could have put them on mannequins for all the talent running around in here."

Terry took a glass of champagne from the waiter's passing tray, then took his seat. "It's just a show, try not to get so caught up in it."

Reka glanced at him. He hadn't looked at any of the women twice. And he probably only looked at them at all to see if their shoes matched their ensemble. Tacoma was openly surveying and critiquing them while Terry was conservative and reserved. Khalil and Keith were quiet, which meant they were enjoying it. Reka simply shook her head. This was going to be a long night.

An hour and a half into the evening, after the dinner and all the talking were done, it was time to get a drink and party. And the gang from Page & Associates did just that until Cienna and Reka begged for a breather and went back to the table, sending their men to get them drinks while Tacoma and Terry danced the night away.

"You and Khalil look good together," Cienna commented when they were alone.

"That's because we're all dressed up," she quipped.

Cienna waved a hand. "No, you look good together beyond your clothes. He really cares about you, you can see it in the way he looks at you."

Reka toyed with a napkin. "Does it look like love to you?"

Cienna was startled for a moment. Reka had told her about the majority of her relationships in the seven years that she'd known her, but never once did she recall hearing her question a man's feelings. "Do you think he's in love with you?"

Sitting back in the chair Reka looked around the room, avoiding Cienna's piercing gaze but feeling it on her just the same. "He says he is."

"Oh really? And what did you say when he told you that?"

Twisting her lips, Reka debated her answer, then figured if she couldn't share her reservations with one of her best friends she'd share them with the other. "I told him I loved him." She chanced a look at Cienna then and was amazed to see her smiling. "What?"

"I think you really are in love with him." Cienna continued to smile. She was happy for Reka, happy that she'd found a piece of what had sustained Cienna for the last four years. "That's why you two look so good together."

"But do you think it's for real?"

"Why do you think it's not?"

"Do you ever just answer a question, Cienna? We're not in a courtroom and I'm not your client. I just want to know what you really think."

Cienna sighed. "Okay, okay. I definitely think he cares a great deal about you and I can see that you care about him. But that's not what you want to hear, is it?" Reka was silent. "You want me to tell you if it's going to last. If you can start planning a wedding, like Tacoma."

Reka shook her head negatively. "No. I just don't want to get my hopes up."

Reaching across the table, Cienna took her friend's hand. "I know you've had some tough hands dealt to you in the past, and I know it's hard for you to trust in something that's so new to you, but that's exactly what you have to do. You have to believe in the love that you and Khalil share. If you don't, then it's destined to fail."

Sighing heavily, Reka sought him out in the crowd. He was at the bar with Keith. They were talking seriously about something and she simply stared at him. At his strong build, his bearded face, his stature among all these important men. He was hers, all hers, and she couldn't believe it.

"I don't want it to fail," she said quietly.

Cienna continued to smile. "Then don't let it. Don't let anything come between you and what you want. If it's Khalil, and I believe it is, then you do what you do best. Stand your ground and make it happen."

Reka would have had a smart retort for that except that she was moved by the unwavering support Cienna always seemed to give to her and for the first time really, truly gave thanks for having her as a friend. "You know me too well," she said instead.

"Looks like you went against my advice," Keith said while they waited for the drinks.

Khalil had hoped to avoid this conversation, but now that Keith had brought it up he was kind of relieved. "I don't suspect her of sending the emails."

"What about someone she knows? Did you rule that out beforehand?"

He hadn't, and there was no use lying. "No. I didn't."

Keith sighed. "So what if it is an ex? What are you going to do then?"

"An ex is not Reka, so it doesn't matter. Besides, I think it's someone who works for either you or Peterson."

"Yeah? What gives you that impression?"

"They're close to both companies. They have to be, else why even waste time harassing the employees there. In the last month Sensuality, Inc., has had just as many of Jack's messages as Page & Associates. But the emails aren't going anywhere else. Jack's a perv, right? So why not join the porn sites or those little chat groups they have? Why impose yourself on the employees of a law firm and a lingerie company? He has to have a connection to one or both of them."

"Okay. I can go along with that." Keith sipped his drink. "But I won't go along with you hurting Reka."

He was getting kind of tired of Keith's assumption that he would hurt Reka. He wasn't a womanizer, and he didn't have a track record of hurting women across the state of New York, so he was having a hard time understanding why Keith was being this way with him. "Do I have a sign on my forehead that says I'm dangerous?"

"Don't try to be funny, man, you're not good at it. All I'm saying is she's been through a lot and—"

Khalil held up a hand. "And I've heard this all before. I know she's been through a lot. I know that she's never had a really good relationship. All the more reason for me to want to give her one, don't you think?"

Keith eyed his friend. He looked serious, and Khalil wasn't the type of guy to purposely go around hurting women. But with Reka one never knew what to expect. "You think you can give her that? She's different from the women you're used to."

"Yeah, that's what makes me want to try harder." Turning his back to the bar, he looked toward the table to find her.

"What do the senior Franklins have to say about her? Cienna said she spent Thanksgiving with you."

Khalil chuckled. "That was something. Sonya showed up."

"You're kidding?"

"Nope."

"Tell me Reka didn't hit Sonya? Tell me I wasn't at Cienna's parents enjoying the game when I could have been in Greenwich enjoying one hell of a chick fight."

Laughing, Khalil slipped a hand in his pocket, his eyes still roaming the room for Reka. "Nah, man. Reka was cool. A little too cool, actually. She had me scared for a minute there when she wanted to talk to Sonya alone. I thought for sure somebody was going to need an ambulance."

"That's my Reka," Keith laughed.

Sobering when he finally spotted her, Khalil forgot all about Thanksgiving. "No. She's my Reka now."

Cienna had prodded Reka into dancing with Barkley. She knew how much Reka detested him, yet she'd made her case by referring to the upcoming Christmas bonus. Never one to turn away from money, Reka pasted a smile on her face and let Barkley Peterson lead her onto the dance floor. The music was up tempo, the best that the six piece band could do, yet Barkley insisted on rubbing his body against hers as if it were a slow song.

She'd backed away from him on two occasions, putting her palms on his chest so that he would keep his distance. But the moment she'd turned her back, because she was tired of his leering glances, he'd grabbed her at the waist and started grinding against her like a dog in heat. She was no stranger to this type of behavior, having experienced it in the clubs on numerous occasions. Generally, if she liked the guy she'd keep the dancing going. In the event she wasn't particularly feeling him, she'd waste no time breaking the contact and explaining her reasons why.

But this was the son of a big client. This was the launch party for that client's biggest line. This was a formal event at the Waldorf Astoria. Bottom line, this wasn't the place to act ugly. So she continued with Barkley's rhythm until she managed to turn herself back around and slip out of his clutches. Each time he made another attempt to dance up on her after that, she carefully maneuvered herself out of his reach until the song was over.

At the end of the dance, she didn't wait for him to say anything. Instead, she turned and made her way off the dance floor. Barkley was right on her heels.

"I wasn't finished dancing," he said, grabbing her by the arm.

She turned to him with a polite smile. "The song was finished."

Pulling her close to him, he glared down on her. "We can make our own music."

Reka pushed against him. "No. We can't." Flashbacks of pushing Donovan out of her face yesterday surfaced and she wondered what it was about the male population and their refusal to accept the word 'no.'

"Don't be a tease. You liked it a few minutes ago," Barkley insisted.

She'd had enough. Client or no client, job or no job, she was tired of him. She wrenched her arm free of his grasp and took a step back. "For your information, I didn't like it. I was being polite."

"Bull," he spat.

"Whatever." Waving a hand, Reka turned to leave again and he grabbed her arm again. Pulling back her other arm, Reka took a swing that landed on his nose with a sickening crack.

"Reka!" Khalil yelled. He'd watched them on the dance floor and had followed them with his eyes as they made their way back towards the table. He hadn't heard their exchange but he had seen the man grab her.

Barkley stumbled back, his hand to his face as blood spewed through his fingers. Keith was right behind Khalil and turned his attention to the man who was now yelling like a female.

Khalil grabbed Reka at the waist, pulling her away from Barkley, afraid she was going to hit the man again. "What are you doing?"

Her hand hurt like hell, but she didn't regret her action. "He wouldn't leave me alone and I was tired of being nice."

"Did he hurt you?"

She shook her head, stealing a glance around him to see how bad Barkley was hurt—not that she really cared, he had it coming. "No. I'm fine."

"What happened?" Cienna came over, followed by Jonathan Peterson and his soon-to-be ex-wife Eleanor.

"My God, Barkley. What happened to you?" Eleanor gasped, going to her son immediately.

It seemed as if the moment she swung, all the music, all the chatter in the room stopped. It was now deafeningly quiet and all eyes were on Reka.

"Somebody should teach your son some manners," she told the Petersons, then looked at Khalil. "I'm ready to go."

He followed her towards the door. He didn't know exactly what had happened. All he knew for sure was that a few moments ago she'd been dancing rather cozily with the guy, then he'd grabbed her and she'd punched him. She wasn't in any mood to talk right now so he'd wait until they were alone. "Wait here, I'll get our coats."

She nodded in agreement, folding her arms over her chest as she waited. Her heart was beating rapidly. She couldn't believe she'd actually hit him. She'd been trying so hard to hold back, to behave appropriately, but he just kept pushing and she just wanted him to get away from her. She wondered what Cienna's reaction was going to be, and the moment she heard the clicking of heels behind her, she knew that she was about to find out.

Keith put a hand on her shoulder, jostling her against his big chest. "Hey slugger, you all right?"

"I'm fine."

Cienna paused in front of her with one hand on her hip. "Barkley wants to press charges."

"Great," she sighed, "another court date."

"His mother wants to sue the firm."

Reka rolled her eyes. She wouldn't beg for her job no matter how much it meant to her. Barkley Peterson was a spoiled jerk and he deserved to have his butt kicked instead of a simple bloody nose. "I won't apologize."

Cienna cracked a smile. "I wouldn't ask you to." Reaching out, she took Reka's hand, looking down at the rapidly swelling knuckles. "You need some ice."

"It hurts like hell."

Both Cienna and Keith chuckled. "I bet it does," Keith told her.

He still had his arm protectively wrapped around her. She liked Keith. He was a good guy and he tended to look out for her, sort of like a big brother.

"Go home and let Khalil take care of you. I'll take care of the Petersons," Cienna said.

Over Cienna's shoulder she could see Khalil returning with their coats. And while she wouldn't apologize to Barkley, she respected Cienna and Keith and appreciated all that they'd done for her. "I'm sorry if I embarrassed you guys," she said quietly.

"Girl, please. I know Barkley's a creep. I've seen the way he eyes you and I've heard some of his remarks. So don't give it another thought. If she wants to press charges, then so will we, for sexual harassment. And after the last sexual harassment scandal Page & Associates was involved in, I don't think they even want to go there."

Keith agreed.

Retrieving her from Keith's grasp, Khalil wrapped the coat around Reka's shoulders. "Let's get you home."

"Take care of her hand," Keith added as they began to walk away.

"I will." Khalil looked down at Reka. She wasn't shaking, as women usually did when they were upset. She didn't seem nervous or even slightly agitated. She was steady and focused as she waited by the curb for the valet to bring his car around.

They rode in silence and, instead of him taking her home, they went to his place. Reka wasn't really paying much attention to their surroundings. Her mind was focused more on Khalil's quietness. Had she embarrassed him? That was her biggest concern. Even though she didn't regret what she'd done, she did regret the place in which it had occurred. But he hadn't spoken so she wasn't quite sure what he was thinking about the situation. He seemed more than a little tense. Still, the mere fact that they were at his place and not hers said something.

Slipping the key into the door, Khalil stepped to the side to let her in. Once inside he took her coat and watched as she went directly to his kitchen. After hanging their things in the closet he quickly followed behind her.

"Do you have tea?" she asked when she heard him approach from behind.

"Third cabinet on the right." Slipping onto a stool at the breakfast bar, he watched her hips move with the slightly shimmering gold material. "Sure you don't want something a little stronger?" he asked, attempting to lighten the mood.

Her head turned and she tossed a warning glare over her shoulder. "If I have something stronger I might get in your car and head back to the Waldorf to finish the job with Barkley."

Khalil grinned. "Oh, I think he was finished. For the night, at least."

Turning back around, Reka chuckled. "You're probably right." She found the tea bags and filled the stainless steel kettle sitting on the stovetop with water before putting it over the blaze.

"So what happened?" Khalil asked when he figured she'd moved around enough to be comfortable with him again. In the car she'd sat close to the door, deep in thought. He hadn't wanted to bother her, yet he'd wanted to reach out to her, to let her know that he was there.

Folding her arms over her chest, Reka slipped out of her shoes, then leaned against the counter. "He's always been a pest, coming on to me and thinking he's all that." She shrugged. "I guess tonight I just got tired of it."

She looked vulnerable, fragile, even as she stood amongst the cold décor of stainless steel and light wood in his kitchen. "I saw you dancing with him." And he hadn't liked it. The moment he'd spied the man's hands on her he'd been instantly angered. He'd watched them on the dance floor with Keith standing beside him telling him it was only a dance. Still, he hadn't liked it. She'd been smiling while the man's hands were on her waist, her hips—she hadn't pushed him away then. He wondered why.

Tilting her head, Reka surveyed him. Was he jealous? Or was he angry? She couldn't quite tell but figured her next response would give her the answer. "He's the son of the client. The VP of Sensuality, Inc., in training. The reason why we were at that party." He didn't respond, and she was betting there were equal amounts of jealousy and anger soaring through him at this very moment. "He asked me to dance. I didn't want to, but Cienna insisted. We danced."

"It looked like more than dancing to me."

Oh, yeah, anger and jealousy, two dangerously ugly creatures daring to rear their heads simultaneously. It was funny because she'd never really imagined Khalil upset or anything besides his normally serious self. "He got a little carried away. I didn't want to make a scene so I finished the dance and tried to walk away."

"And he tried to stop you."

"Yes, he was very persistent." She was getting the impression that he wanted to say something else. "You saw us, is that what it looked like to you?"

Khalil thought about his answer, waited, gauging the moment, the level of tension rising in the air and decided that honesty was best. "No. It looked like you were having a good time until he grabbed you."

Her eyes widened. "Then you do acknowledge that he grabbed me? Twice?"

"I'm telling you what I saw."

"And I told you what happened."

They were at a standoff. Reka didn't know what to say next. Truth be told she didn't quite trust herself to say anything. Her own anger was rising with the speculation and doubt she saw in Khalil's eyes.

"You danced with me similarly when you took me to the club. Do you always dance like that?"

What the hell kind of question was that? "Are you serious?" she asked incredulously.

"I'm asking a serious question."

"You're being a jerk!" she retorted. "Look, I danced with a client because my boss asked me to and because I didn't want to make any waves. Dancing does not give permission for anything else. And I don't care how the dance looked to you. I told him to get lost and he declined so I answered him more affirmatively with my fist."

Khalil did not waver under the heightened pitch of her voice. "You danced with him like you enjoyed his attention, then you walked away. I'm figuring he wasn't quite finished and tried to convince you of that fact. I'm not saying you were wrong to defend yourself against unwanted advances. I'm simply pointing out that the dance itself was like an invitation."

Oh, she was pissed now. Anger had flown out the window about two sentences ago. Pushing away from the counter, she moved until she stood on the other side of the breakfast bar, about two feet away from him. "You're calling me a tease?" Her fingers clenched on the back of the stool, the knuckles on her right hand still burning.

Khalil looked down at her hands, saw the red swollen digits and got up from his stool. Moving to the refrigerator, he took out an ice tray, then found a dish towel and wrapped a couple of cubes in it. He went to stand beside her, reached out and touched the package to her hand.

Reka pushed his hand away, and ice skittered across the pristine white floor. "Answer my question, Khalil. Are you saying that I asked for his advances?"

Clenching his teeth, Khalil knelt to pick up the pieces, tossing them into the sink. "Again, I'm telling you what I saw."

That was like answering 'yes' to Reka. Turning from him, she grabbed her shoes and slipped them back on, then walked out of the kitchen.

He followed her out into the living room. "Where are you going?"

She stopped at the closet, turned to him with an icy glare. "Home. I wouldn't want to be accused of teasing you as well." Pulling out her coat, she hastily slipped her arms inside.

Khalil was beside her in an instant, grabbing her shoulders, turning her to face him. "You're misunderstanding what I meant."

"Am I?" she yelled. "Am I misunderstanding that you saw me dancing with Barkley and immediately assumed that I liked his slimy hands on me? That I wanted him to feel me up in a public place? Tell me something, Khalil. Why is that assumption so easy for you to make?

Is it because I'm not the pampered, rich goddess that Sonya is? My 'hood rat persona makes me a tease *and* an easy lay?"

If she had smacked him, or even punched him as she had Barkley, it wouldn't have hurt or shocked him more. That was not what he'd said to her and that was definitely not what he'd meant. "I didn't say that, Reka. You're reading way too much into this." He put his hands on her shoulders.

It seemed as if she was constantly pulling away from men, and she was frankly sick and tired of them putting their hands on her. She wrenched away from him. "You see, I didn't ask you to grab me but you did! But I guess since I'm in your apartment I've given you the impression that it's allowed! I don't have time for this drama, Khalil." Turning, she made her way to the door.

As soon as she opened it, Khalil reached around her and planted his palm firmly on the door, effectively closing it.

"I want to go home. Are you going to hold me hostage?" she said without turning around.

Khalil closed the small distance between them, pressing his body against her back until she was trapped between the door and him. "No. But I won't let you go until you understand what I meant."

She didn't want to be aroused, didn't want to feel the heat pooling in her center at his closeness, but her body betrayed her anyway. "I already understand," she said in a slightly tortured voice.

Moving his hands from the door, he let them fall on her shoulders, then moved them up and down her arms. "I didn't like seeing his hands on you," he said quietly, closing his eyes to the vivid memory. "I didn't like him rubbing so close against you."

Reka sighed, resting her forehead on the door. "We were only dancing."

Lowering his head, Khalil whispered directly in her ear. "I didn't like it."

Slowly, he peeled her coat away, let it fall to the floor. She didn't resist him, but she didn't turn to him either. "He was the client and Cienna asked me to do it," she told him again.

He kissed her earlobe. "Then I'll make sure she doesn't ask you to dance with clients in the future." Her skin was soft, warming beneath his touch and he felt his own blood heating, his breath raging.

"So I'm not allowed to dance anymore. Is that a condition of this relationship?" Damn, he smelled good. His hard body against her back felt good.

His hands moved from her arms to her waist. Dragging them roughly down her hips and thighs, he grabbed at the material of her dress, pulling it up and over her hips. He kissed her neck, bit her shoulder. All while his hands slipped beneath the rim of her stockings and her panties until he felt the soft curls at her center. "You're not allowed to feel this way with anybody else. Ever." Grinding his arousal against her back, he let his fingers slip between her moistened folds, reveling in the gasp he brought from her.

"Khalil," she whispered. Tonight's incident, the ride over here, the conversation in the kitchen, all became a foggy haze with his touch.

"That's right, baby." Plunging his finger inside her Khalil continued to kiss the bare skin of her neck and shoulders. "Say my name." His tongue ran a long hot path from her neck up to her jaw and around to her lips where hers quickly joined in the tussle.

"Khalil." Reka couldn't help it. She said it again and again as he stroked her persistently, lovingly.

"Mmmhmmm, I'm the one that makes you feel like this. Not the client and not anybody else. Say it again!" he urged her as he pressed another finger inside her.

Reka's palms flattened on the door, and her nails clawed against the surface. Her knees bending slightly, she rotated her hips to match the movement of his hand. He was absolutely right. Nobody had ever made her feel this way before. "Khalil." This time it was a helpless whimper, one that undoubtedly told him that he'd made his point because in the next minute his hand moving quickly to pull both her panties and stockings down to her knees and spread her legs open wider.

"Say it again!" he told her as he dropped scorching kisses on her buttocks, the backs of her thighs and then with a helpless groan, to her center.

"Khalil!" She moaned and squirmed with his ministrations. His tongue was loving her, stroking her. The room was spinning, time stood still. She moved against the pressure, the wetness that seeped from her, the heat he was fueling.

The orgasm hit her like a tidal wave, crashing against her with a violent, refreshing force. Her legs trembled even as he held her open, held her in place. She whimpered and moaned his name over and over again but he didn't stop. He continued licking and sucking, consuming her climax as if it were the sweetest honey. She went limp, her entire body succumbing to his will and when she thought she'd simply fall to the floor, he was there, lifting her, carrying her to his bed.

16

Reka had lain next to Khalil all night. He'd watched her sleep, watched her quiet beauty in a state of pure relaxation. There were no words to adequately describe the way he'd felt when he awakened that morning with her curled up next to him. The moment was so precious he'd breathed deeply to let all that it implied sink in. He'd stroked her skin, touched her hair and cuddled against her, and graciously accepted that she was exactly what he needed.

Her feelings for him seemed to be mutual as she'd made love to him that final time in the wee hours of the morning. She'd whispered promises to him that he wanted desperately to believe. But Sonya's words echoed in his head. And after seeing Reka with Barkley Peterson, he'd succumbed to jealousy.

Khalil had to acknowledge that he wanted her all to himself. For the first time in his life, selfishness was an active part of his personality where she was concerned and he wasn't ashamed to admit it.

For her part, Reka was on top of the world, celebrating an emotional euphoria she'd never believed possible. Khalil was breath-taking. Their night together had been more than she could ever explain. For the first time in her life she was secure in a relationship. Khalil had made his feelings known from day one. He'd kept his word and he'd proved her wrong. While she wasn't normally up to admitting that she was wrong, this time she was glad to concede.

Khalil returned to her apartment with her and helped prepare brunch alongside her and Grammy in the kitchen. Then he happily subjected himself to being the only male at a table of opinionated women. Reka laughed and talked and simply enjoyed the time with him and with her family. After brunch her mother went to take a nap. Grammy remained at the kitchen table playing dominoes and talking to anyone who admitting to listening to her. Wanting a little bit of privacy, Reka and Khalil moved into the living room.

When the phone rang, Reka dragged herself away from him to answer it. After a brief conversation she returned to the living room. "Cienna says she and Keith are cooking on the grill and that we should come out and join them." Dropping onto the couch beside Khalil, she let her hand fall to his thigh.

Snapping back from his thoughts, he looked at her and grimaced. "Cooking on the grill? It's November."

She shrugged. "That's what I said and she just laughed, claiming that married people had to do strange things to keep the spark alive."

He figured she probably had a point and realized he could share some more thoughts on the email matter with Keith if they went. "So do you want to go?"

Cuddling against him, Reka laid her head on his shoulder. "As long as we're spending the day together just as we planned, I don't mind."

Wrapping an arm around her, Khalil kissed the top of her head. "Then let's go. The change of scenery will do us good. Besides, I heard Grammy say that Cletus was coming over after Janell left."

Reka sat up quickly. "Oh no! Then we have to hurry up and leave because if I see my grandmother and that man doing the nasty again, I swear I'm going to hurl."

Standing, Khalil laughed, grabbed both her hands and hauled her up with him. "As much as I like Grammy, I have to say I agree with you."

The huge grill, which looked more like an outside stove to Reka, sizzled and smoked as Keith turned steaks and barbequed chicken over on it. They were on the glass-enclosed deck of the Page home overlooking the tiny lake that lay quietly beneath the sunny sky on this crisp autumn day.

Tianna with her chubby little legs and thick ponytails played at her tiny table with dolls and fake food, immersed in a world all her own, while the grown-ups talked of the person disrupting their office.

"What I still don't understand is his purpose," Cienna remarked after checking on Tianna for the third time.

Reka sat in a high-backed, cushioned chair sipping on an iced tea. "I don't think he has a purpose. I think this is simply entertainment for him."

"Then that's even scarier. That means he gets some type of enjoyment from doing this, and that makes him sick." Cienna rolled her eyes.

Keith chuckled. "Not sick exactly. There happen to be some people that are into erotic talk and fantasies. So I wouldn't conclude the man's out of his mind. I'm just questioning his reasons for sending the emails to a law firm."

Khalil shared his latest information. "The messages have slacked off at Sensuality. In the last three weeks they've only received one message, and that one was to the management asking them to review their stock value because that could be the reason Jill was being so frigid to him."

"So does that mean Jill works for Sensuality, Inc.?" Reka asked.

"Why would you say that?" Keith was curious.

Reka took another sip from her glass before speaking. "Well, if the fall of Sensuality stock is bothering her, then she must either own stock or participate in the company's profit sharing program, which would make her an employee."

Cienna shook her head. "No. I think she's fictitious. I don't think Jack has a woman at all."

"Maybe he's simply looking for female attention," Keith suggested.

"Then why address the emails to everyone in the office? He's smart enough to only email the women." Khalil thought instantly of the message to Reka and, when he caught her glance, figured that she was thinking the same thing.

Cienna stood, walked over to the corner where her daughter sat and rubbed the little girl's cheek before continuing toward the table where fresh fruit and veggies had been laid out. Grabbing a carrot stick, she turned to the other adults. "Well, he's putting a damper on my day. I don't want to discuss this anymore. I actually called you two here to discuss Tacoma and his upcoming nuptials."

Reka groaned. "Oh, please. I am so sick and tired of this wedding. I wish Christmas Eve would hurry up and get here."

"That's the date they picked?" Khalil asked.

Keith nodded his head. "Tacoma is forever the romantic. He wanted to do it on Christmas Day or New Year's Eve but Terry was against it, hated the idea of intruding on everyone's holiday. So they settled on Christmas Eve."

"They're ah," Khalil searched for the word, "a different type of couple."

Cienna laughed. "Do you mean that literally or figuratively?"

Khalil returned her smile. "I mean they almost fit the mold of 'opposites attract' perfectly." The other difference was clear, but seemed unimportant to everyone in the room.

"Tell me about it. Terry is so steady, so mature and so grounded. Tacoma would be lost without him." Tilting her head, Reka thought for a moment. "But then, Tacoma brings out a side of Terry that's funny and adventurous. I think it's a healthy mixture."

Khalil watched her as she spoke, thinking more of them than of Tacoma and Terry, and sensing she was doing the same. "I agree."

Cienna and Keith didn't miss the exchange.

"So last night was a trip, huh?" Keith asked, shaking his head at his now moon-eyed friend. Who would have thought that Khalil would fall for Reka? He looked to have some really genuine feelings for her. He'd seen the jealousy etched across his face last night and, while it appeared the two of them had worked through that, Keith sensed something was still going on in that department.

Reka instantly looked weary. "I don't know what got into Barkley. Normally, he does his thing and I do mine. But last night he seemed pretty determined."

Cienna was chuckling again. "Yeah, determined to get knocked out."

Reka frowned, then let a small smile slip to her lips. "That wasn't planned."

"Oh, I don't doubt that. But it was executed with the efficiency that only you can deliver, my girl. That's why you're my assistant."

All four of them laughed at that, but Khalil's was a little forced. Thoughts of Barkley touching Reka still bothered him.

"What do you think his father will do?" Reka asked cautiously.

Cienna waved a hand. "Jonathan called me this morning apologizing profusely for his son's misconduct. The papers are having a field day with it, which will only increase their sales, so he's not bothered in the least."

"Eleanor Peterson was another matter entirely," Keith added. "She seemed serious enough about pressing charges until Cienna informed her that Barkley had been harassing you for quite some time and that your actions could be construed as self-defense from a stalker."

"A stalker?" Reka hissed. "Barkley? Please, he's a boy scout compared to the stalkers I've heard of. But something about him last night was different."

"He was high," Khalil added.

"What?" the others asked simultaneously.

Khalil grinned. "I saw him in the bathroom shortly after we arrived. He went into one of the stalls and lit up."

Reka nodded her head. "Come to think of it, when we danced I did pick up a little scent."

"Ah, yeah, the dancing thing," Khalil began to Reka's consternation. "Cienna, in the future—"

Shaking her head, Cienna grinned. "Don't even say it. I got an earful from him last night about that. You don't have to worry. Reka won't be asked to go above and beyond for the job again."

Reka was embarrassed. The thought that she was now prohibited from dancing with someone was more than a little disconcerting. But she knew enough not to address that issue here and now; she'd made enough scenes this weekend. Still, she wasn't going out like that. "Well, just the Barkley sort of clients. A little mingling never hurt anyone." She smiled sweetly but Khalil's grim gaze said he didn't agree.

Keith saw the exchange and thought it best that they move on to another subject, quickly.

They decided to throw a small dinner party for Terry and Tacoma the weekend before Christmas as sort of their bachelor/bachelor or pre-wedding or bridal shower, but they didn't actually figure out what to call it. Reka and Cienna agreed to iron out more of the details at work the next day, since the men looked as if they'd been handed a death sentence simply sitting there listening to them.

On the drive home Reka sat back in Khalil's car enjoying the scenery again. She could live in Greenwich. It seemed really out of character for her, she knew, but she was beginning to like the serenity of it all, the quiet streets, the thick trees and green grass. Winter was quickly going to change that but it didn't matter. The complacency of the entire scene calmed her, made her think that happily ever after might make an appearance in her life after all.

Khalil, however, was having other thoughts. The Donovan Jackson thing still nagged at him. How would Sonya know a man like Donovan, and how would she know that he knew Reka? Unless she'd seen them together.

His fingers gripped the steering wheel as he prayed that was not the case. It seemed highly unlikely since Reka and Sonya clearly did not run in the same social circles. But Sonya knew the man's name, knew that he had been involved with Reka. There was a connection somewhere and he was frankly tired of trying to figure it out on his own.

"Do you remember when you mentioned that you realized I had a past before you, and that was okay?" he started, not looking at her.

Still in her daze, resting her head comfortably against the headrest, Reka turned to look at him. "Mmmhmmm. Why? Do you have skeletons you want to tell me about?" she joked.

"Actually, I wanted to talk about your past."

Reka paused. "You said you didn't want to hear about all the mistakes in my relationship catalog."

"I don't want to hear about all of them per se, just one in particular."

He was serious, she quickly realized, and she sat up. "Oh really? And which one is that?" She wondered if Keith had told him something. Surely Cienna wouldn't have said anything, unless she told her husband, which was probably the case.

"Do you know a Donovan Jackson?"

At the sound of his name Reka cringed a little. For nine months Donovan had been out of her life until a few weeks ago when he'd paid her that visit at the office. Damn, how office gossip moved. "You already know the answer to that, so why not ask the real question?" This jealous side was new to her where Khalil was concerned, and she wasn't quite sure she liked it.

He spared her a glance, saw her studying him seriously and thought that maybe he shouldn't have brought this up. Oh well, it was done now. "Are you still seeing him?"

Reka took a deep breath, released it and put a hand on Khalil's leg. His worries were apparent, although she wasn't quite ready to accept that he wanted her so totally that he'd be jealous of someone else, especially Donovan. But she was going to put those fears to rest right away. "Donovan and I were involved. We broke up, close to a year ago. He was no good for me and I was tired of pretending otherwise." He didn't say anything, so she continued. "Last week he paid a surprise visit to the firm."

Khalil looked at her questioningly. He hadn't known that.

"He talked about going to lunch and I told him that was a bad idea. He didn't quite get the message then, so he appeared at my apartment the day after Thanksgiving. This time I told him in no uncertain terms that we were through. I have no interest in sharing a meal, or anything else, with Donovan for that matter. So there, that's that," she said with a smile.

Khalil relaxed a bit, still wondering how it was that Sonya knew the man, but determined now to let it rest. He wasn't an adolescent. He'd asked her straight out and she'd answered him. He really had no reason to doubt her, to think that she was running some type of game on him. Besides, that was in direct contradiction to the woman he knew he was in love with.

It was dark when he pulled up in front of her house. She saw lights on inside her apartment and groaned. "My roommate's still there."

Khalil grinned, putting the car in park but not turning the ignition off. "I think you should probably face the fact that she's not going back to Sunny Days."

Reka frowned, then smiled. "You're probably right." Turning to him, she took his hand. "You're not walking me in tonight?"

Twining his fingers through hers, he reveled in the warmth, lost himself in those glittering eyes. "No. I have some leads on Jack that I want to follow up. Time to put him and his emails to rest once and for all."

He looked tired and more than a little thoughtful. Reaching over with her free hand, she cupped his cheek. "You work too hard."

Khalil sighed. "I know, that's why I have you to help me relax. Which is exactly what we're going to do as soon as this is over with."

"Promise?"

"Promise." Leaning over, he lightly kissed her lips.

Reka sighed, knowing instinctively that Jack was not the only thing on his mind. Just as she'd had doubts looming in her mind when she first saw Sonya and learned that she had been engaged to Khalil, she suspected that whatever his knowledge of Donovan was, doubts were still niggling at him despite her answer.

"My past is my past," she whispered against his lips, her eyes capturing his in the dimness of the car. "I can't change it now. Donovan and I, that's over and done with. It's just you and me now, believe that."

She kissed his lips once lightly, then again with her tongue stroking over his mustache and his top lip. Khalil pulled her closer, desperate for the contact, the confirmation. Deepening the kiss, he poured his soul into that intimate action. She moaned into his mouth and he sighed with contentment. "I believe it," he said when he finally managed to pull away.

Khalil had been in his office since seven, having felt the need to wrap this email case up quickly. He'd been running code and scanning the messages for the last three hours when his screen suddenly blinked green, then black. Lines of code ran quickly until they were like blurred streams of white. A smile spread across his face.

A login name, signal location, internet identification and, finally, an email address blinked like that infamous light bulb over a cartoon character's head.

Hitting the print button, he listened as the information made its way from the screen to the blank sheet of paper. With a sigh of relief he picked up his phone to call Cienna. They would both celebrate with a responsive message to their friend Jack.

He'd just left a message on Cienna's voice mail when there was a knock at his door. "Come in," he yelled jubilantly even as he thought of the fancy restaurant he was going to take Reka to this afternoon for a celebratory lunch.

"This package just came for you," Tacoma said, stepping into the office. "I was going in this direction so I told Clara I'd drop it off."

"Thanks, Tacoma." Khalil took the package and clapped the smaller man on the back.

Tacoma looked at him with a weird expression. "Are you okay?"

Khalil couldn't stop smiling, he was so happy. But the look on Tacoma's face reminded him that he had yet to share his good news. "I just got a break in the emails," he explained.

"Really?" Tacoma's face lit up. "That's fantastic. Who is it? Do they work here? It's probably that freaky Nicole in the bankruptcy department."

Khalil chuckled. "No, it's not freaky...I mean, it's not Nicole." Shaking his head at Tacoma, he went to take a seat behind his desk again. "I have to talk to Cienna first. Then I suspect she'll make an announcement."

"She's in the conference room with some bigwigs. I guess I'll have to wait for the news then." Tacoma sighed, walked towards the door, then paused. "We should go out for drinks tonight to celebrate."

Comfortable with Tacoma and finding himself enjoying the time he spent around other couples, Khalil considered the suggestion and nodded. "That's a good idea. I'll tell Cienna about it when I talk to her."

"Great! I'll go call Terry and I'll stop by Reka's office on my way."

"Okay. I'll see you later." Khalil was already looking down at the package on his desk so he didn't notice Tacoma had left the office until he heard the door close.

Pulling the tab on the FedEx package, he leaned back further in his chair, letting the reclining mechanism move in accordance with his long frame. He was actually humming a tune, that new Brian McKnight song that seemed to be on the radio every time he and Reka were in the car. Did that mean that it should officially be their song? He smiled at the thought, then stuck his hand into the envelope and pulled out the contents.

Suddenly he sat bolt upright, his eyes riveted on the material he now held. His first thought as he flipped through the numerous shots of naked bodies in explicit sexual positions was that Jack had stepped up his game.

Then a pair of eyes stared at him with alarming clarity and all the blood in his body froze. He actually cringed. His hands shook as he moved from one photo to the next over and over again until the images seemed to blur together.

His phone rang but he ignored it. Trembling, Khalil set the pictures on the desk and brought his hands up to his face. Taking deep steadying breaths, he prayed that when he opened his eyes and looked down again he'd be wrong. He was tired, he'd been working since really early this morning. And he'd been thinking about her. For weeks now she'd clouded every part of his mind until his thoughts were completely of her. That was it. That was why he was seeing her.

Relaxing back in the chair he rubbed his hands up and down his thighs. Spinning the chair around, he turned his back on the photos, focused his eyes on the brisk fall day outside. He wasn't thinking clearly—he couldn't possibly be thinking clearly. It wasn't her. In his gut he knew she couldn't do this to him. In his heart, he prayed she couldn't do this. But his mind, his mind was clear on what he had seen. Turning again, he picked up a picture and looked first at the face of the man. A man he'd never seen before in his life until late last night when he'd received an updated email from Garland. Donovan Jackson.

The woman, the first woman, was familiar as well. He'd seen her in the office every day. Her light, almost white complexion and that long straight dark hair were unmistakable. Her breasts were huge as Donovan palmed them. Her face distorted with pleasure, it was Tyrese Buchannon.

But he didn't give a damn about either of those figures. With rapid heartbeats his eyes scanned down to the final woman, the one with her face between Tyrese's legs. Her face wasn't completely visible, but the hair was the same. He flipped to another picture. Donovan lay on his back, Tyrese straddled over his face and the woman Khalil thought he was in love with, the woman he thought was in love with him, was riding this other man, cupping her own breasts as she sat atop his penis.

In one long ragged movement, everything on Khalil's desk hit the floor, pictures included. He stood, slamming a fist into the wall with such fury the picture shook and the drywall gave way, leaving a hole the size of his hand. He wanted to scream, wanted to yell the roof off that building. Then he wanted to kill. Red blurred his vision, tinting everything around him with the fury that he felt. He wanted to break Donovan Jackson's body in two, wanted to watch the man suffer for a long time before finally killing him. Tyrese was a slut, this Khalil had already surmised. The pictures only validated that point. But for her part in this, for her treachery, he could wrap his hands around her pretty little neck and send that rail thin body splattering across a cold hard floor.

And Reka...Falling to his knees, he felt a jagged moan escape his chest. What could he do to her? What could he possibly do to this woman who had come to mean so much to him? Holding his head between his hands he knew he could never hurt her, could never cause her the type of pain she was now causing him. But he couldn't forgive her either. He couldn't, wouldn't, let this go.

Scooping the pictures up from the mess on the floor, he found the FedEx envelope and dropped them inside. Standing, he moved to the door, took a deep breath, then opened it and walked towards her office.

Reka was at her desk finalizing an email she was sending to Khalil. This weekend had been so wonderful and so emotional at the same time. She'd realized just how much she cared about him and had decided to put everything else in her past aside because he was different. They were different and, because of that, their relationship had a chance. Last night she'd lain in bed believing that she and Khalil could have what Cienna and Keith had. They could have a big house filled with kids and lazy Sunday afternoons. They could have the love and trust that was so apparent between Cienna and Keith.

They could be happy.

With a smile on her face she hit the send button and sat back, wondering what his reaction would be to her written words. It was almost lunch time and she hadn't heard from Khalil yet. Tacoma had told her about a half hour ago that Khalil had discovered Jack's identity and that he was waiting to talk to Cienna first, so she assumed that's where he was because when she'd just called his office he hadn't answered.

She had work to do, but couldn't quite concentrate. Her thoughts were focused on one thing, one person, one man.

And at that precise moment that man walked through her office door.

Her heart took that butterfly leap it did each time she saw him, then plummeted with a loud thud as she scanned his face. His lips were set in a thin line, the muscles in his jaw visible through the thin beard and clenching fiercely. His eyes were dark, ominous, as he glared at her. With a fluid motion he shut the door quietly, in blatant contrast to the look of a dark storm on his face.

"Hey, baby. What's the matter?" She made a move to stand, to go to him, but he held up a hand, stopping her.

"No. You need to sit down for this."

His words were cold, almost unrecognizable. He moved closer to her desk and she noticed his chest heaving through the stark white dress shirt he wore. Those thick muscles she'd come to love rubbing her hands and her mouth over rose and fell in sudden spasms, his arms bulging until, for a minute, he looked like the Incredible Hulk about to burst right out of his shirt.

"What's going on?" He didn't look sad, so the thought of someone dying or being hurt didn't immediately come to mind. What he looked was angry enough to kill.

"You tell me, Reka." He tossed the envelope onto her desk before dropping down into the chair across from her, leaning forward, his elbows on his knees. "I thought you and I were in a relationship. I thought we were working towards something real here." He looked away from her then, because today, of all days, she was more beautiful than ever. Her hair hung straight down, resting between her shoulder blades. Her face was smooth, the prettiest shade of brown he'd ever seen, with that bold beauty mark at the corner of her mouth. But then there were those eyes, that molten color that was a toss up between hazel and green on any given day. That was the betrayal, the one thing he couldn't handle.

"Khalil, I don't know what's going on with you, but you're really scaring me."

She didn't make a move for the envelope, he noticed when he turned back to her. "Pick it up and look at them," he said slowly, each word laced with pain.

Sitting up in her chair, Reka reached for the envelope, a sense of dread building in her gut. Grabbing the stack from inside she pulled out the pictures and gasped as the images became clear. Donovan and Tyrese and…and…"Where did you get these?"

"Does it matter?" He grimaced. Where was the denial? She should have been screaming and yelling her innocence. Instead she simply looked at the pictures, then up at him.

Reka couldn't believe what she was seeing, what she was experiencing. In an instant Khalil's anger and the source of it registered with her. In that same instant her own anger began to rise. She tossed the pictures back onto the desk. "So let me guess. You're here because you think I cheated on you. You think I lied to you."

"Let's not play childish games, Reka. I don't have time for them."

She blinked, astonished at the pain his words caused. "Oh, now you want to emphasize the age difference. I seem to remember a time not too long ago when you told me that age didn't matter."

"Age doesn't. Maturity does."

It was a staredown. Dark brown eyes holding hazel flecked ones. The tension in the room was so thick either of them could have choked from it.

"You're right, Khalil. So the mature thing to do is to put all our cards on the table." Dropping her hands to the arms of her chair, she crossed her legs and glared at him. "What do you have to say to me about these pictures?"

Was she turning the tables? Again his vision blurred with rage. She was the one in those photos, she was the one performing a number of explicit acts with her ex-boyfriend and her co-worker. She should be the one doing the talking. "Are you even going to deny it? Aren't you going to try to plead your case, to tell me I'm mistaken?"

Why should she? He already believed the worst of her. Reka shook her head, shook away the tears that threatened to erupt. She'd been through too much in her young life to be baited into a yelling match with him. His mind was made up. Whatever she did or did not say wouldn't matter. It never mattered. Her college degree, her new title at work, her new clothes, none of it mattered to the woman inside. She was who she was, Reka Boyd, born and raised on the streets. She should have never let herself believe that a man like Khalil could see past everything else and truly love a woman like her.

"What I'm going to do is tell you this one time and one time only." She took a deep breath and stood, folding her arms across her chest because she didn't know what else to do with them. "I loved you. I never lied to you about my past or about my present. You knew who and what I was the moment you met me, the moment you talked to Keith about me. You pursued me, even when I told you I was no good at relationships." She paused, those damned tears getting too close to the surface.

"You said our backgrounds didn't matter to you. But you lied. These last few weeks you've been convincing yourself that I was a woman you could be with when in truth, you want a woman like Sonya, the socialite that your family will approve of, the perfect looking bitch to appear on your arm. The other side of you, the carefree, almost human side, wants to live a little dangerously, to break the rules. That's where I came in. But in your mind you knew I'd never measure up. So you sat back, watching, waiting for something to happen, something to prove your point."

"That's not how it was," he interrupted. Standing, he concentrated deeply to keep from going to her, from wrapping his arms around her. Couldn't she see how much this was hurting him? Couldn't she see what she'd done to him?

"Oh yes, it was. There's no use denying it. I was a fool, too, because I thought…I believed you when you said you were different, that you could show me how a man loved his woman." She lost the battle and one tear found its way down her cheek. She quickly wiped it away, then leaned over the desk to scoop the pictures up and put them back inside the envelope. Holding it out to him, she summoned her resolve and looked him straight in the eye. "You never trusted me. That's why you questioned me about Donovan. And if you never trusted me, then how could you love me?"

Khalil had never felt so broken before. This last hour of his life had seemed like a hundred years of hard labor, of solitary confinement in which he was starved and beaten. No. Even that didn't seem to explain what he was feeling. He snatched the pictures from her. "I didn't cheat on you!" he yelled.

She shook her head. "No, you didn't. Cheating would have been the easy way to hurt me. Gaining my trust then letting me down took a lot of work and effort on your part. For that I give you an A+." He stared at her incredulously. He was expecting something else. A scene, a tantrum. That was more like the Reka he presumed she was.

With a chuckle she shook her head, finally giving in, a little. "And for those bullshit pictures you have, you and the pervert who took them can go to hell! Now get out of my office before I call security." She did raise her voice then because the sight of him was literally breaking her heart. She felt the ripping, the searing pain of the separation and wanted to lash out at him. But he'd gotten all he was going to get from the ghetto receptionist turned college prepped paralegal. She wouldn't give him another minute of pleasure.

To prove her point she lifted the receiver of the phone.

Khalil wasn't afraid of security. He wasn't afraid of anyone in the office hearing what was going on between them. He was so beyond that point. What he was afraid of was that he'd take her in his arms and tell her he forgave her, that they could work past this, that he still loved her. He didn't want her to have that type of control over him; she didn't deserve that type of loyalty and dedication, since she was incapable of giving the same in return.

"You disappoint me," he said on his way to the door.

"No, Khalil." Her breath was ragged now, the tears inevitably about to flow. "I didn't make promises, you did. And you didn't keep them. So you let me down." The last was said quietly.

He didn't turn to her again, didn't look at her one last time, simply walked out, closing the door soundly behind him.

Reka sank back into her chair, dropping her head onto the desk, those pesky tears flowing fiercely.

17

Cienna was still in her meeting, and that was just fine with Khalil. Everything, including those damned emails, had taken a backseat in his life the moment he opened that envelope. He stopped by his office only long enough to shut down his computer and grab his suit jacket. Then he was on the elevator, headed out of the building.

He drove with no awareness of the other drivers on the road, and only by sheer luck did he make it to his destination without causing an accident. Switching the ignition off, he attempted to calm himself, resting his head on the steering wheel. Inside he was in turmoil, his emotions so confused, twisted and distorted that he could barely tell right from wrong. He needed to vent, to clear his head. Grabbing the envelope from the passenger seat, he stepped out of the car intent on doing just that.

He was inside the courthouse, was checked and checked again because he'd left his keys in his jacket pocket. Now he was on his way down the marble hall towards the judge's chambers.

"Good afternoon," Gayle said cheerfully from behind her desk.

"Hello," Khalil offered with no hint of a smile. "I'm here to see Judge Page. You can tell him it's Khalil Franklin."

Keith was opening his door, on his way out to lunch, when he saw his friend standing at the desk. "Hey, man. You're just in time. I was about to go out and grab a bite to eat. Join me."

Khalil took Keith's outstretched hand, shook it then shook his head. "Nah, we need to talk. Let's go in your office."

Khalil's voice was grave, and Keith knew instinctively this was going to be bad. "After you," he said extending his arm towards his office. "Gayle, I'm out to lunch. Don't disturb me unless it's my wife."

Gayle nodded her understanding.

Khalil sat down in a high-backed leather chair after dropping the envelope on Keith's desk. Keith watched as the man he'd known for years sat defeated, his shoulders slumped, his head down.

"What's going on? Is it your parents?"

"No," Khalil said quietly.

Keith had known that but asked anyway. The look Khalil had said one thing: woman problems. "Reka?"

Khalil inhaled deeply, sat back in the chair and looked at Keith. "Open the envelope."

Keith did as he was told, but was in no way prepared for what he saw. "What the hell? Where did you get these?"

"They were sent to me at the office this morning."

"Is this Tyrese?"

"Yes." Gritting his teeth, he continued, "The man is Donovan Jackson, Reka's ex. And the other woman is?"

Keith held up a hand. "Don't." This had to be the hardest thing for any man to swallow. Pictures of the woman you're in love with in bed with another man…and a woman. He didn't envy Khalil one bit. But he did sympathize.

"When were these taken?" Was Keith's first question.

Khalil shrugged. "I don't know."

"It could have been before you two got together."

Khalil hadn't thought of that, but agreed. "It could have been. Does that make it all right?"

Still holding the pictures, Keith looked at his friend. "Are you judging her based on these pictures?" Khalil was silent. "Or had you judged her before?"

Khalil stood, throwing his hands up in the air. "I don't know." He walked towards the window, then turned back to Keith. "What kind of woman does something like this?"

Keith rocked back in his chair after setting the pictures on the desk. His fingers steepled beneath his chin, he studied the man he called a friend. Khalil was a good guy, but he'd been raised with blinders on. He was from an affluent family, who lived, breathed and existed a certain way. They believed in black and white; there was no room for gray. And Reka was definitely gray. "What you should be asking yourself is, what type of woman is Reka? That's all that matters here."

Dragging his hands down his face, Khalil felt the weight of the world on his shoulders. He was so conflicted. There was a part of him, a strong part, that told him from the moment he saw those pictures up until now, that Reka couldn't do this. Not before she met him, and certainly not after. But he was faced with irrefutable proof, or so the logical side of him believed. "She didn't deny it," he said quietly.

"She shouldn't have had to."

He shook his head. "I loved her."

Keith raised a brow. "And you don't anymore? Can you honestly say that once you looked at these pictures everything you felt for her disappeared?"

Khalil didn't even attempt to kid himself. "No. I guess that's what makes this so bad."

"I could go into how you should trust her, how I told you not to hurt her, how I explained to you that she was different from the women you were used to, but that would be futile and might turn into a pretty ugly scene in my place of business." Keith stood, walked over to his friend. "So I'm going to be the judge here."

Khalil looked at him peculiarly.

Keith cracked a smile. "Humor me," he said, clapping Khalil on the back.

Khalil nodded, not sure where Keith was going with this but desperate for anything that would shed some light on this situation.

"What I look for first is a motive. Who would want to see you and Reka apart? Because there's no doubt in my mind that's the purpose of these pictures being sent to you. And if you weren't drowning in your own emotions right now you'd see it, too. But since you are, I'm going to help you out."

"Man, I don't feel like doing this right now." Khalil's fists clenched at his sides as one of the pictures popped into his mind.

"Ever heard the saying, 'Hell hath no fury like a woman scorned'?" Keith asked simply.

Khalil paused, closed his eyes, then re-opened them, his thoughts shifting from Reka to Sonya. "She couldn't. How would she have even known?" Then he remembered her phone call the day after Thanksgiving. He remembered her mentioning Donovan Jackson.

"Second, ask yourself who had the most to gain by your breakup. Now I recall hearing about Donovan and Reka's relationship. He seemed all right on the surface, but he loved money and would do just about anything for it. He sold drugs, stole cars. Anything he could do for money, he did it. That's the reason Reka ended it with him. That and the fact that he was pimping women out, then making them sleep with him when they didn't get all his money." Keith shrugged. "Think about it. Put one and one together."

"But in this instance one and one don't go together. How in the hell would Sonya know a guy like Donovan?" He didn't have the answer to that but he knew that she did, she'd told him as much.

"Don't put Sonya on a pedestal, man. She's still a woman, the woman you refused to marry. Imagine how embarrassed she was when you broke things off with her and then took another woman to your mother's house on Thanksgiving. And she still wants you. You even said yourself that she was willing to settle for a loveless marriage for the sake of money and prestige."

"All this is well and good, but pictures don't lie."

"Khalil." Keith was becoming more and more frustrated by the minute. "You know, for a computer geek you sure are stupid when it comes to matters of the heart."

Khalil shot him a heated glare.

"You're into private investigating. Look at these pictures again and tell me they couldn't have been tampered with." Moving to his desk Keith picked up the pictures, then thrust them into Khalil's hands. "Now at first glance you would think it was Reka. But give it a closer look. I mean, I haven't seen her naked so I can't be one hundred percent positive, but there is a strong possibility that this could have been airbrushed. Reka can't stand Tyrese, so there's no way in hell she'd be licking on her or being licked by her, for that matter."

Khalil had no choice but to take the photos even though he was beginning to think that coming to Keith was a bad idea. His friend wasn't exactly soothing his broken ego. He looked down at the photos.

This was the shot of her riding Donovan. The hair was the same, the skin tone was the same. His eyes traveled down further and stopped. Reka had two dimples at the base of her back. The picture didn't show any, but then the lighting wasn't all that great.

He flipped through the pictures, looking for one that would show her face. He would know if it were her face. She was lying down, her legs spread wide, with Donovan between them and Tyrese playing with her breasts, breasts that looked a lot smaller than he recalled. Her eyes were closed in this shot but her lips were puckered as if she were moaning. Then his heart stopped. He lifted the picture closer to his face, studying it earnestly. Where was the beauty mark?

It should be there, just below her bottom lip on the left side. But it wasn't.

Lowering the picture, he sighed. "I messed up, didn't I?"

Keith grimaced. "Big time."

It was almost time to go home and Tacoma hadn't heard a peep from Reka all afternoon. That was unusual, since they normally talked a billion times during the day. He knocked on her door, then opened it without waiting for an answer. "Hey, where've you been hiding all afternoon?" He talked as he entered, then stopped abruptly when he saw her sitting in her chair, swinging it from side to side. Her face was somber, her eyes a little swollen from what he could see. The situation, he surmised, was bad. "What happened to you?"

She'd been closed in this office for the last four hours. First, immediately after Khalil had gone, she'd cried and then cried some more. It was well after lunch by the time she'd used up all her Kleenex and felt a burning in her nostrils from blowing too much. Then she'd found her resolve and thought about the situation seriously. Tacoma had come in at just the right time. "Close the door," she said solemnly.

He did so quickly, then moved around the desk, taking her hand. "Tell me what happened, sweetie. You look absolutely beaten and downtrodden."

His words interrupted her thoughts and she looked up at him strangely. "What the hell is downtrodden?"

Tacoma continued to rub her hand with his. "Oh, did I say that? I've been reading those historical romances again. You know, the ones that Terry absolutely hates." He smiled.

Reka tried to reciprocate but couldn't hold the grin. "You're crazy."

"And you're upset. What happened?"

Reka took a deep breath, then went into the whole sordid spin her life had taken this morning. For a moment Tacoma was absolutely quiet, which in itself was a miracle. That confirmed that this was not a good thing.

"So what are you going to do?" he asked finally.

"I can't change his mind. Whatever he thinks about me he's going to think regardless of what I do or don't do. I was honest with him, so I've done enough in that regard. The rest is up to him."

"Yeah, but seeing those pictures had to be hard for him." Tacoma surprised himself with that statement.

"He should have known it wasn't me," she retorted. "He should have known I couldn't do something like that."

"Calm down, chicky." Tacoma continued to stroke her hand because she was getting riled up, and when Reka got riled up the next step was usually her swinging on you. "I'm not saying he's right for being mad and confronting you. All I'm saying is that you need to put yourself in his shoes for a minute. Imagine if you'd opened up a package of pictures of him and that uppity woman you met. You would have been ready to rip him a new…"

"Tacoma! I get the picture," she interrupted. Taking another deep breath—all this therapeutic breathing she was doing made her feel as if she were about to give birth—and closed her eyes. "I guess I would have been upset initially. But I really believed he wouldn't hurt me. He made me believe that."

"Sweetie, he can't make you do anything. Don't forget I know you, if nobody else does. You believed he wouldn't hurt you because you loved him. You wanted to believe in him and the relationship you had. And there's nothing wrong with that. Sometimes a person's first reaction is more emotional than rational."

"He never even asked me if it were true," she said in a small voice. "He just believed it. Just like that. I think that's what hurt the most."

Leaning over, Tacoma wrapped her in his arms. "I know, sweetie. But everything's going to work out. You just wait and see."

"I don't think so, Tacoma," she said as he released her.

Tacoma waved a hand. "Sure it is. Because we're going to work it out."

"Oh, goodness, slow down, Rambo."

Tacoma was moving about the office now. "Uh-uh, there's no slow down now. Not this time. We're going down that hall and we're going to snatch that little hussy right out of her chair and beat her little ass!"

Reka was already shaking her head. "We can't do that."

"What do you mean, we can't? Are you crazy? Has falling in love permanently distorted your mind? The Reka I know would be about handling her business."

She stood. "I am going to handle my business, just not in the office." She picked up the phone and dialed a number. "Sit down," she instructed him. "Watch and learn. This is how a real woman works."

Tacoma frowned, plopped his bony body into a chair and crossed his legs. He was ready to go, ready to snatch Tyrese bald, but he'd wait for now. Reka was his partner in crime, his road dog, his very best friend in the world. He'd do anything to keep her happy, and right now that included beating down a woman.

"Donovan, this is Reka. Give me a call as soon as you get this message." She hung up, then sat back in her chair. "Somebody paid him. I know they did. Donovan loves money, and if the price was right he'd do just about anything." She was tapping her finger against her chin. "What I can't figure out is who would pay him to do this. And why would he do it with Tyrese?"

"That's simple. The Fifth Avenue Ho," Tacoma said matter of factly.

A knock sounded on the door and Cienna walked in. "Hi, I was looking for Khalil. I got his messages and just managed to get a moment to see him. Do you guys know where he is?"

Tacoma looked at Reka, who tried her best not to cry all over again. Cienna looked at the two of them and knew something was going on. "What's happened?" She was in the office with the door closed behind her in no time.

"Do you want to do the honors or shall I?" Tacoma asked.

With another deep breath she told Cienna the story.

"You have got to be kidding." Cienna put a hand to her forehead. "I swear this firm must be a magnet for crazy sexual antics. Tyrese? Are you sure it was her?"

Reka nodded. "Positive. I did a double take myself. But then there were so many pictures that her face became clearer in each one. She's definitely not the stuck up ghetto I-married-well-so-now-I'm-all-that twit we thought she was."

Tacoma grinned. "Ain't that the truth. But she is a bimbo, so I say we treat her like one and put the smack down on her." He was up and out of his chair again.

"Sit down, Tacoma," Cienna sighed. "No fighting in the office."

"Then you go down there and fire her skinny ass," Tacoma rebutted as he took his seat again.

Cienna shook her head. "Fire her for what? Having a sex life outside of the office? She'll sue Page & Associates so quick we won't have time to get to the unemployment line."

"But isn't it insubordination or something to bring photos like this into the workplace?" Reka asked. The thought of seeing Tyrese every day from here on out made her sick.

"Not unless you can prove that she brought them here. And you said they were in a FedEx envelope. It's easy enough to find out who sent the package, but if it wasn't her there's really nothing I can do."

"Well, she's not getting off that easy!" Tacoma was up again.

"Sit down, Tacoma!" Reka and Cienna yelled in unison.

Tacoma frowned.

"I can't fire her," Cienna said thoughtfully, "but if she were to resign I'd have no problem accepting it." She looked at Reka.

"So what does that tell us? She's not going to quit and you know it," Tacoma fired back.

Reka kept her eyes on Cienna, getting her meaning and smiling. "Oh she's going to quit. It'll just take a little convincing." She turned to Tacoma. "I know you're up for convincing her, aren't you?"

A smile spread across Tacoma's face. "You know I am," he said, rubbing his hands together happily.

Khalil breathed a heavy sigh as he let himself into his apartment. It was after seven and he was tired from driving around the city trying to get his thoughts together. Keith had pointed out something he hadn't even considered. As a result he'd looked at the pictures over and over again until he almost had them memorized. Was he wrong?

He dropped the infamous envelope onto his dresser, for the first time looking for the sender's address. There was none. But finding out the identity wasn't a problem. Taking the envelope into his office, he booted up his computer. Rolling his head around, he tried to crack his neck in the hope that some of the tension would be relieved. When that didn't work he opted for a shower. He could research the package when he finished.

Hot water streamed over his honey-toned skin as he stood beneath the sprinkler, head bowed, eyes closed. He loved her, of that there was no doubt. And if these pictures weren't of her, which he was now reasonably sure they weren't, then he had two problems. Who would go to such drastic measures to separate them, and how would he win Reka back?

He remembered the look on her face when he walked into her office: concern. But when he spoke to her, when he instructed her to open the envelope, that concern had quickly faded. Shock. Confusion. Then realization. He recalled the exact moment that the pictures and their impact settled into her mind. The usual gleam in her eyes had shifted. Anger was clear, disappointment presumed, but hurt, that was definite. As if he thought he'd been in enough pain, remembering the look she'd given him only squeezed his heart tighter. Could a woman who was caught in her lies still manage to look that way?

He hadn't verbally accused her, but then he didn't need to. The pictures and his attitude most likely spoke for themselves. Cursing again, he washed, then stepped out of the shower. He'd dried off and was just slipping on a pair of shorts when his doorbell rang. He paused, looked toward his bedroom door and felt a jolt of his heart. Was it Reka? Had she come to talk about this?

His feet moved him to find out even as he thought it would be more likely for Reka to be stopping by to finish the argument. She'd wanted to say more to him; he'd seen her struggle to hold back. But now he was probably about to receive the full brunt of her anger.

Swinging the door open, he looked into familiar eyes, but not the ones he wanted to see. Before he could speak she'd brushed past him. "Hi, darling. I hated the way we ended things the last time we talked, so I thought I'd stop by."

For a moment Khalil still held the door open, shocked at seeing her and amazed at her casualness. But then, she had no idea he suspected her of being involved with those pictures. That could play to his advantage. "Ah, yeah, I've been thinking a lot about that, too." Closing the door, he walked into the living room where she'd already shed her coat, dropping it on the chair. She looked good in her ivory pant suit and shoes. Her hair was perfect, her face the picture of a model, but in her eyes—you could always tell the truth of a person through their eyes—he saw a spark of triumph.

"You look tired, Khalil. Are you sleeping okay?" Sonya asked.

Yeah, she was enjoying this. What she didn't know was that he was about to have some fun himself. "Actually, no. I've been thinking about a lot of things. Re-evaluating, I guess you could say." He moved until he was standing directly in front of her, lifting his hand to toy with a strand of her hair.

Her smile warmed as she touched a palm to his cheek. "Oh, poor baby. Can I do anything to help?"

"I don't think so. I'm just so confused right now."

Sonya took a step closer, her victory all but bubbling over inside. He was naked except for his shorts, and she realized with a start how truly handsome Khalil was. All that smooth golden skin, the small splatter of dark curls on his chest, the tight muscles of his abs. Her mouth actually watered. With both hands she felt the strength in his shoulders, then let her hands roam the length of his torso. "I can make it better, Khalil. Remember how we were together?" she whispered into his ear. She remembered, but had a feeling that tonight with him would be different.

"I'm not sure sex is the solution for what I'm going through." Khalil restrained himself, allowed her to touch him, though every second she spoke convinced him she was definitely in on the picture scheme. He wished he'd had the opportunity to find out who the sender was, but this might be even better. But how to get her to confess? Her hands wrapped around him, cupped his buttocks, and he found his answer.

"I can make you feel so much better, baby. If you let me." She kissed along his chest, laving his nipple before slipping her hands beneath the band of his shorts.

Closing his eyes, Khalil convinced himself that this was the only way. He wrapped his arms around her, pulled her closer. "You're the only one I can trust, Sonya."

She sighed. "That's right, baby. I am."

His hands moved up and down her back, stopping just before her bottom. "I just feel so betrayed right now. I feel like every time I give my trust it's thrown back in my face."

"You can trust me, Khalil." She kissed his neck, the line of his jaw, then hovered momentarily over his lips. "I love you."

"You do?" he asked, amazed at how well she lied.

"Yes, baby, I do. I'd do anything to keep us together, Khalil. Just tell me what you want me to do." She traced her tongue over his bottom lip, was about to delve inside when he grabbed her hair roughly. Every bell inside her body rang, and heat and moisture soared to her center. "What do you want?" she whispered.

He tugged on her hair a little harder, until she arched backward, her throat bared, her pulse quickening. Her eyes had darkened, and he realized it was because his roughness had aroused her. This was not the Sonya he'd known. "Tell me how you know Donovan Jackson."

Sonya blinked. "What? Who? What does he have to do with us?"

She grasped his arms, her nails skimming his skin. "If you want us to be together again I have to know how you know him. I have to make sure that it's just me and you."

Sonya licked her lips. "Yes, it's just me and you, Khalil. I've never really wanted anybody else."

"Did you want Donovan?"

"No."

He pulled her hair a little more. "The truth, Sonya." Then he lightened his grip. "Or we can't get back together."

Her breathing was erratic, her nipples hard and straining against her blouse. He looked positively dangerous, and his hands on her were rough and hard. She wanted him, oh she wanted him badly. "Just for a while. Just while you were running around with her. I needed somebody."

A muscle in his jaw twitched. "Where did you meet him?"

"At a party or something." She was wiggling in his arms, trying like hell to increase the contact of their bodies. "Baby, let me take my jacket off."

"Not yet. I like how you look right now."

She smiled. "Is it over between you and her?"

He prayed it wasn't. "I found out she was cheating."

A smirk slipped over her lips. "I told you she wasn't good enough for you. She's just a tramp, just like Donovan. I knew you'd see that the moment..." Her words broke off.

Lifting a hand, Khalil rubbed the pad of his thumb over her bottom lip. It quivered. "The moment I what?" he whispered.

It was a good thing he was holding her up or Sonya would have melted right then and there. Why hadn't he showed her this side of him before? "I already knew she was still sleeping with him when I saw you on Thanksgiving. Donovan is into a lot of kinky stuff."

"Kinky?" Khalil purposely rubbed his chest against hers and watched as her eyes fluttered. She was clearly aroused, and to a point that he'd never seen before. When had she become so wanton? "What do you know about kinky, Sonya? I thought you were a good girl."

She purred. "I am a good girl, baby. I'm *your* good girl." His finger was still close enough that when she extended her tongue it touched the lone digit. "But I can show you so many bad things."

"Really?" He wanted nothing more than to throw her to the floor. A sick and disgusting feeling was roiling through him. "What can you show me?" She opened her mouth to speak and he quieted her with a finger over her lips. "Shhh, let me tell you what I want you to show me. I want to have you," he dragged his finger down the line of her neck, watched her smile, "and another woman. I want us all in bed. Together."

Her eyes lit up. "And then I want somebody to take pictures. No, better yet, I want it videotaped. Can you do that for me, baby?"

Sonya cooed. Marrying Khalil wasn't going to be so bad after all. "Oh yes, baby, I can do that. I know just who to call."

Khalil released her abruptly. "Then make the call."

She looked startled for a moment, then moved to the phone. He walked behind her, watched as she dialed, committing the number to memory. He was so close to her he could hear when the woman answered the phone. Then he yanked the phone cord right out of the wall with one hand and grabbed Sonya's shoulder with the other.

"How much did you pay them?" he yelled.

"What? Baby, I don't know what you're talking about. I was just going to make your fantasies come true." She reached out for him again.

"My fantasies were coming true, but you put a stop to that, didn't you? How much did you pay Donovan Jackson? How much did you pay Tyrese?"

Pulling her hands back, she stepped away from him. "I don't know what you're talking about."

He grabbed her by the shoulders, pushing her until her back slammed against the wall. "You know damned well what I'm talking about, and if you don't tell me exactly what you did, your father is going to know as well!"

She was silent.

"You can't live without his money, his prestige. He'll disown you. You know how he hates a scandal. And what's a bigger scandal than a sex one?"

With all her strength she pushed him away from her. "Get your hands off me!" she yelled, moving towards the sofa again to retrieve her coat. "You know what, Khalil? You're not even worth it. I would say I wasted my money, but that would be a lie. I enjoyed it. And even though the outcome wasn't what I had in mind, it's okay. There's so much more out there than you."

"More like Donovan Jackson? More like the group sex you seem to be so into?" Against his upbringing and for the second time today, Khalil felt as if he could actually hit a woman. "Reka would never be involved in something like that."

Sonya grinned as she slipped her arms into her coat. "Oh dear, you are truly taken by her, aren't you? Well, didn't you see the pictures, darling? Didn't you see your little slut? She enjoys Donovan almost as much as I do."

Like a flash he was across the room, his hands wrapped around her neck. She swatted at him even as she gasped for breath. "You are a cheap trick! I can't believe I ever entertained the idea of marrying you. You fixed those pictures so I'd break up with her! You wanted me to believe it was her but it wasn't, was it?"

She couldn't feel the floor beneath her; the room was beginning to spin. "Stop! Khalil! Stop!" she croaked.

With one last bout of rage he dropped her to the floor. Looking down, he watched her crumble. He didn't need her to admit it. He didn't need her words.

"Get out of my house!"

Reka and Tacoma pulled up in front of the huge house in the wooded area. How many times had she seen pictures of the wood being nailed together to build this fortress? It was beautiful, she had to give her that much. But it was also empty on so many levels.

Tyrese lived alone, her husband having left her just last month for another woman. Her family had long since disowned her because of the change she'd made in her personality upon marrying well. She'd been the princess for a while, and now she was simply pathetic.

Even with those thoughts Reka still found it hard to believe that she'd be a part of this scandal. What made a woman do the things she'd done? And how had she known Donovan?

"Here we are," Tacoma announced.

It was dark outside, the secluded neighborhood even darker. "Let's do it."

Getting out of the car, they made their way up to the door and knocked. They'd gone home and changed, realizing that this was the best course of action. Cienna couldn't fire Tyrese, but they could certainly make sure she no longer wanted to work at Page & Associates.

Tyrese frowned as she opened the door. "What are you two doing here? This certainly isn't your neck of the woods."

Oh, she was smug. She was uppity and she was still looking down on them. With a look to Tacoma, who simply nodded his head, Reka pushed the skinny twit inside the house and listened as Tacoma closed and locked the door.

18

Raising his hand to knock on the door, Khalil was prepared to grovel for her forgiveness. He'd tossed and turned all night after throwing Sonya's behind out of his house. Going to the computer to trace the package was pointless since he already knew who'd sent it. So instead he'd gone straight to bed. Only to lie there and think about the colossal mistake he'd made with Reka.

Keith was right, he should have trusted her. He should have believed in what they had. He'd thought about her words as well. She'd told him that he'd wanted to believe the worst about her, that she wasn't the type of woman he really wanted to be with. She couldn't have been further from the truth. From the start she'd been exactly what he needed. Reka Boyd was not your ordinary woman. She'd been dealt a bad hand repeatedly in life, yet she'd prevailed. She'd gone to school, gotten her degree and was making something out of her life; something that meant a lot to her.

She had great friends. Cienna, Keith and Tacoma would go to the ends of the earth for her, and she for them. She had a good family, albeit strange. The closeness of those three women was unquestionable. Their love and support for each other made each a strong woman. Truth be told, he'd envied her. She knew what she wanted and didn't let anybody stop her from achieving that, not even him.

Her tolerance for men, he knew, had been exceeded. He'd promised to treat her like a woman ought to be treated and he'd hurt her just like the rest of them had. It really didn't matter that his actions had spun from his own hurt and misunderstanding. The bottom line was that he'd let her down. And before he did another thing today, he had to set that straight.

"Mornin', handsome." Grammy wore a colorful robe as she opened the door to greet him.

"Good morning, Grammy," Khalil spoke as he walked into the apartment. "Is Reka up yet?" As much as he enjoyed his talks with Grammy, he wanted to see Reka more.

"She's up and gone, chile. Came in late last night and got up early this morning." Grammy moved to the couch and took a seat, immediately picking up the remote to switch the channels. "She was in a mood too. Yelling at people and mouthing off. I was about to put her over my knee, but then she came to her senses and apologized."

Khalil sighed. Looking at his watch, he surmised she was on her way to work. Where else could she be going at this hour? "All right. Well, I guess I'll see her at the office." He was about to go to the door when Grammy held up a hand to stop him.

"You two have a fight?"

Khalil didn't answer.

"I thought so. Look, you sit down and let me tell you how to make it right."

"Grammy, I really don't have time to talk right now," Khalil said, his exasperation evident.

"Sit down!" Grammy said more forcefully. "Chasing her around the city ain't goin' make her take you back no faster."

With deep resignation, Khalil sat down.

"Now, you listen. Reka's a stubborn girl. She likes things her way but she'll give for the right person. You don't seem like those other guys she's been with. No," Grammy shook her head, "I knew you were different that first time I met you."

Khalil tried to smile.

"She knows you're different, too, and that scares her. You scare her. You and the thought that maybe she can finally have it all."

"Have it all? What does she want?"

"She wants what most women want. What her mother and I never had. I see it in her eyes every day and, for a minute there, I thought you were the one who was going to finally give it to her." Looking at Khalil as if he should have already known, Grammy sighed. "She wants to fall in love, to get married, to have some babies. That's her fantasy, the ultimate happy ending for her."

Khalil let his head fall back against the chair. All the things he'd wanted for himself. He could picture their kids, his and Reka's. They'd have her exotic good looks, her vivacious personality. Their sons might follow in his footsteps, their daughters in hers. But it really didn't matter as long as they were together, a family. He stood abruptly. "Thanks, Grammy. I really have to go now."

"All right, handsome. You go and get her."

Not waiting for Grammy to walk him out, Khalil headed for the door, rushed down the steps and to his car. That's exactly what he planned to do.

Reka stepped off the elevator and moved to the closet. Dropping her purse on the counter of the front desk, she undid her coat and hung it up. Memories of last night still floated in her mind. A smile crept over her face as she remembered Tacoma tying Tyrese up, then dropping her onto the couch in her den. Reka had purchased a porn flick and turned the TV on so Tyrese could watch it.

The scene was of three people, one man and two women. For hours she and Tacoma had talked about the picture and what it would be like to participate in a threesome of their own. All the while Tyrese squirmed and struggled to speak through the silk scarf Tacoma had stuffed in her mouth. When the movie was over, they pulled out porn magazines and asked Tyrese if she thought she'd be a good model for them since she was so photogenic.

Reka offered to send copies of her photos to the magazine and to the local newspapers as well, saying that the exposure would be a great kickoff to her new career as a porn star. Tyrese's eyes had bulged, and Reka hadn't been able to resist. She took the scarf out of her mouth and listened to a steady stream of curses before stuffing the scarf back in to keep her from babbling anymore.

By the end of the night, Tyrese was in tears, partly because of Reka's plan for her new career and partly because of the huge chunk of hair Tacoma had cut from her head. All things had gone well.

There was one last person for her to deal with, and she'd handled that this morning. Donovan had been asleep when she used the key she still had and slipped into his apartment at six A.M. She stood over him in his bedroom; a sheet barely covered his naked body. When she switched on the light, he didn't budge. But she'd come prepared. Pulling away the sheet completely, she then poured the hot fudge he'd always been so fond of all over him, starting at his limp penis, then going up to his chest. By that time he was up and yelling.

Emptying the container, she hissed in surprise, "Oh, I'm sorry, was that too hot?"

"What the...Reka? What...what are you doing here? And why the hell are you trying to scorch me?" He was out of the bed now, his dark skin coated with darker chocolate.

It might have been arousing if the mere sight of him didn't make her utterly sick. "I thought I'd stop by and thank you personally."

Donovan grabbed the sheet, wiping at the chocolate on his skin. "Thank me for what? Damn, Reka! Look at this mess! If you wanted to get some, that's all you had to say."

"I don't want any of what you have, Donovan. That's for damned sure." She rolled her eyes at him and his arrogance. "Like I said, I'm here to give you my gratitude."

He frowned at her. "For?"

"For those lovely pictures you took. I really appreciate you sending me a copy, although I never would have imagined you with Tyrese. And who was the other woman?"

"So that's what finally got you here? It took seeing me with other women to make you realize what you'd given up?" Donovan smiled, then shrugged. Sonya had told him this would work to get him and Reka back together. For a minute he'd doubted the crazy broad, but all those zeroes on the check she'd handed him had taken that doubt away. "I told you you'd come back. Come on over here and give daddy a kiss." He held his arms out to her.

Reka took a step closer to him, then another, all the while loathing the man she'd once thought she was in love with. He was a freak. A money hungry, ignorant freak. Still, she plastered a smile on her face as she approached him, reached out a hand and grabbed his now erect penis. "That's right, baby, I came back."

"Mmmmm," Donovan moaned. "That's what I'm talking about." Lifting his hands to fold at the back of his head, he spread his legs in a stance that gave Reka full control.

His eyes closed and with her free hand she reached into her purse and pulled out her stunner. Releasing his penis, she shifted and positioned it, reveling in the sound of the electric shock as it connected with his manhood.

"Aaarrgghh!" Donovan roared.

"Now you can take your money and get as far away from me as you possibly can before I do something we'll both regret!" With one last stun she turned on her heels and left him standing there, buck naked, covered in chocolate, yelling like a maniac.

Her revenge had been sweet. In her mind she knew that Donovan would have never done something like this on his own, and for that matter neither would Tyrese. But they were both pitiful creatures, driven by money and all its glory. It was so sad. Sonya Davenport and her big bank account had accomplished exactly what she set out to do. But Reka wouldn't bother her. She wouldn't seek revenge on her. Any woman who had to go to such lengths to get a man deserved all the pain and misery she was sure to encounter in the future.

Grabbing her purse, she was about to go to her office when Clara came around the corner. "Oh, Reka, you're are in. It's a good thing, too, because Mr. Peterson is early for your nine o'clock meeting. I just sat him in the conference room."

Reka frowned. "Good morning, Clara. Did you say Mr. Peterson? I don't recall having a meeting with him this morning."

It was Clara's turn to frown now. "I checked the computer," the older woman said as she made her way around her desk to punch the keys again. "Here, it's right here on the firm's calendar."

Reka walked around the desk, astonished to see that it was true. "Oh, well, I guess I must have forgotten. I'll go right in."

Walking down the hall towards the conference room, she was baffled. She never forgot a meeting. She kept her own personal handwritten calendar as well as the one she had in Outlook, all in sync with the firm's calendar. Oh well, she thought, she'd get this over with and continue with her day. Jonathan Peterson probably wanted to go over the hike in his sales since the party. He'd called her at home personally to say that he didn't hold any hard feelings against her for what happened with his son. She'd appreciated that and thanked him.

So when she opened the door that's who she fully expected to see. Not the younger, debonair son.

"Good morning, beautiful." Barkley smiled.

Damn, he was just too fine for his own good, even with the bandaged nose. She entered the conference room, set her purse and briefcase on the table, and stared at him, knowing instinctively that she did not have an appointment with *him* this morning. "What are you doing here?"

He arched a brow. "Now is that anyway to treat a client, Ms. Boyd?"

Reka caught his drift and changed her tone, a little. "What can I help you with, Mr. Peterson?"

Barkley moved around her without saying a word. Reka stood perfectly still as he approached, then passed her, knowing that if he touched her, she'd punch him again. Then she heard the door close and the clicking of the lock. Turning quickly, she saw him smiling, no, leering at her, and felt dread churn in her stomach.

"We could make a lot of money together, Reka." Barkley stood about two feet away from her, his hands thrust into his pockets. She was a very attractive woman and, while he'd had others, and could get more, something about this one made the chase more exciting.

"First of all, I make my own money. Second, this is my place of business so I don't handle personal stuff here." She was still standing. She picked up her purse and was about to grab her briefcase and leave him in the conference room when he stepped forward, grabbing her shoulders.

"You can stop playing that little hard-to-get game now. It's worked. I want you so bad I can hardly see straight." He ground his pelvis against her so she wouldn't mistake his meaning.

Reka struggled to break free of his grasp. "I don't play games, Barkley. But when I have to, I play dirty." She lifted a knee to his groin but he was quick, backing just out of her reach.

He laughed. "You are so sexy when you're angry. Did you know that your eyes look like molten lava when you're aroused?"

"How would you know? You've never aroused me," she spat. He still held her shoulders, his grip much stronger than she would have imagined. Tiny beads of sweat appeared on his forehead as his frantic eyes moved over her.

"Oh, really? Tell me something, Reka. Did you like my messages?"

Reka stilled as confusion gave way to acknowledgment in a few quick seconds. "You're Jack?" she whispered.

A slow smile slid over Barkley's face. His gray eyes glittered like a madman's. "And you're Jill. I've watched you for so long now. And I personally handpicked all the samples that Sensuality sent to the office because I knew Cienna was giving them to you."

Should she be afraid? She wasn't sure, because right now all she felt was repulsed. Barkley Peterson, son of a multi-millionaire, was nothing more than a perverted stalker. "Thanks for the info. I'll be sure to throw all that stuff away as soon as I get home."

He shook her roughly until strands of hair fell from the ponytail she wore. "Don't get smart with me! I've had enough of that! It's time for the game to stop. It's time for us."

She kept looking into his eyes, trying to decipher if he was high again. Khalil had mentioned him smoking something in the bathroom, but she didn't think Barkley had smoked anything before coming here today. He didn't look lethargic at all. He looked crazy as hell. Intensifying her struggle, she managed to break free of his grasp and back away from him. "There is no us, and after this little stunt I'm sure Cienna's going to tell your father and his company to take a hike. You are so beyond sexual harassment here." She kept moving backward, not wanting him to get close enough to touch her again.

Barkley followed her, his blood pumping fiercely through his veins now. She was so worth the wait. This chase, this master plan he had to bring them together, had been brilliant. And while it started out as revenge against his father, he'd managed to finagle a way to please himself, as well as his mother, in the process. Jonathan Peterson was embarrassed by the emails and afraid that company stock would plummet once they became public. His mother, on the other hand, was gaining lots more in the divorce settlement because his father was so desperately trying to keep the peace. As for him, he wanted Reka. "We've been in this conference room so many times. You sitting on one side of the table and me on the other." With every step he took, she took two more. Her eyes were ablaze, with desire, he was sure. Her blouse wasn't buttoned completely and he could just see the swell of her breasts. He licked his lips. "I've so often imagined you on top of this table, open and waiting for me."

"You have a very vivid imagination, then, because I wouldn't be caught dead waiting for you." She was on the other side of the room now, debating if she could make a dash for the door. Maybe if he hadn't locked it she'd have a chance, but since she'd undoubtedly have to fiddle with the lock he'd be on her in an instant. If she screamed for help, would anyone hear her? There had to be plenty of people in the office by now. Maybe she could get close to the phone and call the front desk.

Barkley removed his jacket, undid his tie and the first few buttons of his shirt. "That's okay, I knew you wouldn't be compliant. That makes it even more exciting."

"No, that makes you a rapist, among other things." She watched the shift in his eyes and had enough forewarning to duck when he lifted a chair and threw it in her direction.

"Don't call me names! I'm a very rich man, and you'd be lucky to sleep with me. They all are!" he roared.

Okay, whereas before she was mildly irritated by this little scene he'd created, now Reka was feeling the first jolts of real fear. Barkley was definitely unstable. But she wouldn't cower, she wouldn't beg him to leave her alone. And she wouldn't give up without a fight. Standing again, she folded her arms over her chest. "Then maybe you should go and chase one of them around a table."

In a move that looked too smooth and too easily accomplished, Barkley jumped up on the table, came across with a few steps, and landed directly in front of her. Reka backed into the wall at his approach, her heart thudding in her chest, a scream stuck somewhere deep in her throat.

"I don't want them. I want you." With his hands planted firmly on the wall on either side of her head, he boxed her in. "And you want me too." Leaning closer, he licked the line of her jaw because she turned her face before he could get to her lips.

Her stomach roiled at his closeness, at the fact that his tongue was on her. Her palms went to his chest to push him away.

"That's right, touch me, baby. We are going to be so good together." His tongue trailed down her neck towards her collarbone.

Reka pushed against him. "You are going to be so good to some man while you're rotting in a jail cell!"

Barkley grabbed her wrists, squeezing them tightly as he dragged her away from the wall and turned her so that her bottom was now pressed against the table. "Maybe so, but I'll have you first." He pushed her back.

Reka struggled, swinging her fists wildly and thrashing her feet as much as possible. Anything to keep him off of her. He was touching her, his hands pawing at her breasts, moving down to the hem of her skirt, pushing it up to her thighs. "Stop it! Get off of me, you idiot! Get off me!" she yelled.

"You like it!" Barkley breathed heavily. "You know you do!" He groaned and lifted her hands above her head.

"No!" The scream she'd been holding back escaped, resonating throughout the office.

Khalil walked into his office with a handful of pink message slips. Cienna wanted to see him immediately. With a sigh and a curse, he remembered the emails and the break in the case he'd had yesterday before his life had fallen apart. Moving quickly to his desk, he retrieved the papers he'd printed out, dropped his bag on the chair and headed back for Cienna's office.

She was on the phone when he walked in, but she motioned for him to close the door and take a seat. He did and waited impatiently while she finished the conversation. He wanted to see Reka as soon as possible. He'd take care of this business with Cienna, then go straight to her office. Everything else was second in his mind to making things right with her.

Cienna finished talking to one of her clients while keeping an eye on Khalil. He looked tired, antsy and broken-hearted. A part of her felt sorry for him. Another part wanted to tell him that's what he deserved for being such a jerk. She'd probably go with the latter part the moment she hung the phone up.

"Yes. That sounds fine. I'll have that ready for our meeting next week," she was saying when Khalil caught her looking at him. And in that instant he knew this meeting wasn't going to go well.

Cienna hung up the phone, closed the file she had opened, then sat back in her chair, surveying him. "You want to tell me how you managed to come into my office to find an email stalker, fall in love with my assistant, then break her heart, all in the span of two months?"

Khalil took a deep breath, expelled it. "Which explanation do you want to hear first?"

"Let's go with the personal, since I don't think I'll be able to discuss business with you until I've gotten a few things off my chest."

Khalil shook his head. "Married people really do tell each other everything, don't they?"

"Everything," Cienna conceded. "Especially when their best friend messes up royally."

He sighed. "You didn't see the pictures," he began. "Imagine how you would have felt opening a package of pictures like that with Keith in them."

Cienna took a minute to do just that. "I would have seen red. I would have gone to his office and thrown the pictures in his face."

"My point exactly."

Cienna held up a hand. "But then we would have talked about it. I would have given him the chance to explain. I would have listened."

Because he knew her, because he knew the point she was trying to make, he relaxed a bit. "And then?"

Cienna cracked a smile. "And then I would have beat his ass and the trick who was in the picture with him."

"My point exactly," Khalil repeated. "I went to her. I showed her the pictures. I waited for her to explain. But she never did."

"Did you want her to explain or confirm?"

"It's the same thing."

"It's not, and you know it. You went to her believing that she'd done this horrible thing to you, to your relationship. You didn't stop to think that there was a possibility that you were wrong. She was guilty before proven innocent," Cienna said matter-of-factly.

Khalil lifted a brow. "Do I get the chance to rebut that statement, counselor?"

"By all means." She nodded. He was suffering, she could tell. Just as she suspected Reka was doing. She only hoped that Khalil was ready to do battle, because with Reka's stubbornness that was exactly what he was going to need to do.

"I was quick to believe the pictures, even though a part of me said she couldn't possibly have done this. And when I saw her, when she didn't, not once, say that it wasn't her, I was crushed. She treated me like I was the fool all along."

"You were the fool for believing she'd cheat on you. Had she ever given you reason to believe she'd do something like that, Khalil? Reka, of all people, would be the last to cheat on a man. With as much as it's been done to her, you can bet that she'd dump you first before betraying your trust like that."

He let his head fall into his hands. "I know. I know. That's what she said. She said that she never cheated on me. But I couldn't see past the anger, the hurt."

Cienna stood then, walked around her desk and put a hand on his shoulder. "Love's a painful thing. I know, I've traveled that road before."

"Then you should have warned me."

"It wouldn't have been worth it if you didn't experience it for yourself. Besides," she said, still rubbing his shoulder, "it's worth it."

He lifted his head. "Is it?"

Cienna smiled down at him, seeing the hope in his eyes. "Definitely."

Khalil managed a smile.

"Now, tell me about Jack."

"Oh, yeah. I forgot all about him." Khalil lifted the papers he'd put in the chair beside him and gave them to her. "Read for yourself."

Cienna stared down at the papers in disbelief. "Are you sure, Khalil? This can't possibly be true. Why would he do this?"

Khalil shook his head as he watched her go back to her desk, her eyes riveted on the papers. "Yes, I'm sure. Positive, actually, because I ran a second check. I was hoping you'd have an answer as to why."

Cienna sat in her chair, shaking her head. "No, I don't have a clue."

Her phone rang. She hit the intercom button. "Yes?"

"Mrs. Page, ah, I think we have a situation," Clara stammered.

Cienna looked up from the papers. "A situation? Clara, what are you talking about?"

"Um, it's in the conference room. There's something going on in there."

"What's going on in the conference room, Clara?" Cienna gave Khalil a puzzled look.

Khalil shrugged.

"I walked by there a moment ago and I heard yelling and a lot of commotion."

"What? Who's in there?"

Clara hesitated. "It's Reka. She came in this morning and her nine o'clock was already here and she went on in. But something's, wrong, Mrs. Page, something is definitely wrong."

Khalil stood the moment he heard her name. "Who's in there with her Clara?"

"Ah, it's, it's Mr. Peterson."

With knowing glances Khalil and Cienna's hearts stopped.

"Jonathan Peterson?" Cienna asked hopefully.

"No, it's the son. It's Barkley Peterson."

Khalil was out of the office before Cienna could disconnect.

Somebody pounded on the door, and her heart leapt with joy. Barkley looked toward the door and Reka took advantage of the moment. She twisted and wriggled until her knee gained enough leverage to slam into his groin.

Barkley growled, released her hands and stepped back a bit. She hadn't kneed him hard, but it was enough to get him off her. She quickly slipped off the table and was headed towards the door when he grabbed her by her ponytail, pulling her across the floor.

"I like a little chase, Reka! But you're beginning to piss me off!" he yelled when he had her in the corner. "Now you'll have to pay for that."

Barkley stood over her, a knife in one hand while the other hand worked at his zipper. The sleek silver blade looked way too sharp.

She felt sick and knew that at any moment now she was going to vomit all over the conference room. Never in a million years would she have pegged Barkley for a nut case. An arrogant mama's boy maybe, but never a sex-crazed stalker. "Barkley, wait a minute. Let's talk about this," she pleaded.

"We can talk afterwards," he snickered. "I know how you women like that."

His voice sounded desperate, just on the edge of complete lunacy. She tried to get up, but he swiftly bent over and touched the knife to her throat. "All you have to do is cooperate," he told her.

He was serious. The prick of the blade against her skin told her that. "Barkley, no," she whispered desperately.

"I want you, Reka. I've waited so long, baby. Please, " he moaned.

"No," she moaned, tears streaming down her face.

"I'll kill you, bitch! Don't you understand that? I'll kill you!" Barkley yelled, the knife shaking in his hand.

With his free hand he was touching her, violating her. Against her will, Reka whimpered. Some people said their whole life flashed before their eyes before they died. But hers didn't. Only the last few weeks did. She thought of meeting Khalil, of their first night at the bar, of him seeing her safely home, of him kissing her. Her mind reeled with memories of her and Khalil and she cried, not for herself, but for the love that would be forever lost before she had the chance to really claim it. For once in her life she wasn't fighting. She felt the warm tears streaming down her cheeks, heard her own pitiful moans and then felt the sting of the blade.

Suddenly the door crashed open with a loud splintering sound and Khalil was across the room in two seconds flat, yanking Barkley up by his collar. "You sick bastard!" he roared as he tossed Barkley into the wall.

Khalil didn't see him push off the wall and come at him with the knife. With a flash of silver blade, Barkley sank it into Khalil's shoulder.

"Aarrgghh!" Khalil roared. He struck Barkley with all the strength in him and Barkley slid to the floor, unconscious.

Then Khalil fell to his knees, scooping Reka up into his arms and hugging her tightly to his chest. "I'm so sorry, baby. So sorry for everything," he said as he rocked back and forth. "I should have found out who he was sooner. I should have protected you."

Reka continued to cry, although it wasn't out of fear or loss anymore. She wept now because she knew love, real love, and it was wrapped securely around her. "I didn't cheat on you, Khalil. I would never betray you that way," she whispered.

"Shhh, baby. It's okay. We'll talk about it later." Suddenly he noticed that she was bleeding. "Get the paramedics!" he yelled over his shoulder.

Keith arrived then, as did the police and the paramedics. As Barkley was being cuffed, Keith bent and put a hand to Khalil's shoulder.

"I hired you to get to the bottom of some emails, not have blood drawn in my office," he said lightly.

All at once Khalil realized that his shoulder hurt like hell. Then the paramedics were beside him, pulling Reka away and looking at his wound.

"Sir, you're losing a lot of blood. We need to get you to the hospital."

Khalil reached for Reka.

Cienna put a hand out to restrain him. "She's going to the hospital, too."

He didn't want to be away from her, not for a minute, not for a second. Guilt weighed heavily on him. He'd told her he would protect her. She had doubted him, but he'd been persistent. He'd told her she let him down, but, in truth, he'd let himself down. He loved this woman and how had he shown her? By judging her and not believing in her, in their love. He'd spend the rest of his life begging her forgiveness.

After getting his thirty-seven stitches, Khalil went to the examining room where Reka was. Just before he pushed the curtain aside he heard her say something to Grammy and smiled to himself. From the sound of Reka's voice she was tired of Grammy and Janell and their warnings and musings about today's events, so he didn't hesitate to enter.

"And you, handsome," Grammy never missed a beat as she looked from Reka to him. "You like jumping in front of knives, too, I see. Come here and let me see if they fixed you up good."

Khalil's eyes were riveted on Reka. She held his gaze but he couldn't decipher what that meant. Was she still angry with him? Where did their relationship stand? Grammy made an impatient sound and he quickly moved toward her.

She didn't touch his shoulder but she pulled him down far enough so that she could kiss his cheek. "Thanks for protecting my baby."

The guilt Khalil had already been feeling magnified.

"Yeah, I knew you were a good one the first time I met you," Janell added. "Come on, Mama. Let's go outside and get the car. These two need a ride home."

"Ah, actually I think my sister's around here somewhere," Khalil added.

"Nope. We told her to go home to that baby. We'll take you home and then take Reka and get her all tucked in."

Khalil didn't argue. The more time he could spend with her the better. He suspected he was going to need more than a few hours to make this up to her.

They were alone. Reka had both dreaded and feared this moment. What would she say to him? What would he say to her? How would they go on from here?

"What did the doctor say?" he asked as he took a seat on the edge of her bed.

He was so close and yet, she sensed, so far away. Where had things gone wrong with them? "It wasn't deep enough to do serious damage, thank goodness. So they gave me ten stitches and some pain killers and told me to get the hell out of here before they charge me for the sheets too." She gave a wan smile.

His heart tightened at that simple action. With no makeup, her hair tousled, dressed in an ugly hospital gown and wearing a huge white patch taped to her neck, she was beautiful. There was so much he needed to say to her, so much they needed to resolve but he couldn't seem to find the words.

It didn't seem that he was in a hurry to get their showdown over with, so Reka, in her signature fashion, jumped right in. "I meant what I said to you. I didn't cheat on you. I don't know how those pictures were made, but it wasn't me."

Khalil shifted on the bed and took her hand in his. Bringing it to his lips, he kissed it and closed his eyes. Inhaling deeply, he let the fact that she hadn't pulled away settle inside. "I should have trusted you," he said, then looked at her. "I should have trusted the person I knew you were. But I saw the pictures and I just reacted." He shook his head because there was no other excuse he could offer her. "I was wrong and I apologize."

She tilted her head to the side and watched him carefully. "You were jealous, weren't you?"

Khalil laughed. "That's an understatement. I was crazy out of my mind jealous. I'm not sure what it is about you, but the thought of you being with someone else drives me crazy. I've never been the jealous type. I've never had insecurities. But with you..." He couldn't even begin to explain something he didn't understand himself.

"You don't have to be," she said quietly.

"I don't?"

She shook her head. "No. I'm a one-man woman. And I'm in love with you."

Khalil sighed. All this time he was supposed to be rescuing her, showing her how it felt to be truly loved, and here she was teaching him. "I just love you so much," he said before leaning down to hug her. Because his shoulder still hurt like hell and she was still in a fair amount of pain herself, it was a restrained hug. But the love between them was still intense, still strong and everlasting.

Reka sighed at the sound of his words. He loved her. Somebody, a real man, loved her. Not that she needed that to be sure of herself, but it was a damn good feeling. "This is going to work."

Khalil pulled slightly back and looked deep into her eyes. "Of course it's going to work. Just try to get rid of me."

She smiled even though she hadn't realized she'd spoken the words aloud. "We don't have to worry about that, since I'm not going to let you go."

EPILOGUE

The Wedding

Something old, something new, something borrowed, something blue. Reka ran down the checklist one more time.

"Our briefs match, they're ice blue." Tacoma smiled at her in the mirror.

"It figures," Reka chuckled. "Okay, I think we're all set. You ready for this?"

Tacoma grinned from ear to ear. "I'm more than ready."

On impulse she hugged him, inhaling his expensive cologne and feeling a wave of emotions she couldn't quite explain. "You really are ready, aren't you?" she asked when they pulled apart.

Tacoma looked at her and figured out what she was thinking. "Sweetie, you know when it's right. Me and Terry, we've been together for a long time, but now, at this very moment, I'm ready to make him my lifelong partner. For better or for worse." He cracked another smile.

Reka smoothed his eyebrows, let her hand linger on his cheek. "I'm so jealous," she admitted.

"Don't be." Tacoma held her in his arms. "You and Khalil are ready. I can see it."

Because she'd been wondering that very thing, and because it was so like Tacoma to have known that, she lost her grip on her emotions and one tear slipped down her face. "I hope so."

Catching the tear with the pad of his thumb, Tacoma sighed. "Now we're gonna have to fix your face, you big baby."

They were laughing, holding each other, sharing these jumbled emotions when Khalil walked in.

"Hey, hey, you're about to be a married man. Get your hands off my woman." He smiled as he walked towards them, knowing that their friendship had been strengthened by the events a few weeks ago. Hell, his relationship with Reka had been strengthened.

True to their word, Grammy and Janell had taken Reka and him home. He'd wanted to be with Reka so he'd asked her to stay at his place. When she declined, his heart had suffered another blow. But she'd called him first thing the next morning and they'd begun healing their relationship, spending lots of time together since they were both on sick leave. They weren't yet where they needed to be, but he was sure that in a little more time they would be.

Tacoma released her. "She's only your woman because I allow it," he shot back at Khalil. "Don't forget, I'm always watching you."

Extending a hand to Tacoma, Khalil nodded. "I'm sure you won't let me forget. Congratulations, man. This is your big day."

Tacoma shook his hand, then pulled Khalil's larger frame into a big hug. "Thanks. It'll be your day soon," he whispered so that only Khalil could hear him.

Reka smiled at her two favorite men hugging, her heart so full of joy she thought it would burst. "If we don't get moving we're going to miss it," she announced.

"Oh, no. I've worked too hard and look too damn good to miss this day. C'mon, y'all, let's go."

Tacoma was already out the door when Khalil turned to her, crooking his elbow. "Shall we?"

Tucking her arm into his elbow, she said, "I guess we shall."

Reka stood at the aisle watching the two men recite their vows.

Khalil sat in the second pew watching her. Without a doubt she was the woman he wanted. What had been missing from his life just months ago had been found. He felt complete, but only when he was with her, only when he knew she was near. Barkley Peterson was in jail. Sonya had taken his advice and moved out of state to run one of her father's companies. His parents had reluctantly come around to accepting Reka; his sister was ecstatically happy for him. All he needed now was the promise from Reka that this would last forever.

Later at the reception, after Tacoma and Terry had their first dance as a married couple, the DJ invited others to dance. Khalil instantly grabbed Reka's hand. She went with him willingly, wrapped in the euphoria of a perfect wedding day. Tacoma and Terry were handsome as ever in their matching winter white suits and ice blue ties that coordinated perfectly with their underwear that no one was privy to see. Keith and Cienna looked happy, the news of her second pregnancy surrounding them in a glow of wedded bliss. Grammy and her mother were there but they'd been at the bar since arriving so she didn't have to worry about them until it was time to lug them out the door.

With her hand in his, she let Khalil lead her to the floor. His arms went around her waist and he pulled her close, smiling down at her as he did. She was in love. She'd realized it only a few weeks ago but there it was, like a halo around her heart. He was a good man, a strong man, an honest man. But best of all, he was her man. She trusted him completely and knew that he had only her best interest and happiness in mind. Wrapping her arms around his neck she held on tightly, never wanting this moment to end.

But end it did when Khalil suddenly backed away from her, going down on one knee. Silence fell over the room as a hundred pairs of eyes watched them. Reka's heart thudded and tears filled her eyes. For her, there were only the two of them and this moment, this one precious moment that she'd remember for the rest of her life.

"I promise to be the best man for you. I promise to cherish you and to hold you above all others. I promise to take care of you until our dying days. But most of all, I promise to love you with all my heart, my mind and my soul." Reaching into his jacket pocket, he pulled out a small blue box, lifted the lid and presented it to her.

Through tear-blurred eyes, Reka caught a glimpse of the magnificent stone but didn't give it too much attention. She'd have time to savor it later. For right now, she had something to say, a promise of her own to make. "I promise to be the woman that you need, the woman you deserve. I promise to cheer you up when you're down, to relax you when you're tense." Khalil smiled and her heart melted. "Until the end of time, I promise to love you like you've never been loved before."

With resounding applause from the guests, the DJ went into another ballad. The room was full of cheer. Couples hugged and kissed each other while tossing congratulations their way. Khalil took the ring from the box and slipped it onto her finger.

"Hot damn! I can see that bling blingin' from all the way over here!" Grammy yelled from her seat at the bar.

Rolling her eyes in that direction, Reka laughed. Khalil had risen and was now hugging her close to him, their foreheads touching as their bodies began to sway with the music. "What are we going to do with her?" Reka asked wistfully.

Khalil had already given that some thought. "The first of the year you're moving in with me. Leave the apartment to her and Cletus." Khalil and Reka looked at each other and burst into laughter.

"Free drinks for everybody!" Grammy yelled again, this time almost slipping out of her seat.

ABOUT THE AUTHOR

Artist C. Arthur was born and raised in Baltimore, Maryland where she currently resides with her husband and three children. An active imagination and a love of reading encouraged her to begin writing in high school and she hasn't stopped since.

Determined to bring a new edge to romance, she continues to develop intriguing plots, racy characters and fresh dialogue—thus keeping the readers on their toes! Visit her website at www.acarthur.net.

Excerpt from

THE PERFECT FRAME

BY

BEVERLY CLARK

Release Date: February 2007

CHAPTER ONE

Mackinsey Jessup eyed John Victor Townsend Jr., the newly made president of Townsend Stock Brokerage and Investments with curious dislike. One thing for sure, he was a sorry imitation of his father. Mack had worked for the company five years ago under the senior Townsend, but sensed that working for the son would be a different proposition entirely. Townsend cleared his throat. "As I mentioned when I contacted you, Mr. Jessup, I have found discrepancies in several of our premier accounts. I suspect an embezzlement scam is going on within the company. Will you take the case?"

"I'm considering it."

"Look, Jessup, if you—"

Mack watched as Townsend nervously moved his fingers through his thin salt and pepper hair.

"If I take the case," Mack cut him off, "the investigation will be handled my way, with no interference from you. Got it?" He smiled at the look of affronted dignity and controlled anger on the other man's face. He could tell that Townsend was aching to rescind the request for his services. But Mack was sure he wouldn't do that because he knew that Jessup Financial Investigations—specializing in corporate theft—happened to be the best in Los Angeles, in the state, Mack would go so far as to say. It was no brag, just fact.

"All right, Jessup," Townsend conceded through stiff lips. "Handle this your way."

"Good. Now the first thing I need you to do is get me a copy of all the portfolios that have been tampered with, or that you suspect have been tampered with. Oh, and I'll need to check out your account books, personnel files, computer disks, printouts; in essence, everything."

Townsend's exasperated brown eyes suddenly brightened. "Don't you want to know who I suspect is the thief?"

Mack arched his brows speculatively. "You have proof to support your allegations?"

"No, but—"

A sardonic smile curved Mack's mouth. "As I said before, Mr. Townsend, leave the investigating to me."

"How soon do you want the information?" Townsend gritted out.

"Now would be a good time since all of the employees have left for the day."

"But that means that I'll have to personally—"

"Retrieve the information? Exactly."

As she sat eyeing the stack of reports and sales figures yet to analyze, Toni sighed and brushed back stray wisps of wavy black hair that had escaped from her upswept hair style. The thought of working overtime this evening didn't appeal to her at all. She enjoyed her job as personal assistant to the CEO, but sometimes…

Pat Davis, the department's executive secretary, glanced at the clock on the wall. "It's almost quitting time, Toni. You're not working late again tonight, are you?"

Before Toni could answer, Hank Warren, the other personal assistant to the CEO, walked over to them and answered.

"Of course she is. Have to rack up those brownie points. Right, sweetheart? Lucky for you old Townsend conveniently up and died." He smirked. "Damn lucky, I'd say. It was like you arranged it. Sure you didn't knock the old guy off?" He laughed, then cleared his throat and said, "You think you've got it made now, don't you, Miss Efficiency? Save your energy, Toni. That directorship is as good as mine."

"You mean because you're male? That's not a prerequisite to success anymore, Hanky Panky," Toni said in a sugary-sweet voice. She watched his eyes flash and his jaw clench with barely suppressed temper, knowing good and well how much he hated being called that. Toni shifted her attention back to Pat, completely ignoring him, and smiled. "In answer to your question, Pat, not tonight."

Toni's phone buzzed. She picked up the receiver. "Yes, Mr. Clifford. If you need them for tomorrow's conference meeting, then of course I can stay. No problem."

"You'll be here alone with the boss," Hank said thoughtfully. "Could it be those brownie points will be racked up in, shall we say, more personal ways?" The look he gave Toni before arrogantly striding from the office was riddled with amused malice.

"Whew! If looks could kill," Pat quipped.

Toni shrugged. "Do I look like I'm scared?"

"You really shouldn't call him Hanky Panky to his face, even if most of the girls in the company do it behind his back."

"Maybe not, but the man is so full of himself I couldn't resist."

Pat shook her head, then turned off her computer. "I'd better get moving. Joe's waiting for me downstairs, and tonight I don't dare be late. It's Monday. You know what that means."

"Monday night football!" they chorused.

"What it really means is that I'll be relegated to playing waitress and serving my armchair quarterback popcorn and beer while he watches the game. I'm an executive secretary, for crying out loud." A comic pout shaped her lips and mock resentment tinged her voice. "You'd think I'd risen above that. But not as far as Joe is concerned." She glanced at Toni.

"So it looks like you're going to be working overtime after all."

"Mr. Clifford needs my help."

Pat plowed on. "For the last six months, no, make it the last year and a half, you've worked late three or four days out of every week. You bucking for sainthood by way of an early grave?"

"Neither. I don't mind the extra work, so give it a rest, Pat."

"Is the possibility of getting the promotion what's driving you so hard?"

"It's not the only reason."

"You're out to prove something, then."

"No woman starts at the bottom of the success ladder and reaches the position I have in so short a time without drive and ambition."

"And don't forget hard work, above and beyond the call of duty. I hope Mr. Clifford appreciates the sacrifices you're making, like putting your love life on the back burner."

"Joe is waiting for you, Pat," Toni reminded her.

She sighed. "You're right, and he is." Pat grabbed her purse and sweater, then sliced her friend a curious look. "You do have a love life, don't you, Toni? You do go out?"

"On occasion." Toni averted her gaze.

"When was the last time?" Pat asked in a coaxing voice intended to draw out confidences.

"Pat!"

"Oh, all right," she said, slipping her purse strap over her shoulder. "I'm outta here."

As Toni watched her friend leave, a feeling of relief washed over her. She liked Pat, but sometimes…Toni glanced at the clock. If she hurried and finished the requested stock analysis, she could be ready to leave in an hour. Admittedly, she was beginning to feel more stressed lately. Maybe the long work weeks were getting to her, but it would all be worth it once she got the promotion.

Toni had worked for TSBI three and a half, going on four, years. She'd started out as a stock and investment consultant trainee, and in the short span of three years she'd taken classes and had worked her way up to assistant to the CEO, Frank Clifford. He had promised her a bright future if she could prove she was up to the challenge. Despite

Hank's asinine insinuation that she was sleeping her way to the top, they both knew she was doing a damn good job. And that was what really rankled.

It was Toni's dream to carve a permanent niche for herself at Townsend's. Most of the people—the majority of them in the top positions at Townsend's—stayed on until they retired. More than anything, she wanted job security, a feeling of belonging, permanence, something she'd rarely experienced in her twenty-six years.

Toni got up from her seat and walked over to the coffee machine to pour herself a cup. She drank her coffee black, allowing no additives to dull her senses. It was all-important that she be sharp, alert and ready for any challenge. She carried her coffee to her desk, sat back in the chair, and after a few swallows of the strong, steamy stimulant set the cup down and swiveled her chair around to face the computer screen. Then she accessed the accounts portfolio menu, then went right into the Harper Bond Exchange file.

She was ready to begin the sales comparison and stock analysis, but what she saw a minute later made her eyes widen in confusion. The sales figure for the common bonds this month and the previous two should have been recorded on the fifteenth. She checked the codes against the names on the bonds. They matched, but when she punched in confirmation, it showed they had been confirmed on the sixteenth in the two previous months. She would have to ask Pat about these entries. Evidently the dates or the codes or something had been wrongly entered.

How odd.

Pat was too good at what she did to overlook a mistake like this. Toni frowned. There had been similar instances in other accounts, but every time she'd gone in to investigate and shown it to the CEO, he had logically explained them away. So maybe she was going looney tunes.

All right, girl, get back to work so you can go home, fix yourself a quick dinner and relax in a hot tub.

Toni moved on to the next report. But the Harper account continued to prey on her mind. She stopped, cleared the screen and brought up the account again to check the percentage figures. According to what she was seeing the bonds had sold at

60% of their market value. But no details of the transaction had been recorded. She shook her head, wondering why they hadn't been.

"I'm ready to leave now, Toni," Mr. Clifford announced. "Have you finished the report?"

At the sound of her boss's voice, she shifted her gaze away from her computer screen and glanced up at him. "I have a few more things to check out before I'm done, sir. It won't be much longer."

He smiled, easing his hip onto her desk. "I've asked you to call me Frank." He cleared his throat as he continued to watch her. "You're certainly a conscientious young woman. It's a rare quality these days. I can tell you. I intend to see that you are amply rewarded."

She smiled. "Thank you, sir."

"Now, none of that sir business. Call me Frank."

Toni's smile faltered and she hurried to complete the report, waited for it to print, then handed it to him.

He took the report and checked through it.

Toni watched him. Something about the man disturbed her, even though she couldn't quite put a name to it. He seemed fair and supportive of his employees, her anyway. And he was an attractive older man, but there were times when she felt weird vibes coming from him.

He smiled, nodding his head. "As usual, you've done an excellent job. Come on, let me walk you out." He waved his hand for her to precede him.

Toni ached to examine the Harper account in more depth, but it would have to wait.

❧

Several days after the monthly board meeting, Toni was in the hall outside the boardroom when she noticed the rigidity in Mr. Townsend's steps as he walked over to the elevator. She felt sorry for the man. His latest proposal had been shot down. It had to be a humiliating experience for a company president. He was certainly not the force to be reckoned with that his father had been. For one thing, he lacked the man's innate ruthlessness. Even though the senior Townsend was dead and his son was now president and chairman of the board, it was as though he were pulling strings from the grave.

"Maybe I was wrong about you playing hot and heavy with old Frank to get the promotion, Toni," Hank said, walking up behind her. "The way you were eyeing his son just now leads me to believe that you're setting your goals higher these days. Maybe it's Nina Townsend who should be worried."

"Has that thing you call a brain taken up permanent residence in the sewer, Hanky Panky? To you nothing is sacred, is it? You must want that promotion awfully bad."

"And I'm going to get it, too, never fear. No one, especially a woman, has ever beat me out of anything. And I don't intend to let a new trend get started."

"There's always a first time for everything. And you won't always be able to stop the wave of the future, Hanky."

"Don't call me that, damn it!"

The look in his cold, black eyes and harshly handsome African-American features chilled her to the bone. The menacing look on his face was so frightening she jumped when he shifted the subject to the death of the elder Townsend.

"I wonder if a stroke was what really killed the old man. Maybe he was having an affair with you and it proved to be more than his body could handle." A nasty grin distorted his face. "You were alone with him when he died. I wonder, sweetheart, are you pretty poison or what?"

With that he walked away, leaving Toni seething.

"I'm glad you suggested we eat Italian today, Toni," Pat commented.

"Me too." Toni grinned. "Even if I don't know what I want to order."

"Just the thought of Mr. Angeletti's lasagna makes my mouth

water," Pat confided as they followed the hostess.

The Italian Kitchen was Toni's favorite restaurant. And not because she happened to be part Italian. The prices were reasonable, the pasta the best in town. The hostess showed them to a table near the garden, just off the outside terrace.

Minutes later a waiter arrived with the menus. Pat ordered lasagna; Toni decided on the pasta salad. The waiter had taken their orders and left when Toni saw Mr. Townsend, his wife Nina, and Frank Clifford being shown to a table in the restaurant's VIP section.

Toni's eyes narrowed in barely contained dislike as she studied Nina Townsend's long, brassy-blond, thickly weaved hair style, heavy makeup, and the way she dressed, as though she were a twenty-year-old hoochie mama instead of a forty-something wife of a wealthy black businessman. The overly long fire-engine red nails reminded Toni of dragon claws. And the way the woman flirted shamelessly with Mr. Clifford, with her husband sitting right there, turned Toni's stomach.

"It's enough to make you lose your appetite, isn't it?" Pat wrinkled her nose.

"Poor Mr. Townsend. I wonder how he could have ever married a woman like that."

"Isn't that the way it usually happens? There's just no accounting for taste."

After finishing their lunch, Toni and Pat returned to the office. Toni picked up the report she'd started working on before lunch and was deep into studying it when Hank Warren came storming out of the CEO's office and stalked past her. In his hurry to leave, he just missed colliding with Pat Davis. Toni wondered what had happened between him and the boss.

"What did you say to piss him off this time?" Pat asked.

"Not a thing, I swear," Toni answered. "Forget about Hank. Listen,

Pat, I need to talk to you about the Harper account."

"The Harper account?" She frowned.

Toni swiveled her chair around to face the computer screen and accessed the Harper account, but when she did, she noticed that some of the facts and figures had been altered. What had happened to the mistakes? Who had changed them?

Could it have been Hank? And Mr. Clifford had found out and that was reason he'd stormed out?

"I found some mistakes the other day, but now they seemed to have vanished."

"Mistakes? What kind of mistakes?" Pat glanced over Toni's shoulder at the computer screen, then gave her a confused sidelong look.

"They were there, Pat. I swear to you they were."

"Well, they're gone now." Pat gave her a sympathetic smile. "I think you've been working too hard, girl. Look, I've got a lot to do before I go home. Joe is liable to go postal if I have to work overtime the way I used to. He was really bent out of shape about that."

Toni noticed that a distressed look came into her friend's eyes. Pat let out a definitely strained sigh and added, "I wasn't too crazy about that either." A bitter edge tinged her voice. "Anyway, it only added to our shared opinion that Mr. Clifford is a Simon Legree or worse. And of course everybody knows he works you like a slave."

"But he doesn't, actually."

"Try convincing Joe of that. Ever since I got promoted to executive secretary, he's been impossible to live with."

"That's because Mr. Clifford passed him over for mail room manager when he had assumed that it was in the bag. I'm sure Joe still resents it."

"But why should I have to suffer? My promotion has nothing to do with him not getting his."

"Evidently to Joe's way of thinking it does. I also think he's jealous."

"Joe? Jealous!" Pat made a derisive choking sound. "Of Mr. Clifford? Yeah, right."

"It's possible, you know. You're a pretty girl, Pat," Toni observed, looking her friend over. Pat had huge hazel eyes and wore her short, brown hair in a cute pixie cut. Although petite, she had a curvy figure and looked a lot like the actress Jada Pinkett-Smith.

Pat grinned. "You do wonders for a girl's vanity."

After Pat had gone back to her desk, Toni thought about her friend's reaction to what she'd said about Joe being jealous of their boss, and before that the crack about overtime. At other times there was something in the tone of her voice when her name and Mr. Clifford's were linked in any conversation. Toni wondered what her attitude about that was all about. She shook her head and recalled the look of pure unadulterated murder on Hank Warren's face when he came tearing out of the CEO's office.

Toni was asked to work overtime on Thursday; Mr. Clifford had a meeting in Chicago and was scheduled to catch the red-eye flight, and needed a last-minute analysis done to take with him.

Hank hadn't been back to work since the day he stormed out, which left all the urgent work on her shoulders. Toni had found out at lunch the day before, from Mazie in personnel, that the CEO had "urged" Hank to take a few days off. Anxious curiosity worked through Toni's system. She wondered what was going on and what effect it might have on her getting the promotion.

She finished her work and headed for the elevators. As she got out on the parking lot level and started toward her car, she saw Bill Watkins, head of parking security.

"Been working late again, I see."

"It's becoming an occupational hazard, I'm afraid." Toni laughed, continuing to her car.

"Good night, now," Bill called after her.

Toni stopped in front of her car, setting her purse on the hood, to rummage inside for her keys. She sighed in frustration when she couldn't find them. They had to be there somewhere. After making a more thorough search and still no keys, Toni concluded that they had fallen out of her purse into her bottom desk drawer. Damn it, she would have to go back upstairs to get them.

She saw the knowing smile on Bill Watkins' face when she headed back to the elevator.

"Left your keys upstairs, huh?"

"You guessed it. I should have checked to make sure I had them before leaving the office. Oh well."

The thought of going back upstairs was not in the least appealing to Toni, considering how dead tired she felt. During the ride to the seventh floor, she grumbled, scolding herself for her stupidity. According to the self-defense course she had recently enrolled in, every time a woman left home or work, she should have her keys in her hand with the two longest ones protruding between her fingers to use as a weapon against a possible attacker. Ms. Kymoto, her instructress, would be far from pleased by her carelessness.

Toni stepped off the elevator and strode into the office. Once inside, she made a beeline for her desk. Slipping her purse off her shoulder, she tossed it onto the desk, then pushing her chair back, opened the bottom drawer. She didn't have to search for the keys. They were in plain sight, gleaming up at her like the mocking grin of a lighted jack-o-lantern.

Toni's shoulders slumped and she groaned tiredly. She grabbed her keys and was ready to leave when her boss's voice snagged her attention. Maybe the business trip wasn't that urgent after all and he would be catching an early morning flight. She wondered who was with him. When she didn't hear any answering replies, she assumed he must be on the phone. His next words not only confirmed the fact, but stopped her cold.

"She's finally left for the day. Our Miss Carlton is thorough, I'll give her that. Yes, we have almost everything we need. It's a good thing, too, because I think she's getting suspicious." A short pause. "No, not if we're careful. When the time comes everyone will believe our hard-working Miss Carlton is a clever, over-confident thief. The trail of evidence I've set up will lead right to the ambitious little lady's desk. The net will drop on her, completely entangling her." He laughed. "It's the perfect frame, don't you agree?"

He laughed again. "I am becoming eloquent in my prime, aren't I?

You know, the gullible little bitch hasn't a clue why she's been singled out to work overtime all these months. She thinks it's because of the whole-hearted confidence I have in her abilities. Isn't that a hoot?"

Toni swallowed around the lump in her throat and blinked several times. Mired in shock, she lost the rest of the conversation. This just couldn't be happening to her. All this time her boss had been using her to steal from the company. And was setting her up royally to take the blame! A hot anger came to life inside her and began to build in her blood. As she started shaking with the intensity of it, the keys slipped from her fingers and hit the floor with a loud clink, alerting her boss that he was not alone.

Toni heard the phone receiver crash down on its cradle and seconds later her boss came rushing into the outer office. He stalked over to her desk and stood glaring at her.

"Little girls who have big ears hear things they really shouldn't."

Toni's anger dissolved into stomach-knotting fear and her heart started pounding furiously in her chest. Every self-protective instinct she possessed screamed at her to take to her heels and run, but the numbing effect of shock slowed down her reaction time.

"What are you doing back here?" he demanded. "Were you by any chance spying on me?"

When she could answer, her voice came out sounding like a rusty hinge "No, I came back because I left my keys."

He shook his head. "That's unfortunate. Too much is involved to let you mess things up at this late date. If you happen to have an accident…"

Fear for her safety propelled Toni into action. She pushed her chair into Clifford and made a mad dash for the door.

"Why you—" He growled, then angrily thrust the chair aside and started after her. Moments before she could make it to the door, he grabbed her arms.

Toni tried to twist out of his grasp, but he was too strong for her. Then her self-defense training kicked in. Glad she had mastered at least a few basic moves, she ground the heel of her pump into his instep, then jabbed her elbow into his ribs with all her strength. When his grip loosened and she heard him groan in pain, it was all the opportunity she needed, and she wasted no time in fleeing from the office.

Toni ran to the elevator and pounded frantically, desperately, on the down button.

"Come on," she cried in mounting agitation and fear.

As luck would have it, all four elevators were downstairs in the lobby. She didn't have time to wait for them to come back up. Frank Clifford had recovered and was coming after her. Toni darted toward the stair exit.

He was hot on her heels!

"You might as well stop this, Toni. You can't hope to get away from me. It's going to be my word against yours. Can you guess who'll be believed?" he taunted.

Chest heaving and her breaths coming in hard jerky gasps, Toni ignored his words and sped down one flight of stairs, then the next. Clifford's long, menacing strides cut in half the distance her shorter, frightened ones made.

Toni stepped up the pace, but by the time she reached the third floor she could barely catch her breath. She could hear Clifford's labored breathing, but it seemed far away. Maybe he was tiring. She could only hope. He was, after all, a middle-aged man. She wrenched open the door leading to the floor of offices. If she could only find a place to hide. The hall lights had been dimmed, which meant that all the offices were probably closed. The dismal thought doused her hope of escaping Clifford. Could the cleaning people have left a door open?

"Oh, God, please, let them have forgotten to lock one. Please," she prayed.

Toni raced down the hall, trying one door after another, finding each one locked. When she'd given up hope of finding an unlocked door, the last one at the end of the hall opened and she rushed inside.

Toni turned the lock and leaned back against the door, allowing her breathing time to slow down to normal. She was safe for the moment.

The door to Toni's left eased open and the shadowed silhouette of a man filled the space.

"Oh, God, no!" she cried and slid to the floor as everything went black.

2007 Publication Schedule

January

Corporate Seduction
A. C. Arthur
1-58571-238-8
$9.95

A Taste of Temptation
Reneé Alexis
1-58571-207-8
$9.95

February

The Perfect Frame
Beverly Clark
1-58571-240-x
$9.95

Ebony Angel
Deatri King-Bey
1-58571-239-6
$9.95

March

Sweet Sensations
Gwendolyn Bolton
1-58571-206-X
$9.95

Crush
Crystal Hubbard
1-58571-243-4
$9.95

April

Secret Thunder
Annetta P. Lee
1-58571-204-3
$9.95

Blood Seduction
J.M. Jeffries
1-58571-237-X
$9.95

May

Lies Too Long
Pamela Ridley
1-58571-246-9
$13.95

Two Sides to Every
    Story
Dyanne Davis
1-58571-248-5
$9.95

June

One of These Days
Michele Sudler

$9.95

Who's That Lady
Andrea Jackson
1-58571-190-x
$9.95

2007 Publication Schedule (continued)

July

Heart of the Phoenix
A. C. Arthur
1-58571-242-6
$9.95

Do Over
Jaci Kenney
1-58571-241-8
$9.95

It's Not Over Yet
J.J. Michael

$12.95

August

The Fires Within
Beverly Clark
1-58571-244-2

Stolen Kisses
Dominiqua Douglas
1-58571-248-5
$9.95

September

October

November

December

Other Genesis Press, Inc. Titles

A Dangerous Deception	J.M. Jeffries	$8.95
A Dangerous Love	J.M. Jeffries	$8.95
A Dangerous Obsession	J.M. Jeffries	$8.95
A Dangerous Woman	J.M. Jeffries	$9.95
A Dead Man Speaks	Lisa Jones Johnson	$12.95
A Drummer's Beat to Mend	Kei Swanson	$9.95
A Happy Life	Charlotte Harris	$9.95
A Heart's Awakening	Veronica Parker	$9.95
A Lark on the Wing	Phyliss Hamilton	$9.95
A Love of Her Own	Cheris F. Hodges	$9.95
A Love to Cherish	Beverly Clark	$8.95
A Lover's Legacy	Veronica Parker	$9.95
A Pefect Place to Pray	I.L. Goodwin	$12.95
A Risk of Rain	Dar Tomlinson	$8.95
A Twist of Fate	Beverly Clark	$8.95
A Will to Love	Angie Daniels	$9.95
Acquisitions	Kimberley White	$8.95
Across	Carol Payne	$12.95
After the Vows	Leslie Esdaile	$10.95
(Summer Anthology)	T.T. Henderson	
	Jacqueline Thomas	
Again My Love	Kayla Perrin	$10.95
Against the Wind	Gwynne Forster	$8.95
All I Ask	Barbara Keaton	$8.95
Ambrosia	T.T. Henderson	$8.95
An Unfinished Love Affair	Barbara Keaton	$8.95
And Then Came You	Dorothy Elizabeth Love	$8.95
Angel's Paradise	Janice Angelique	$9.95
At Last	Lisa G. Riley	$8.95
Best of Friends	Natalie Dunbar	$8.95
Between Tears	Pamela Ridley	$12.95
Beyond the Rapture	Beverly Clark	$9.95
Blaze	Barbara Keaton	$9.95

Other Genesis Press, Inc. Titles (continued)

Blood Lust	J. M. Jeffries	$9.95
Bodyguard	Andrea Jackson	$9.95
Boss of Me	Diana Nyad	$8.95
Bound by Love	Beverly Clark	$8.95
Breeze	Robin Hampton Allen	$10.95
Broken	Dar Tomlinson	$24.95
The Business of Love	Cheris Hodges	$9.95
By Design	Barbara Keaton	$8.95
Cajun Heat	Charlene Berry	$8.95
Careless Whispers	Rochelle Alers	$8.95
Cats & Other Tales	Marilyn Wagner	$8.95
Caught in a Trap	Andre Michelle	$8.95
Caught Up In the Rapture	Lisa G. Riley	$9.95
Cautious Heart	Cheris F Hodges	$8.95
Caught Up	Deatri King Bey	$12.95
Chances	Pamela Leigh Starr	$8.95
Cherish the Flame	Beverly Clark	$8.95
Class Reunion	Irma Jenkins/John Brown	$12.95
Code Name: Diva	J.M. Jeffries	$9.95
Conquering Dr. Wexler's Heart	Kimberley White	$9.95
Cricket's Serenade	Carolita Blythe	$12.95
Crossing Paths, Tempting Memories	Dorothy Elizabeth Love	$9.95
Cupid	Barbara Keaton	$9.95
Cypress Whisperings	Phyllis Hamilton	$8.95
Dark Embrace	Crystal Wilson Harris	$8.95
Dark Storm Rising	Chinelu Moore	$10.95
Daughter of the Wind	Joan Xian	$8.95
Deadly Sacrifice	Jack Kean	$22.95
Designer Passion	Dar Tomlinson	$8.95
Dreamtective	Liz Swados	$5.95
Ebony Butterfly II	Delilah Dawson	$14.95
Ebony Eyes	Kei Swanson	$9.95

Other Genesis Press, Inc. Titles (continued)

Other Genesis Press, Inc. Titles (continued)

Indigo After Dark Vol. II	Dolores Bundy/Cole Riley	$10.95
Indigo After Dark Vol. III	Montana Blue/Coco Morena	$10.95
Indigo After Dark Vol. IV	Cassandra Colt/	$14.95
	Diana Richeaux	
Indigo After Dark Vol. V	Delilah Dawson	$14.95
Icie	Pamela Leigh Starr	$8.95
I'll Be Your Shelter	Giselle Carmichael	$8.95
I'll Paint a Sun	A.J. Garrotto	$9.95
Illusions	Pamela Leigh Starr	$8.95
Indiscretions	Donna Hill	$8.95
Intentional Mistakes	Michele Sudler	$9.95
Interlude	Donna Hill	$8.95
Intimate Intentions	Angie Daniels	$8.95
Ironic	Pamela Leigh Starr	$9.95
Jolie's Surrender	Edwina Martin-Arnold	$8.95
Kiss or Keep	Debra Phillips	$8.95
Lace	Giselle Carmichael	$9.95
Last Train to Memphis	Elsa Cook	$12.95
Lasting Valor	Ken Olsen	$24.95
Let's Get It On	Dyanne Davis	$9.95
Let Us Prey	Hunter Lundy	$25.95
Life Is Never As It Seems	J.J. Michael	$12.95
Lighter Shade of Brown	Vicki Andrews	$8.95
Love Always	Mildred E. Riley	$10.95
Love Doesn't Come Easy	Charlyne Dickerson	$8.95
Love in High Gear	Charlotte Roy	$9.95
Love Lasts Forever	Dominiqua Douglas	$9.95
Love Me Carefully	A. C. Arthur	$9.95
Love Unveiled	Gloria Greene	$10.95
Love's Deception	Charlene Berry	$10.95
Love's Destiny	M. Loui Quezada	$8.95
Mae's Promise	Melody Walcott	$8.95
Magnolia Sunset	Giselle Carmichael	$8.95

Other Genesis Press, Inc. Titles (continued)

Other Genesis Press, Inc. Titles (continued)

Path of Thorns	Annetta P. Lee	$9.95
Peace Be Still	Colette Haywood	$12.95
Picture Perfect	Reon Carter	$8.95
Playing for Keeps	Stephanie Salinas	$8.95
Pride & Joi	Gay G. Gunn	$8.95
Promises to Keep	Alicia Wiggins	$8.95
Quiet Storm	Donna Hill	$10.95
Reckless Surrender	Rochelle Alers	$6.95
Red Polka Dot in a World of Plaid	Varian Johnson	$12.95
Rehoboth Road	Anita Ballard-Jones	$12.95
Reluctant Captive	Joyce Jackson	$8.95
Rendezvous with Fate	Jeanne Sumerix	$8.95
Revelations	Cheris F. Hodges	$8.95
Rise of the Phoenix	Kenneth Whetstone	$12.95
Rivers of the Soul	Leslie Esdaile	$8.95
Rock Star	Rosyln Hardy Holcomb	$9.95
Rocky Mountain Romance	Kathleen Suzanne	$8.95
Rooms of the Heart	Donna Hill	$8.95
Rough on Rats and Tough on Cats	Chris Parker	$12.95
Scent of Rain	Annetta P. Lee	$9.95
Second Chances at Love	Cheris Hodges	$9.95
Secret Library Vol. 1	Nina Sheridan	$18.95
Secret Library Vol. 2	Cassandra Colt	$8.95
Shades of Brown	Denise Becker	$8.95
Shades of Desire	Monica White	$8.95
Shadows in the Moonlight	Jeanne Sumerix	$8.95
Sin	Crystal Rhodes	$8.95
Sin and Surrender	J.M. Jeffries	$9.95
Sinful Intentions	Crystal Rhodes	$12.95
So Amazing	Sinclair LeBeau	$8.95
Somebody's Someone	Sinclair LeBeau	$8.95

Other Genesis Press, Inc. Titles (continued)

ESCAPE WITH INDIGO !!!!

Join Indigo Book Club©
It's simple, easy and secure.

Sign up and receive the new releases
every month + Free shipping and
20% off the cover price.

Go online to www.genesis-press.com
and click on Bookclub or
call 1-888-INDIGO-1

Order Form

Mail to: Genesis Press, Inc.
P.O. Box 101
Columbus, MS 39703

Name _____

Address _____

City/State _____ Zip _____

Telephone _____

Ship to (if different from above)

Name _____

Address _____

City/State _____ Zip _____

Telephone _____

Credit Card Information

Credit Card # _____ ☐ Visa   ☐ Mastercard

Expiration Date (mm/yy) _____ ☐ AmEx   ☐ Discover

Qty.	Author	Title	Price	Total

Use this order
form, or call
1-888-INDIGO-1

Total for books _____

Shipping and handling:
  $5 first two books,
  $1 each additional book _____

Total S & H _____

Total amount enclosed _____

Mississippi residents add 7% sales tax